"With *Shattered Sanctua*... herself a master of suspense at the top of her game. Fans of edge-of-your-seat thrillers will find themselves eagerly awaiting the next installment—like I am!"

—Lynette Eason, award-winning, bestselling author of the
LAKE CITY HEROES series

"*Shattered Sanctuary* is a masterpiece! This suspenseful mystery gripped me from the first sentence and kept me turning pages. Readers will be riveted by this non-stop, twisty thriller set deep in the Smoky Mountains. Highly recommended!"

—Elizabeth Goddard, bestselling author
of *Storm Warning*

"Kaely Quinn is back! Nancy Mehl's new book—the first in this exciting new series featuring Quinn and Erin Delaney—will have readers flipping the pages as the two race to discover the killer before one of them becomes his next victim."

—Patricia Bradley, award-winning author
of the PEARL RIVER series

SHATTERED SANCTUARY

BOOKS BY NANCY MEHL

ROAD TO KINGDOM

Inescapable

Unbreakable

Unforeseeable

THE QUANTICO FILES

Night Fall

Dead Fall

Free Fall

FINDING SANCTUARY

Gathering Shadows

Deadly Echoes

Rising Darkness

RYLAND & ST. CLAIR

Cold Pursuit

Cold Threat

Cold Vengeance

DEFENDERS OF JUSTICE

Fatal Frost

Dark Deception

Blind Betrayal

THE ERIN DELANEY MYSTERIES

Shattered Sanctuary

KAELY QUINN PROFILER

Mind Games

Fire Storm

Dead End

SHATTERED SANCTUARY

NANCY MEHL

BETHANYHOUSE

a division of Baker Publishing Group
Minneapolis, Minnesota

Published by Bethany House Publishers
Minneapolis, Minnesota
BethanyHouse.com

Bethany House Publishers is a division of
Baker Publishing Group, Grand Rapids, Michigan

Printed in the United States of America

Library of Congress Cataloging-in-Publication Data
Names: Mehl, Nancy, author.
Title: Shattered sanctuary / Nancy Mehl.
Description: Minneapolis, Minnesota : Bethany House, a division of Baker
    Publishing Group, 2025. | Series: The Erin Delaney Mysteries ; 1
Identifiers: LCCN 2024036360 | ISBN 9780764243363 (paper) | ISBN 9780764244568
    (casebound) | ISBN 9781493448944 (ebook)
Subjects: LCGFT: Detective and mystery fiction. | Christian fiction. | Novels.
Classification: LCC PS3613.E4254 S52 2025 | DDC 813/.6—dc23/eng/20240812
LC record available at https://lccn.loc.gov/2024036360

This book is a work of fiction. Names, characters, places, and incidents are the product of the author's imagination or are used fictitiously. Any resemblance to actual events, locales, or persons, living or dead, is coincidental.

Cover design by Christopher Gilbert, Studio Gearbox
Cover image of cabin by Stephen Mulcahey / Trevillion Images

Baker Publishing Group publications use paper produced from sustainable forestry practices and postconsumer waste whenever possible.

25 26 27 28 29 30 31   7 6 5 4 3 2 1

What is a dog? A dog is a being who loves you
no matter what you do. No matter how many
mistakes you make. If only we could see ourselves
and each other through the eyes of a dog.

It was my privilege to be loved by a wonderful dog
named Watson. I dedicate this book to him.
When you left, you took a part of me with you. I know
that when I see you again, I'll be whole once more.
I love you more than words can say.

Until then, my dearest friend.

William Watcher slew his wife.
Slit her throat with his butcher knife.
Now she wanders Watcher Woods,
A ghastly visage in a cloak and hood.
If you should hear her mournful cries,
You will be the next to die.

PROLOGUE

He stood over the rough-hewn wooden coffin, gazing at the face of his mother—the only person who had ever loved him. Who had ever understood him. A heavy hand rested on his shoulder.

"The angels done took her away, boy. We cannot contend with heaven. The angels know what's best."

He looked up at his grandmother, a hard woman who had spent her life trying to crush her free-spirited daughter with her heavy-handed judgments and religious bondages. A daughter who should have been adored, cherished. Who had spent her brief life searching for joy in a world that had refused to embrace her. They'd taken away her pretty shoes and forbade her to wear makeup, jewelry, or ribbons in her hair. Slowly but surely, the light in his mother's eyes faded, and eventually she forgot about him. Forgot that he needed her. Left him here alone with his grandparents, people he loathed.

In that moment, he made a decision. He *would* contend with heaven.

And he would spend his life finding a way to make the angels cry.

ONE

Erin stood in the street outside a large dirty brick building that housed too many people in small rooms decorated
with mold-infested etchings on crumbling pus-green walls.
Human beings should not live like this. And tonight, some
were not. Living, that is.

She felt something on her shoes and cast her gaze down-
ward. The street where she stood was beginning to flood. The
nearby streetlight flickered in the night, and she suddenly
realized she was standing in blood—dark, thick, gooey. She
wanted to run, but her feet were stuck. She couldn't move.

"Erin!" someone yelled. "Erin!"

She looked up and saw her partner, Scott. He stood several yards away. She could barely make him out through a
strange fog that swirled around them, but it was obvious he
was struggling. He held his arms out toward her.

"Erin, save me. You're my partner. You're supposed to
have my back."

She watched in horror as the same crimson flood that held
her fast swept him away. She fought as hard as she could to
reach him, but it was impossible.

"Scott," she called out to him. "Scott!"

And then he was gone.

Erin sat up in bed sobbing, her face wet with tears and her sheets soaked with sweat. She swung her legs over the side of the bed and put her face in her hands. When would these nightmares end? Would she ever heal from that night?

She looked at the clock next to her bed. It read 3:33 a.m. Again. Why did she wake up so many nights at the same time? It was eerie. Gave her the shivers. She got out of bed and walked over to her closet. After sliding the door open, she glanced up at the locked box on the top shelf. Her gun. She hadn't touched it since . . .

Every morning when she woke up, her feet led her to the closet as if they had a mind of their own. Why? She was drawn to the gun and yet repelled by it. It wasn't the one she'd used that night. She'd turned that one in—along with her badge—when she quit the force. Erin stared at the box as the clock on her nightstand ticked loudly in the quiet room. It was as if the sound was a reminder that her life was slowly ticking away.

She shook her head and closed the closet door. Then she made her way to the kitchen. Maybe a cup of chamomile tea would help. Her doctor had prescribed sleeping pills, but they remained untouched on her nightstand. She was afraid to open the bottle. Afraid she . . .

"Stop it," she said to herself as she flipped the kitchen light on.

Erin finished brewing her tea and thought about going back to bed, but her sheets were still damp, and she didn't feel like changing them. Even if she did, she wasn't sure she had any clean ones. She hadn't done laundry for a while. She'd finally hired someone to come in and clean her house. It was embarrassing. She was basically unemployed, had nothing else to do, but she couldn't take care of the relatively small space where she lived. Correction—where she existed. She used to pride herself on being able to do everything. Cooking, cleaning, taking down bad guys. But now she spent her time watching too much TV and trying to dodge calls from her editor, who wanted more books. She wasn't sure she had another book in her. As it was, the one she'd written only existed because she needed something to do. A way to focus on anything besides that horrific night. Her novel was simply a way to release the dream she'd had inside for so many years. A dream that died the same night Scott had.

She sat at the kitchen table and stared out the window at the falling rain that streaked the glass. The light on her deck caused the rivulets of water to shimmer and dance. She stayed focused on the world outside until she finished her tea. She got up and grabbed the package of Mallomars from her cabinet. She hadn't cooked for a long time. Some days all she ate were Mallomars. Her favorite food. She carried the package into the living room and laid down on the couch, turning on the TV. What should she watch this time? No cop shows. Those were too painful. Strangely, comedies made her angry. Seeing people laugh felt so wrong. Scott was dead. Her career was over. And she was lost. Utterly and completely lost. The life she had now was unsustainable. The only time she'd felt alive was when she was writing that stupid book. And that was fiction. Not real.

She glanced at her coffee table. *Dark Matters* by Erin Delaney. She'd been able to live vicariously through her protagonist, Alex Caine. Alex was the FBI behavioral analyst Erin would never be. Alex lived out Erin's dead dream. The FBI didn't want a broken ex-cop. The book had made a lot of money and even shot up to the top of the *New York Times* bestsellers list. But it hadn't made her happy. All it did was make it clear how empty her life really was.

She knew how to write. She'd taken creative writing courses in college—along with her real interest, criminal justice. She'd even written a couple of novels distributed by a small publisher. She hadn't made much money. She'd just written them for fun. But *Dark Matters* had caught the interest of a large publisher, thanks to the retired FBI behavioral analyst who had been her source—and had become her friend. She'd hoped writing the book would be cathartic. She wrote about a police detective whose partner died in front of him. But it didn't help. It only caused more trauma. Now, her editor wanted three more books. Not only did she have nothing else to say, she couldn't face the additional pain that writing them could bring. Why did her editor keep calling? Why wouldn't she take no for an answer? Money? Prestige? Nothing that Erin cared about.

She'd just popped a Mallomar into her mouth when her cell phone rang, causing her to jump. She quickly chewed and swallowed. There was only one human being alive who knew she woke up at the same time most nights.

"Hello, Kaely," she said when she answered.

"Now you've got me waking up at 3:33," Kaely said. "I felt like this was one of those nights."

"You were right. I'm sorry. I'm sure Noah doesn't appreciate being disturbed this early."

Kaely Quinn-Hunter had walked Erin through the details of *Dark Matters*. Without her, Erin couldn't have written it. As they shared things that only those in law enforcement could understand, they had bonded in a way she couldn't with any of the therapists she'd seen. She'd been through three already, including the one the police had recommended. None of them had helped.

Kaely laughed. "Noah sleeps like a log. Nothing wakes him up." She hesitated for a moment before saying, "Same nightmare?"

"Yeah, it's like some kind of dysfunctional friend who won't go away."

"Not sure it's your friend." She paused again.

"Okay, spit it out. I can tell you have something on your mind."

Kaely sighed loudly. "I hope the day doesn't come when I'm actually trying to keep something from you."

"Why would you want to keep something from me?" Erin asked.

"You're taking this way too literally." Kaely cleared her throat. "Look, I . . . I have a proposal."

"If this is another invitation to fly to Virginia for a visit, you're wasting your time. You know I can't leave my apartment."

"Erin, you *can* leave your apartment. You just choose not to."

"Says you."

"Yeah, says me," Kaely said. "I'm not asking you to come here, but I am asking you to walk out your front door. You can't spend the rest of your life holed up in that place."

Erin really did want to venture out, but she couldn't stand the idea of being in a situation she couldn't control. She was safe here. She could have anything she wanted delivered. She actually had left her apartment a few times, but just to go to the doctor, the therapist, or to pick up fast food. She'd just bought a new car, but only because she discovered she could do it online. The dealership delivered it to her door. Life had certainly changed over the last several years. Now, it was pretty easy to cut yourself off from the rest of the world.

"So, just what *are* you asking me to do?"

"I want you to get into that nice new car you bought and drive to the Smokies. I have a friend who owns a cabin in a town called Sanctuary."

"You're making that up."

Kaely snickered. "No, I'm not. That's really its name. Anyway, I'm proposing a week in an isolated cabin, just you and me. We can talk, cry, yell, do whatever we want with no one to bother us. I'll even pick up groceries, do whatever I need to do. All you have to do is be there. The countryside is beautiful. You'll love it. What do you say?"

Erin searched for an argument, but as she gazed around her kitchen, realizing how tired she was of looking at these same walls, she heard herself agreeing to go. She could drive there without the trauma of the close quarters on a plane, so it shouldn't be too bad.

After getting more information from Kaely, Erin hung up her phone. What had she just done? She wanted to call Kaely back and explain why she couldn't join her in Tennessee this weekend, but suddenly, the image of that box in the closet flashed in her mind. She had the distinct feeling that if she didn't meet Kaely at the cabin, one of these nights she'd finally unlock it.

TWO

"I want to try again."

Noah scooted his chair closer to his wife and took her hands. "Kaely, we've tried three times. It's not just the cost of the treatments, it's what I see happening to you. Every time it fails, it crushes you. I think it's time to talk about adoption."

"But I want your child, not someone else's." As soon as the words left her lips, she regretted them. She knew what it felt like to be unwanted. Giving a child without parents a home was a wonderful thing to do. But she also wanted Noah's baby. She wanted to look into the face of their son or daughter and see themselves reflected back. Was that wrong? It didn't feel wrong, but dismissing the idea of giving a home to children who needed a family made her feel ashamed.

"Kaely . . ."

She shook her head. "No, don't say it. I'm sorry. I didn't mean that. Maybe you're right. But I'm just not ready to give up. Not yet, anyway."

Noah squeezed her hands and smiled. Now Kaely felt even guiltier. He was so patient and understanding. Maybe he was right. Perhaps they should at least look into adoption. She gently pulled her hands from his and took a sip of her coffee. Sunlight streamed in from the kitchen window, reminding her that it was getting late. They'd both slept a little later than usual and had just finished breakfast. Noah had to get to work at the FBI's Behavioral Analysis Unit, and she needed to pack for her trip.

"Look," he said. "You're getting ready to spend a week with Erin in the Smoky Mountains. Why don't you just take a break from thinking about this? Have some fun. We'll talk again when you get back. I find that when my mind is quiet, it's easier to hear from God. Maybe being in new surroundings will help you."

Kaely leaned over and kissed him. "Maybe it will, but being away from you will be hard. I depend on you more than you know."

Noah smiled. "I love being here for you, but even though I'm pretty perfect, I'm not God. You need to find out what He wants you to do."

Kaely laughed. "Let's not get carried away. You're not really perfect, my love."

He grinned. "Now that's just mean."

Kaely shook her head. "You're a pill, you know that?" Her smile slipped. "I really will miss you. I hate it when we're apart."

"You'll have Erin. You two seem to really connect."

"That's true," Kaely said. "But she's not a Christian. Not sure how this is going to go. She knows I'm saved, and she's been respectful, but trying to be friends with someone who doesn't share the most important thing in your life isn't always easy. When she's hurting, I want to tell her how much God loves her. And how He wants to help her."

"If you're uncomfortable, then why did you set this thing up?"

Kaely sighed. "Because I felt very strongly that I was supposed to. You know I don't believe in just throwing seed around on ground that hasn't been prepared to accept it. If I trust what I'm feeling, then I have to assume Erin is ready to know God. If that's true, I have to go. I really have no choice."

Noah kissed her on the forehead. "The smartest thing I ever did was to marry you. You know that?"

Kaely chuckled. "Yes, I absolutely do know that."

"Now who's being a pill?"

Kaely got up from the kitchen table. "I'm just trying to stay up with you, honey."

She heard him laugh as she headed toward the bedroom to pack for her trip. "I really do want to hear from You," she whispered to God. "And whatever you want to do in Erin's life? Please use me. Just help me to not mess it up."

Even with Kaely's directions, Erin had gotten lost twice. GPS didn't work here. It only got her off the main road. She drove through Sanctuary on her way to the cabin. It really was a small town. Reminded her of her grandmother's town in Nebraska, except it was old and rundown. Sanctuary was old—but charming. The ancient buildings had been painted and updated with wonderful wooden sidewalks made of painted slats. Even though she didn't plan to leave the cabin while she was here, she had to admit that the idea of exploring Sanctuary was tempting.

She was grateful she'd been able to drive from St. Louis.

Ever since the night Scott died, she couldn't stand the thought of getting on a plane, trapped inside an enclosed metal structure filled with people. The idea terrified her. With stops, her drive was just a little over eight hours. She decided to break it into two days, although she could have done it in one. She was concerned about having to drive on rural roads in the dark. Everything had worked out well. She'd found a nice hotel about halfway between home and Sanctuary. Today she felt rested as she completed her trip.

After taking two wrong turns, Erin decided to turn left instead of right and finally found herself headed in the correct direction. A few minutes later, she pulled up in front of a lovely, large, cabin-like home. It was much nicer than what she'd imagined. The November air was crisp, and the smoke curling up from the brick chimney made it look even more appealing.

There was a large black truck in the driveway. The owner of the cabin. Kaely wasn't getting in until tomorrow, so the owner, Steve something, said he'd meet her and let her inside.

As she got out of her car, the front door opened, and a large man with brown hair and a mustache stepped out onto the front porch. He waited for her to reach him.

"You must be Erin," he said, sticking his hand out.

To add to her other phobias, germs had joined the list. She shook his hand, thinking about the hand sanitizer in her purse.

"I'm Steve Tremont," he said. "Glad to meet you." He offered her a wide smile. "We don't get many celebrities in these parts."

Oh, great. Here we go again. "I'm really not a celebrity, Steve," she said. "Just a writer who got lucky."

He appeared to size her up. "Good for you. Talented and humble." He held the door open for her. "Loved your book, by the way. Can't wait for the next one."

She just smiled. *You may be waiting a long time.*

Erin stepped into the large living room. A fire sputtered in the huge stone fireplace. On both sides there were built-in brick firewood boxes. The mantle was long with a big off-white clock in the middle, and pictures and plants on either side. Matching chairs flanked an overstuffed brown leather couch. A large glass and wood coffee table sat on top of a colorful rug. The walls were made out of what appeared to be stained wood, and the floors were the same. The high ceiling held a huge hanging light, brass, shaped like branches, with crystal sparkling lights. Floor-to-ceiling glass panels offered an incredible view of the tall trees that surrounded the cabin. It was breathtaking. She caught herself before she actually gasped.

The open concept led into an incredible kitchen with white marbled counters, gleaming appliances, and a built-in booth that made her want to curl up with a cup of coffee and a great book. This certainly wasn't the rustic cabin she'd expected.

"Thank you so much for allowing Kaely and me to stay here," she said, turning back to Steve. "It's beautiful. If I were you, I'd want to stay here year-round. But Kaely says you live in Gatlinburg?"

He nodded. "I bought this a couple of years ago. Decided to update it and rent it out."

"I imagine you're pretty booked up in the summer. I guess things are slower in the fall?"

A furtive glance to the left and a twinge in his jaw told her that she'd just said something that made him uncomfortable. What was that about?

Steve reached into his jacket pocket and took out a card. "You can call me here if you have any questions. I doubt that you will. The cabin has electricity as well as a backup generator in case you need it. If you lose power, it will kick on automatically. The fridge is stocked, and you're welcome to help yourself, although you may want to go into town tomorrow to pick up your favorite foods. You should be good for quite a while though."

"Thanks," she said. "The generator. Do you think we'll need it?"

He smiled, but it didn't reach his eyes. Erin had learned a lot about reading people from Kaely. There was something wrong here. "Usually, I'd say no, but it's possible we may be in for a snowstorm. Don't usually have them in November, and our weather forecasters are frequently wrong. But you have nothing to worry about. If for any reason you lose electricity, just wait." He hesitated a moment, and the thick mustache on his upper lip quivered almost imperceptibly. He cleared his throat. "Be sure you stay indoors at night. There are bears in the woods. Generally, they'll leave you alone. They're used to people, but it's important to remember that they're wild animals. In the dark, they might see you, but you may not see them."

"Okay," Erin said slowly. Did that really make sense? If bears could see her at night, didn't that mean they'd go the other way? She'd read once that bears weren't really looking for a confrontation with humans. This guy was beginning to make her a little nervous.

He took a set of keys from his coat pocket and handed them to her. "Tell Kaely I'll stop by sometime in the next few days. We haven't seen each other in a long time. I'd like to say hi."

"She didn't mention how she knew you."

"I'm actually friends with her husband, Noah. We went to college together. I met Kaely at their wedding. Wonderful girl. It was clear that Noah found his soulmate in Kaely." This was the first thing Steve had said since she'd met him that was from the heart. His body was relaxed, and his smile was genuine.

He said good-bye and started to leave, but he hesitated at the last moment. "Be sure you lock this door securely at night. And the door to the deck as well."

"The bears here know how to pick locks, Steve?" She didn't mean to sound combative, but this guy was spooking her.

He laughed nervously. "Funny," was all he said before pulling the door shut behind him. Erin gazed out the window and watched as he got into his truck and drove slowly away. What was going on? Was she just being paranoid? It was possible, but the physical clues she saw made her suspicious.

Erin went to the kitchen sink and washed her hands. Then she went outside and started unloading her bags. It only took a few minutes to bring everything inside. Even though she fought the urge, she found herself looking around, peering into the woods. Once she shut the door again, she breathed a sigh of relief.

"Stop it," she said to herself. "This is stupid." She walked over to the refrigerator and opened it. "Wow," was all she could say. Steve was being modest. The fridge was stocked with several premade meals that included burgundy beef tips, glazed salmon, chicken tikka masala, and stuffed pork chops. Each meal included fancy veggies and either rice or potatoes. Not plain rice or potatoes, either. Rice pilaf, brown rice, saffron rice, grilled potatoes, garlic mashed potatoes, or garlic-infused potatoes.

The bottom bin contained several kinds of fruits and ingredients for salad. There were trays of sliced cheeses, sausage, and different kinds of deli meats. There was enough food here for at least a week. Erin closed the fridge and found a door that led to a stocked pantry. Breads, cereals, condiments, and different kinds of wines. She was certain Kaely didn't drink, and neither did she. Not for any kind of religious reasons. She didn't drink because she'd seen too many families torn apart by alcohol. Besides, the idea of giving up control to anything or anyone was something she had no desire to do. Especially now.

She decided to check out the rest of the cabin, although again, the word *cabin* didn't really fit this place. She and Kaely certainly wouldn't be roughing it here.

Downstairs there was a luxurious bathroom with a soaking tub and a separate shower. Upstairs there were three bedrooms and two more bathrooms. The largest bedroom led to a deck. Erin unlocked the sliding glass door and pulled it open. When she stepped onto the stained wood flooring, this time she did gasp. She looked out over acres of pine trees shrouded in mist as far as she could see. Mountains framed the landscape, making the astounding view more magnificent than anything she'd ever experienced. The sun hung low in a sky painted in pinks, yellows, and blues. She looked around the large deck and found several Adirondack chairs as well as a table and a large fire pit. It was so inviting that she didn't care how cold it was. She and Kaely would have to spend some time out here. She felt tears spring to her eyes, but she quickly wiped them away. Silly. She suspected it wasn't because of the deck or even the view. For a few minutes, the past couple of years took a backseat in her mind. And that made her emotional.

She stood outside, shivering from the cold, until reluctantly, she decided it was time to get inside where it was warm. As she turned to go, she thought she heard something, almost like a woman crying. She stood still for a moment. Was she imagining things? As she waited, there was only silence. Her body began to tremble from more than just the cold, and she hurried inside, pulling the door closed behind her. Remembering Steve's words, she quickly locked the door. Suddenly, the cabin didn't seem quite as inviting. As she stared out into the dark, an all-too-familiar chill of fear slid down her spine.

THREE

Once she'd returned downstairs, Erin checked the front door again. Of course she hadn't actually heard a woman sobbing. There were all kinds of animals in the woods. It was probably a bird of some kind. For a split second, she thought about calling the police—or even Steve—but she didn't want to sound like some kind of silly city person who jumped at every noise. Besides, it could easily be her imagination. The nightmares and a lack of sleep had caused hallucinations before. She'd seen things in her room—or thought she had. Heard voices threatening her. Blaming her for Scott's death. She'd never told anyone about them. Not even the shrinks she'd talked to after the shooting. She struggled with herself for a few minutes, but in the end, she sat down on the couch in the living room and called Kaely.

"Just what did you get us into?" she said when Kaely answered her phone.

"What are you talking about?"

Erin recounted her meeting with Steve and the strange sound she'd heard outside. "Your friend Steve spooked me a little. It was obvious something was bothering him. He kept warning me to lock the doors. Is he always so paranoid?"

Kaely was quiet for a moment. "That's odd," she said finally. "To be honest, I don't know him very well, but I got the impression from Noah that he was pretty stable."

Erin sighed. "I don't know. Maybe it's my imagination. You know how messed up I've been."

"Yeah, I know," Kaely said, "but I trust your instincts. When I get there, maybe I should have a talk with him."

"Yeah, and he'll think you have a bonkers friend who shouldn't be allowed out by herself."

"Well, there's that, but just in case . . ."

Erin laughed. "Thanks a lot. Seriously, this place really doesn't look like anyone's idea of a cabin. Maybe from the outside, but inside it's incredible."

"Sounds great. I'm really looking forward to tomorrow. My plane should be in around two."

"I wish you'd let me pick you up at the airport. Sunday traffic shouldn't be bad. As long as I don't have to get out of the car, I'll be fine."

"No," Kaely said. "The area can be pretty confusing. I can't have you getting lost out there."

"Where did you stay when you were here before?"

"We rented a place about ten miles from where you are now. Steve only bought the cabin a couple of years ago, so this will be the first chance I've had to see it."

"I wish you were getting here tonight," Erin said.

"I wish I were too, but like I told you, we promised to babysit for church friends while they're away on a second honeymoon. They get back in the morning, and Noah's taking me straight to the airport."

Erin sighed. "I know. It's nice of you to do something like that. Not sure I could handle it. Kids drive me up the wall."

Kaely was quiet, and Erin immediately felt awful. She wanted to take back her careless words. Noah and Kaely had been trying for a family for several years now, without success. Why had she said that?

"They're not too bad," Kaely said, filling the awkward silence herself. "But if their teenager rolls her eyes at me one more time, I may show her photos from one of Noah's cases. That should scare her straight."

Erin laughed again in spite of herself. Kaely was like that. Never getting offended. Always kind. Erin assumed it was because she was a Christian. Although Kaely had told her more than once that she prayed for her, she'd never tried to force her beliefs on Erin. If she had, they might not be friends—and they were. Erin had no place for a God that let good men like Scott die—or who could stand by as an innocent girl was cut down because violent gang members couldn't stop shooting at each other. She'd never accept a God like that. Never.

"I'd better go," Kaely said. "I just heard a weird noise from the living room. Hopefully, everything is still standing." She paused for a moment. "Are you going to be okay? I think you're right about the sound you heard, but if you have any doubt, call the police. I'm pretty sure there's a local department even though the closest town is pretty small."

"That's all I need, Barney Fife showing up at my door."

Kaely snorted. "Look at it this way. You might get Luther."

"I'd be surprised and happy to find Idris Elba standing on the porch. However, I have a feeling in a town as small as Sanctuary, the police chief is probably Barney's less sophisticated brother."

"Oh, ye of little faith," Kaely said. "Hopefully, we won't have to interact with the police while we're there. I think we both need a break from law enforcement, profiling, and anything associated with dead bodies."

"Well, dead bodies in my book made me a lot of money, but you're right. Time for bunnies, puppies, and kittens,"

"Not sure we'll find any puppies or kittens running around, but we might be able to find a bunny or two for you."

"I'm looking forward to it," Erin said.

"Well, dear friend, let's say good-night. I'll see you tomorrow around three o'clock. Our first time together in person."

"We've Zoomed several times," Erin said. "I don't think it will be too shocking."

"I did tell you that I'm only four feet tall, right? You can't tell that on your laptop."

Erin grinned. "So, you're a foot taller than I am? I think we'll get along just fine."

Kaely laughed, said good-bye, and hung up. Erin looked around the cabin, wondering what it would be like to spend a week in a different place. She hadn't slept away from home even once since the night of the shooting. She'd written *Dark Matters* in three months. Her agent couldn't believe it, but it's pretty easy to write a ninety-thousand-word book when you have nothing else to do. Nowhere to go. You can't sleep, and you're trying to drown out the grim voices in your head. The editors moved quickly, and a year later her book was released. Her publisher put some bucks behind it, and it quickly became popular. What followed were requests for interviews—written, online, and even from other media outlets. Erin was horrified. She did most of the written in-terviews but turned down the television shows and online interviews. Then her publisher began to talk to her about developing a "media presence." What the heck was that? She was busy hiding from the world, and they wanted her to develop a presence? She was barely present for herself. She halfheartedly joined a few online sites but couldn't keep up with the responses. Finally, she pulled back completely, even though her publisher wasn't happy about it.

In the end, they still wanted more books and were willing to allow her to stay sheltered in the background. She'd told Kaely she wanted to be known as the "anonymous author." Kaely had laughed. "If that's what you want, go for it," she'd said. Kaely, who'd hung in there, walked her through her darkest nights, and answered all of her questions, no matter what time she called. Erin had distanced herself from all her former friends. Now Kaely was the only one left. Would she really want to be her friend once she really got to know her? Realized how messed up she really was? She self-consciously reached up and touched the scar on the side of her face. Sometimes when she was upset or insecure she could swear it burned.

Suddenly, a woeful sound caught her attention. She stiff-ened at the sound until it repeated. A coyote, not a woman crying. Weird. Somehow it made her feel better. She wasn't certain why. Maybe it was because he sounded as lonely as she felt.

He carefully placed her on the dead leaves. He'd dressed her and prepared her. She was his first perfect sacrifice. The others had been flawed, but he still counted them as puzzle pieces, destined to become the picture he wanted someone to see. To understand. It was time for the world to know him. He removed the figurine from his pocket and put it in her hands. Would they know what it meant? He doubted it. People were stupid. After the next one, they'd understand. He wasn't worried about being caught. He'd been careful. No fingerprints. No DNA. Nothing to point back to him. He was smart. Much smarter than anyone around here.

He rose slowly to his feet and pulled his other phone from his pocket. Then he took her picture. He couldn't just walk away and rely on his memory. He wanted to . . . no . . . *needed* to relive this moment. To remember how killing her made him feel. He put the phone back in his jacket pocket and looked up to the sky.

The angels were crying tonight. He could almost swear that he heard them. It made him smile.

FOUR

Erin was awakened by the sound of someone knocking on the door downstairs. She sat up in bed, wondering where she was and who wanted inside her apartment. It took a few seconds for her to remember that she was in a cabin in the Smoky Mountains and that Kaely would be here today. Was she early? Erin jumped out of bed and grabbed her denim jacket. She'd taken the bedroom at the top of the stairs. It was comfortable and nicely decorated. The room had a wood ceiling with exposed beams and white shiplap walls. An antique chandelier was positioned over the queen-sized bed with an off-white tufted headboard, a sky-blue comforter, and a white ruffled bed skirt. Across from the bed was a white brick fireplace with a large mantle. A blue overstuffed chair with a matching ottoman sat in the corner. It was a lovely room, and the bed was so soft, Erin felt as if she'd melted into it.

She'd wanted to light a fire last night but had decided to wait until tonight. By the time she was ready for bed, all she'd wanted was sleep. Thankfully, the nightmares had stayed away, although she was always aware that they lurked in the dark recesses of her mind, ready to attack her at their own pleasure.

She glanced at the antique clock on the mantel. It was almost seven. Now that she was a little more awake, she realized it couldn't be Kaely. She would have called if she was coming this early.

As Erin made her way down the stairs, she was greeted by another round of very insistent knocks. She walked slowly toward the large wooden door that led to the porch and peered out through the peephole. There was a man standing there. She'd noticed an intercom next to the door last night and pressed the button.

"May I help you?" she asked.

"Miss Delaney, my name is Adrian Nightengale. I'm the police chief in Sanctuary. I'd like to talk to you."

"Would you show me your badge please?" If he couldn't produce one, she intended to dial 911. She tightened her grip on the phone she'd automatically grabbed before coming down the stairs.

The man reached into his jacket and pulled out a leather wallet. He opened it and then held it up in front of the peep hole. Sure enough, it was a badge. Erin slipped her phone into her pocket. She pressed the intercom button again.

"Is something wrong, Chief?" she asked.

"I'm sorry to bother you," he said. "But I need your help. Could I come in, please?"

Although his badge looked genuine, Erin felt a stab of apprehension. Research for her book had required her to explore the minds of several serial killers. There were some who'd impersonated police officers to lure unsuspecting women to their deaths. Kenneth Bianchi and his cousin,

Angelo Buono, came to mind. Together they'd raped and killed ten women, but the number could be higher. There were some murders that investigators felt could have been committed by one or both of them, but they were never able to get indictments due to a lack of evidence.

Erin took a deep breath. "If you don't mind, I'd rather come out there and talk to you," she said. "Will you step back?"

"Of course. No problem."

At that moment, Erin wished she'd grabbed her gun before answering the door, but it was upstairs, still locked in the metal box she used to store it. It wasn't loaded, she kept her clips somewhere else, making it legal for her to transport it.

She really was being paranoid, but she couldn't help it. The onslaught of letters, emails, and people on social media who seemed abnormally interested in her since the book had released made her wary. Some of the messages were rather disturbing. She realized taking her gun out of the locked box would keep her safer from the dangers that might be out there in the world, but she wasn't certain it would keep her safe from herself.

Erin fought a feeling of panic that made her feel nauseated. Her throat burned, and she swallowed the acrid bile that tried to push its way into her mouth. Fear had become her constant companion—one that she detested. She used to be so brave. Where was that woman?

Just then she heard a car pull into the driveway. She moved back the drape that hung next to the front door. A patrol car. Two officers got out and hurried up to the porch. She listened as they talked to the man standing there. She clearly heard them call him *chief*. As they turned to leave, she finally opened the door, her body trembling with the effort. This man was clearly who he said he was. He moved back a few feet as she took a deep breath and stepped out onto the porch.

Chief Adrian Nightengale looked too young to be a police chief. His thick dark hair was combed back from his face and curled around his neck. He sported a light mustache and beard, and his thick eyebrows sat over hazel eyes that peered deeply into hers. She felt as if he were seeing too much—more than she wanted revealed. It was almost too personal. Too intrusive. Even though she wasn't happy about being bothered, she took a quick breath. He actually looked remarkably like a character in her book. A police detective she'd named Jake Mallory. How could Jake be standing here in front of her?

Erin suddenly felt a little insecure in her sweats, t-shirt, and jacket. Her hand slipped up to check her hair. Although she wore her light blonde hair short in what some people would call a "messy style," there was a difference between purposely messy and just plain messy. The word *bedhead* came to mind.

She quickly ran her hand through her hair and then dropped her arm. She'd removed her makeup last night and knew her scar was visible. She felt the urge to cover it with her hand, but that would call even more attention to it. Why was she feeling vulnerable? This man had interrupted her sleep. He was the one who should feel uncomfortable. She straightened her shoulders, frowned, and said, "What can I do for you, Chief?"

"I heard you were staying here, Miss Delaney. I read your book."

"You woke me up this early to tell me you liked my book, Chief? Really?" Her discomfort quickly turned to irritation. She'd come to this place to get away from people. "This is highly inappropriate."

The chief frowned. "No, Miss Delaney. I didn't come here because I liked your book. I don't believe I said that. I'm here because your knowledge of crime scenes was spot on. Very impressive. Something has happened, and I'd appreciate your help. This situation is . . . unusual for us, and I'm afraid we might miss something important."

Erin was so surprised she opened her mouth but couldn't find the right words to respond to his ridiculous statement. Finally, she said, "Chief Nightengale, I'm an author, not a police officer anymore, and certainly not a criminalist. You're asking the wrong person for help."

"We're a small department," the chief said. "You *were* a police officer, and you've done a lot of research for your book. I realize that this seems like a strange request, but I need you, Miss Delaney. You see, a young woman has been murdered."

FIVE

As Erin pulled on her jeans and grabbed a shirt, she couldn't believe she was actually getting ready to follow a small-town police chief into the woods to look at a corpse. It was true that before she left the police department, her goal was to become a detective. Her research with Kaely had taught her a lot about reading crime scenes, although she'd also learned a great deal from being on the force. St. Louis was rife with crime and dead bodies. Still, this was something she didn't feel prepared for. She wished Kaely was here. She was the one who should be assisting the chief.

After she was dressed, she ran a brush through her hair and then shaped it with mousse. She carefully applied the cover up makeup she used to hide the scar she'd been given by a gang member's knife while trying to secure him. When she was certain it was concealed as well as possible, she added a little blush and mascara. She stared at herself in the mirror. Scott had told her she was beautiful, and she'd almost believed him. But not anymore. Regardless, she was as ready as she would ever be. She made sure to put her phone in her pocket. She intended to take plenty of pictures. She and Kaely could go through them after she arrived. She'd probably see something Erin missed.

She hurried downstairs and grabbed her coat. November was chilly in Tennessee. She took a deep breath and opened the door. Chief Nightengale was standing next to a ruby-red Jeep Wrangler. Pretty bold for a small-town police chief. Again, she was struck by how much he looked like Jake. Weird. She closed the door and walked up to him. His eyes searched hers, and once again she felt a slight shock as she reacted to him without meaning to.

"Thank you for this," he said. "I realize you don't feel qualified to look over my crime scene, but I truly believe that your time with the St. Louis police department, as well as the research you did for your book, makes you extremely competent for this situation. We've never faced anything like this before in Sanctuary."

"I'm willing to do what I can," Erin said, "but if you don't mind, I'd like to take some pictures. My friend, Kaely Hunter, will be here later today. She worked as a . . ."

"Behavioral analyst for the FBI," the chief finished for her. "I know. As I said, I read your book and saw the acknowledgment you wrote for her. I'd be happy to have her input." He frowned. "Maybe this is just a murder." He shook his head. "I'm sorry, that sounds rather flippant. Any murder is a tragedy. Even though Sanctuary is small, we've had our share of death. But this is . . . different. I'm sure you'll understand why I wanted your feedback when you see the body."

He opened the door of his Jeep and motioned for Erin to get inside.

"We can drive most of the way, but we'll have to walk the

last stretch." He looked down at her boots. "Good thing you're wearing those. You'll need them."

Erin didn't say anything, just climbed into the Jeep, wondering how in the world she'd gotten herself into this situation. She could feel the beads of perspiration on her forehead and tried to remind herself that she was safe. She was with a police chief, in his vehicle, and he would watch out for her. Still, the farther they drove from the cabin, the more uncomfortable she became. She made fists, digging her nails into her palms, trying to stay calm. She had no desire to come apart in front of this man.

When he took a turn down a dirt road that led deeper into the woods, even though she wasn't at ease with the situation, she couldn't help but admire the scenery. The tall trees, with the morning sun sneaking through the branches, were breathtaking. Suddenly, the chief braked. Erin turned her head and watched as a mother bear and her cubs lumbered across the road in front of them. She gasped at the sight.

"There are bears all around here," the chief said. "Always be aware of your surroundings if you're outside, and never confront one."

"Trust me, I have no intention of confronting a bear. I'd turn and run away as fast as I could."

The chief turned his head to look at her. "That's the last thing you want to do."

"Seriously? What do you want me to do? Try to talk it out of eating me?"

The chief smiled. "Back up slowly, talk in a calm voice, and don't look directly at it."

Erin laughed. "And what should I say calmly? 'Please don't eat me, Mr. Bear. I wouldn't taste very good.'"

"It doesn't really matter what you say. Just stay calm."

Erin shook her head. "I'm not sure that's possible."

"To be honest, the bears around her are pretty used to people," he said. "If you ignore them, they'll generally ignore you." He cocked his head toward the mother and cubs in front of them. "A mother bear is the one you have to worry about the most." He sighed. "You wouldn't believe how many tourists get out of their cars and try to approach a *cute* bear cub. You might not see the mother, but trust me, she's somewhere close by."

"I like cats and dogs, but I'm not really interested in making friends with bears. You won't have to worry about me."

They drove for a while before the chief said, "So, did you always want to be a writer?"

"Not really. I wrote a couple of novels in college just for fun. My family and friends bought some copies, but that was about it. I only wrote *Dark Matters* because I had nothing else to do. I always thought that someday I'd work for the BAU, but that's not going to happen now. Writing a book was my way of saying good-bye to that dream."

As soon as the words left her mouth, she wondered why she'd told him that. She wasn't used to sharing private things with people she didn't know. It was too late to take them back now.

"I don't understand. Why can't you work for the FBI? With your police background . . ."

"I don't really want to talk about it," Erin said more sharply than she meant to. "I . . . I'm sorry. Sore subject and very personal."

"I understand," he replied. "Sorry." He slowed down and pulled the Jeep to the side of the road. "We'll have to walk from here."

Erin got out. "Any bears in this area?" She tried to make it sound as if she were kidding, but the truth was, she was nervous. She glanced over at the chief and noticed he was armed. Good. Just in case soft words didn't actually work.

"Do you know the victim?" she asked as she followed him into the woods.

"No. We get a lot of tourists, so that's not a big surprise. My officers are checking with local hotels and B&Bs in the area, trying to find out who she is. So far, we haven't uncovered anything."

"This location seems pretty remote. Who discovered the body?"

"Usually, you'd be right, but hunting season started on the first. Lots of people in the woods. A hunter found her."

Erin shook her head, and the chief obviously noticed.

"Not a fan of hunting?"

"No, I'm not." She held up one hand. "I've heard all the arguments about hunting for food or whatever. But getting joy out of killing an innocent animal is something I'll never understand."

She waited for the inevitable justification for hunting, but instead, the chief said, "I actually agree with you. I have no stomach for it either, but I still have to allow people to do it. I'm always glad when the season is over, though."

Erin was surprised, but glad to see that the chief felt he had the right to have what was probably an unpopular opinion among the people who came here to hunt and the business owners who made money from them.

Although Erin had seen her share of dead bodies, it had been a while. The last one had been the little girl she'd accidentally shot. She felt sick to her stomach at the prospect of viewing another one. The truth was, she'd believed this kind of thing was behind her. Now, here it was again. Death. Writing about it and actually looking at it were two very different things. She felt herself sway, and the chief reached out and took her arm.

"Are you okay?" he asked.

"Yeah, I'm fine." She pulled her arm out of his grasp. "I think I stepped on a branch or something."

He stood still and stared at her, concern written clearly on his face. "I've been selfish. I shouldn't have asked you to do this."

She turned toward him. "I'm an adult, Chief. Not a child. If I didn't want to come, I would have told you. Please don't patronize me."

He held up in hands in surrender. "Sorry, again. We're almost there."

He began walking away, and she hurried to keep up. She was chiding herself for being so abrupt when he suddenly stopped.

Erin stepped around him. In front of them was a woman, lying on the ground. She wore a long white dress, the bodice stained with blood. She held something in her hands. Erin wanted to turn away. Wanted to run back to the cabin. And then back to her apartment. Why had she come here? What was she thinking?

She looked up into the face of Chief Nightengale. There was something in his eyes that unsettled her. It ignited a fire inside her. She stepped around him and went closer to the body, being careful not to contaminate the area. Two officers stood nearby, watching her and staring at their chief as if waiting for instructions.

Erin ignored them and looked over the scene. What she saw made her feel cold inside. She turned around to face the chief.

"Chief Nightengale, I think you may have a serial killer on your hands," she said, trying to keep her voice steady.

SIX

Although Adrian wasn't completely surprised by Erin's statement, hearing her confirm his worst fear made it hard to catch his breath. How could this be? Sanctuary was a small town. The place where he'd grown up. As far back as he could remember, there had only been two killings in Sanctuary. The first one happened almost twenty years ago. A man shot an intruder who broke into his house intending to rob him—and then the incident two years ago. A violent argument between a married couple. The man had tried to beat his wife. She responded by stabbing him in the throat. Adrian had responded to a hysterical call from the wife. He still had flashbacks of the scene. When he'd accepted the job in his hometown, he'd believed he'd left behind the violence he'd witnessed in Chicago, where he'd first been a cop. But seeing the dead man lying on the floor of his home, blood everywhere because the wife had sliced open his carotid artery, Adrian had flashed back to those days. That night he was haunted by the man's eyes, open and staring at nothing. There'd been a look of horror on his face. It was an expression he'd seen before, too many times. Was it there because people who were dying realized their lives were over? If they'd rejected God, did the fear that hell might be real suddenly overwhelm them? There was no way to know, but still, Adrian wondered about it. Sometimes at night, when he was trying to sleep, images from the past would pop into his mind. It would take him a while to push them back into the vault in his mind where he kept the things he didn't want to think about. Both of the killings in Sanctuary had been ruled as justified, although they were still tragedies, but now things had changed. Something evil had come to Sanctuary, and it was his job to stop it.

Finding the body in the woods had created a situation he wasn't sure he could face alone. That's why he felt compelled to contact Erin Delaney. He was relieved to know that Kaely Quinn-Hunter would also be here soon. In Chicago, most of the murders he'd encountered had either been gang shootings or violent thefts. However, he'd never encountered a serial killer. He'd read about them, but he never believed something like this could happen in Sanctuary. Of course, just because Erin Delaney said it was . . .

"Why do you say that?" he asked her.

Erin sighed audibly. "First of all, let me tell you what I see, then we'll get to why I suspect he's not finished."

"How do you know the killer is a man?" he asked. "I know the statistics, but I don't see how you can rule out a woman."

"She'd have to be pretty strong to carry the body here."

Before Adrian could ask her how she knew the woman wasn't murdered in this spot, she crouched down and pointed at the ground.

"It's fall so there are leaves everywhere. The leaves around the body are barely disturbed, but there are broken leaves leading back toward the road. She wasn't dragged. If she had been, there would be drag marks. Whoever put her here carried her, and that's not a short walk. That means you have someone who is strong enough to carry a body. That tells me that it was most probably a man. Moving on, I notice that she was stabbed in the chest. The person who did this knew exactly what he was doing. Most people hit a rib when they try to stab someone in the heart. However, there's just one wound here. He hit his mark right off the bat. This doesn't mean he had medical knowledge. It might just mean that he's perfected his killing, meaning this may not be his first murder. Saying that, it's important to remember that the first death is always the most important. If this is his first, you need to pay special attention to it. But I suspect it's not." She sighed. "She bled a lot, but as you can see, the blood has darkened and there isn't any on the ground around her. She bled out somewhere else." Erin paused and took a breath. Adrian could tell this was difficult for her. "Her eyes are closed. The killer closed them. He has some remorse. Didn't want her staring at him. Have your forensic people look for fingerprints on her eyelids. Some killers forget about that. He didn't cover her, so any reticence he has is minor. He wants everyone to see what he did. I feel like this was some kind of mission. As if he's trying to right a wrong. I think you'll find that she wasn't molested. He wouldn't put her in a white dress if he'd defiled her."

"You think the killer dressed her?" Adrian asked.

Erin nodded. "This woman would never wear anything like this. It's obviously handmade, and not expertly. Whoever sewed this dress knows the basics, but isn't skilled. Look at this woman's hair. It's been expertly highlighted. Her nails are manicured. I'd guess her teeth are in good shape, but I don't want to touch the body. I don't want to disturb any evidence." She paused for a moment. "This white dress reminds me of something a woman might wear to a confirmation. I believe there's some kind of religious symbolism here." She paused for a moment. "In fact, I'm certain of it. I'll explain that in a minute. It will be hard to determine TOD because it was in the twenties last night. Hopefully, your ME will be able to give you a good estimate."

A voice behind them called Adrian's name, causing him to turn around. The medical examiner was here. Dr. Gibson was a local physician who had volunteered to serve in the position. The doctor was what some would call a curmudgeon. Adrian wondered how he'd take having an outsider look over his crime scene.

Gibson walked up next to him. He glared at Adrian, his jaw working hard. Then he cursed under his breath.

"You wanna tell me just what's goin' on here?" he asked.

"Doc, just give her a minute, please," Adrian said. "I asked her to look things over before you take control."

"And just who is this?" Gibson bellowed. "Is she the local ME? If so, I'll just head back to the office."

Adrian took a deep breath, trying to control his irritation. If he ticked Gibson off, he'd have a real problem. "You're the ME, Doc. This lady is someone who has experience with crime scenes. I just asked her opinion because we're not used to something like this. She's almost done." He looked at Erin. "Right?"

It was obvious that she understood his situation. "Yes, I am. Sorry to be in your way, Doctor. Just give me a couple of minutes."

47

Adrian took a few steps away from Gibson and knelt down next to Erin. "Thanks for trying to smooth things over. I apologize."

"It's okay. I believe this woman is a tourist. She's unmarried, but she has a pet. This may not be her dress, but the shoes are hers." Erin pointed at the top of one of her shoes. Sure enough, there were a couple of small white hairs. "You can see that these hairs don't belong to her. Either they belong to her pet—or to his if she picked them up in his car. I doubt that though, because I think the killer was more careful than that. He probably put something under the body. I would guess he used plastic, but your forensic people should check her dress for any kinds of fibers—or hair. Locard's exchange principle." She looked up at him. "Do you know what that is?"

Adrian nodded. He could have been offended, but he wasn't. "The perpetrator of a crime will not only bring something to the scene, he'll leave with something."

She smiled at him. "Yes. Good."

"What else do you see?" he asked.

"Her lipstick was put on before she was killed. I think she was getting ready to go somewhere. Although some women put on makeup in the morning, it's usually light. This isn't. She's wearing foundation, liner, blush, mascara . . . she even shaped her eyebrows. Her lipstick is dark and applied very carefully. Then there are the shoes. Dressy heels. Earrings and a necklace. She was probably going somewhere last night. Look for events in the area. Or maybe she was meeting someone for dinner. I doubt she knew him . . . or her . . . well." She frowned. "The blue ribbon in her hair?"

He nodded.

"I think the murderer added it too. It just doesn't fit with

her makeup, her shoes, or even her hair. It looks forced."
She nodded. "I believe he's responsible for the ribbon, as
well as the dress."

"Okay. So why do you think that if she was meeting someone, she didn't know them very well? "

"Just guessing," Erin said, "but if you haven't gotten a
call from someone reporting her missing, that means anyone she was meeting didn't know her very well. If he—or
she—had . . . they would be concerned about her where-
abouts by now. They probably would have contacted you.
Were there any special events happening in the area last
night?"

Adrian thought for a moment. "Most of the nearby events
are over by the end of October. It picks up again in Decem-
ber. The only thing I can think of is Grits and Grains. It's
in Townsend, about twenty miles from here, but it's really
popular."

Erin frowned at him. "She doesn't look like someone who
would go to something called Grits and Grains."

"You may be pretty perceptive about most things, but
you're reading this wrong. They feature gourmet foods and
fancy drinks. Sounds like it might be right up this gal's alley."

Erin shrugged. "Sorry. Hard to tell from the title."

"Some things aren't that easy to judge. Along with some
people."

Erin paused and seemed to be taking stock of him. Her
green eyes locked on his. It made him nervous.

She frowned. "Do you get many visitors in the fall?"

He nodded. "A lot of people come here to see the leaves
turn."

"But it's pretty cold."

"We're usually in the thirties at night. Close to forty. This cold snap is a little unusual, but it happens."

Erin was silent for a moment. "It's November," she said. "The leaves start changing in October. My guess is that she was probably getting ready to go home. Maybe after the event you mentioned. Look for someone renting a place or a room whose reservation is almost up." She pointed at the object the woman held in her hands. "Did you notice this?"

"Sure. This is why I came to you. I've never seen anything like it before. An angel statue with what looks like red tears falling from its eyes. Looks like whoever painted it wasn't skilled at it." A long line of paint dribbled down the front of the angel.

Erin stood, and Adrian did the same. She stepped closer to him. He could smell her hair. What was that scent? Peaches?

"The angel is a spiritual symbol. Like the dress. It's the killer's signature. The angel is crying. Your UNSUB may be saying that this woman offends him for some kind of spiritual reason. Maybe he thinks her lifestyle makes the angels cry. Or he's trying to make them cry by his actions. I can't be sure of that. There's no way to know what it is that offends him until he kills again and then you should be able to see the connection. And the sloppiness? That's the problem, Chief. This is why I believe you're dealing with a serial killer. I don't think the person who painted this angel made a mistake. In fact, I think he's very, very careful. Extremely organized." She looked around her at the officers and Gibson who would have steam coming from his ears if it were possible. She took a step even closer to him. She clearly didn't want to be overheard. "That isn't a slip-up. It's a number. The number one."

Adrian felt as if all the blood in his body had suddenly frozen solid.

SEVEN

Kaely was relieved to hear the captain announce that they were getting ready to land. She wasn't a fan of flying. She'd heard the statistics, how much safer flying was than driving. But the problem wasn't the flying part. The problem was the falling part.

She fastened her seat belt and prayed that this was the right thing to do. She'd felt led to reach out to Erin. She knew a lot about trauma. God had healed her of so much, and now she wanted to help Erin. They'd become close while working on her book, but would their online relationship endure in person? She wasn't sure. But one thing she did know. If God put this together, He would see it through. She reminded herself of His faithfulness and that He loved Erin even more than Kaely did. She whispered a prayer of consecration.

"Do whatever You want to do through me," she said quietly. "Not my will, but Yours."

In a few hours, she'd be at the cabin. She hoped she and Erin would have a relaxed time together. No stress. Just fun and fellowship.

The chief was cautious when telling Gibson that he needed to be especially meticulous in his handling of the body. Although it was clear he wasn't happy about Erin's access to the dead woman, he seemed to understand how important it was to preserve evidence. Still, she was a little worried.

"You do have people trained in forensics, right?" she asked the chief when they were both back in his Jeep.

"Detective Sergeant Timothy Johnson. He trained at the National Forensics Academy in Knoxville, Tennessee. He'll work with Gibson to get whatever they can from the body and the place where she was found."

A late-model dark blue pickup pulled up behind them and a tall man with dark blond hair emerged. The chief rolled down his window and called him over. When he reached them, the chief introduced Erin. Then he said, "This is Detective Sergeant Johnson. He'll do a great job of looking over and collecting evidence."

Johnson nodded at her. "Erin Delaney?" he said. "Like the author?"

"This *is* the author," the chief said. "But let's keep that under our hats, okay?"

Johnson grinned. "No one will hear it from me, but you know how folks in Sanctuary are. If everyone doesn't know it already, they will soon."

"I'm sure you're right. I just don't want anyone hounding Miss Delaney."

"Got it, boss. I'd better get over there before Gibson has a coronary. He's not the most patient man."

"And that's with a natural death. This is different, Tim.

Very different. We have an unknown subject that needs to be found—sooner than later."

"Okay," Johnson said slowly. "Now I'm intrigued."

"See you back at the station."

"Nice to meet you," Johnson said to Erin. Then he pushed himself off the Jeep and headed toward the spot where Gibson waited.

"So, you think he's up to the job?" Erin asked as the chief started the Jeep and headed back to the road they'd come in on.

"Absolutely." The chief chuckled. "He reminds me of you."

"I'm not sure how to take that."

"I mean it in a good way," the chief said. "He's smart, knowledgeable, and thorough. There's no one better. He graduated top of his class, and he did it on his own, without a family to help him. He won't miss anything."

"Good." Erin sighed. "I wish Kaely was here."

"Seems to me you already know how to read a crime scene. I doubt anyone could have done any better."

"I appreciate that, but she could certainly have helped you more than I did," Erin said. "Hopefully she'll be able to see something in the photos I took for her."

"Thanks for hiding your phone from Gibson. He would have been apoplectic if he'd known you were taking pictures. I hope they help, but if Ms. Hunter is able to add much to your analysis, I'll be shocked. Seems like you learned a lot from her—or from your own research. I'm not sure you should give up your dream of working for the FBI."

In an attempt to steer the conversation away from things she didn't want to talk about, Erin said, "Do you know Steve Tremont?"

"The guy who owns the cabin where you're staying? Sure."

"I met him when I arrived. He seemed . . . nervous. It wasn't because he knew who I was. It was something else. Do you have any idea what that's about?"

The chief laughed. "You'll think it's absurd, but here goes. Steve got a good deal on the cabin, but he's new to the area. Bought the cabin a couple of years ago and only moved here a year ago so he could oversee renovations. He didn't know the cabin's history. I think the locals are having some fun with him. He's a little . . . How do I say this nicely? Pretentious? He moved here from the big city. He finds us . . . quaint."

"Quaint?" Now it was Erin's turn to laugh. "Wow. Yeah, that might make me want to mess with him." She shook her head. "So, about the cabin's history?"

"Are you sure you want to know?" the chief asked. Erin could see from his expression that he wanted to tell her.

"I'm fascinated. Spill it."

"It's pretty spooky. Don't want to give you nightmares."

A scene from Erin's most recent nightmare flashed in her mind. "No," she said more forcefully than she meant to. "Tell me."

"The cabin where you're staying was built in the early eighteen hundreds by a man named William Watcher. He built it for his new bride, Emma. He also bought about fifty acres around the house. That's why it's called Watcher Woods."

"Sounds good so far."

"It was good . . . until it wasn't. About two years after they moved into the cabin, he killed Emma. Then he killed himself. The poem began to circulate not long after that. It's been passed down for generations."

"The poem?"

The chief nodded. "People say they've seen Emma walking through the woods in her dark cape, crying for her lost love."

Erin felt a chill run down her spine as she remembered the sound of sobbing the night before. She realized she was holding her breath, so she let it out slowly. This was silly. There were no ghosts wandering the woods.

"And the poem?"

"You asked for it. It goes like this: 'William Watcher slew his wife. Slit her throat with his butcher knife. Now she wanders Watcher Woods, a ghastly visage in a cloak and hood. If you should hear her mournful cries, you will be the next to die.'"

EIGHT

Erin looked away from the chief, wondering if he could tell how shocked she was by the awful poem. She swallowed hard and forced a smile.

"That's rather gruesome," she said, fighting to appear nonchalant.

The chief's eyebrows shot up. "Your book wasn't exactly tame. I'm surprised that silly poem bothers you."

Erin couldn't tell him about what she'd heard last night. He'd think she was unbalanced. If she thought it had anything to do with the body in the woods, she would have mentioned it. But the woman was dead before she was dumped in the woods. Besides, what she'd heard was probably an animal. Or the wind. She wasn't used to being here and had no idea what the sound actually was.

"So, how long will you be staying?" the chief asked.

"A week. Kaely is joining me later today."

"Brainstorming session?" he asked with a smile.

"No. I just needed some time to chill out. You know, get away."

"I understand," the chief said. "We have quite a few people

who come here to escape the city. It's peaceful here. Tuning out the noise helps you see things more clearly."

"Are you originally from here?"

"Raised here by my grandparents. My mother died when I was three. I never knew my father. I moved to Chicago and joined the police force when I graduated." He shook his head. "It was too much for me. The crime, the awful things people did to each other. Especially the children. I just couldn't take it. Found out the job of police chief was open here, so I applied and was hired."

"Do your grandparents still live here?" Erin asked.

"No, they've passed away. It's just me now. No other family that I know of."

"I'm sorry. My parents are gone too. I have a sister somewhere, but we're not in touch."

"Sounds like we're both short on family," he said.

Erin nodded.

"So, when *is* your next book coming out?" he asked. "You can probably tell that I'm a fan."

The question. One that she was asked constantly. One she had no answers for. Erin shrugged. "I have no idea. To be honest, I'm not sure I want to write another one. *Dark Matters* was cathartic. I wrote it because I needed to. But I've never seen myself as a novelist."

"I'd guess there are a lot of authors out there who would like to be in your shoes. You write a book that goes straight to the bestsellers list, but you don't see yourself as a novelist? Ouch."

The chief was very perceptive. Other authors had reached out to her on social media, but she hadn't reached back. She wasn't comfortable pretending to be something she wasn't.

Some reacted badly to her lack of response, branding her as a snob. Others were very nice—people she'd like to know, if she stayed involved in that community. She didn't feel comfortable explaining herself to a stranger. True, Adrian Nightengale seemed to be a nice person—someone easy to talk to. But the only human being she really shared her feelings with was Kaely—and that had taken some time. Kaely was . . . different. She didn't seem to have an agenda, and she certainly wasn't impressed with Erin's celebrity.

She glanced sideways at Adrian. He really was good-looking. He pushed his hair back with his right hand, and she realized he was wearing a hearing aid.

He turned his head and caught her gaze. Without thinking, she blurted out, "You wear hearing aids?"

He smiled. "Yeah. I have noise-induced hearing loss. Sirens, target training, lots of things that can affect police officers."

"My partner, Scott, suffered from NIHL. He wore hearing aids too. Didn't affect his job performance at all."

Most people didn't realize that police officers couldn't wear hearing protection. They had to always be aware of their surroundings. The general public had no idea how many in law enforcement had been affected by all the noise they had to endure. Thankfully, Erin's hearing was okay. Scott had gotten the worst of it.

The chief nodded. "I do fine as long as I'm wearing them."

"So that's the noise you wanted to get away from? The streets of Chicago?"

"Well, it's certainly quieter here."

The chief slowed down and stopped the Jeep. They were back at the cabin. Erin was surprised they were already here.

"Thanks for the assistance," he said.

"I hope it really did help. Could you . . . I mean, would you . . ."

"Keep you apprised of our progress?" he said.

"I'd like that. If it's okay."

"Of course it's okay," he said.

Erin got out of the Jeep. Before she closed the door, she said, "I hope you catch him, Chief. And thanks for the story about the cabin. Hopefully, I'll be able to sleep tonight."

He laughed heartily. "I hope so too. And it's Adrian. No one calls me *chief* except my officers—and only when we're on duty."

"Okay, Adrian. It was nice meeting you."

"You too."

As Erin walked toward the front door of the cabin, a voice whispered in her head. *William Watcher slew his wife. Slit her throat with his butcher knife. Now she wanders Watcher Woods, a ghastly visage in a cloak and hood. If you should hear her mournful cries, you will be the next to die.*

Kaely checked the GPS on the rental car. A little over sixteen miles to the cabin. She'd been praying. Praying for the baby she and Noah wanted so badly. But this week was about Erin, not her own problems. It was hard not to think about it, though. It was always there in her mind. She asked God to help her put her own needs on the back burner and concentrate on Erin. Her GPS indicated that a turn was coming, so she focused her attention on the upcoming exit. Once she made it, she relaxed some. Spending a week with Erin had sounded like exactly what she needed. She and Erin had clicked from the beginning, and she felt connected to the woman she'd spent so much time with...online. But now they would be face-to-face. Would the easy relationship they'd created stay the same?

She checked her GPS again. Another twenty minutes, and she'd be there. "God, Erin has had so much pain in her life," she prayed quietly. "I understand that. Help me to be sensitive and compassionate. You've brought me so far, and I really want to see her soul healed too. You're the only One who can do that. Help me to not think I can do Your job." She sighed heavily. "And keep reminding me to stay out of Your way, okay?"

This was going to be an interesting week. As she made the last turn toward the cabin, Kaely whispered the same prayer she'd prayed so many times. "Not my will, Lord. Just Yours."

NINE

Adrian dropped Erin off at the cabin and headed to the station. He needed to concentrate on the case he'd just been handed. A murder. He needed to find the killer and bring justice to the poor woman whose body was probably on the way to the ME's office by now. Hopefully, it wouldn't take them long to find out who she was. Surely, someone was missing her.

His thoughts drifted to Erin Delaney. She was guarded. Private. He was usually pretty perceptive about people, but she wouldn't allow him past the wall she'd erected around herself. He tried to shake off thoughts about her, but her wide green eyes kept popping into his mind. He'd seen the pain inside them, and he wanted to ease it. But why? She wasn't his type.

He'd told the truth about her book. He'd enjoyed it. It was realistic. She'd captured the heart of law enforcement and those who carried ghosts inside them. Ghosts who whispered in their minds at night when they tried to sleep. Although the public didn't realize it, they wept over victims and faced confusion when confronted with the evil that human beings could inflict on each other. Although her powerful story had held him in its thrall, it lacked redemption. Hope. He felt certain Erin Delaney didn't know God. Adrian couldn't be involved with someone who didn't share his faith. Yet, he'd felt something. Something he couldn't explain. She really was amazing. Naturally talented. She'd provided him with more information than Dr. Gibson ever could have. She clearly noticed things that others didn't.

When he reached the station, he parked and went inside. Now began the search for the identity of the dead woman. Then, once they knew who she was, he'd have to locate her family. He'd had to notify family members in Sanctuary before, but this was different. This appeared to be a senseless death. Something that shouldn't have happened. There was a very dangerous person in the area, near the town and the people he cared for. Did the killer pick his victim at random? Or was he hunting something specific? Erin hadn't been sure. She'd said that the next victim or victims would tell them more. But there was no way Adrian could allow some maniac to add more bodies to his horrific count.

When he reached his office, his administrative assistant stopped him before he opened his door. Lisa Parrish wasn't a police officer, but she knew as much or more than most of the officers under his command.

"Hey, got a call from Merle Hubbard over at the resort. Seems like some woman who's been staying there didn't check out this morning when she was supposed to. A Chloe Banner. She left last night to go to the Grits and Grains event. Should have been back by now. He went into her room. All her things are still there, and it appears that her bed wasn't slept in. It's possible this could be your victim."

"Or some tourist who drank too much and didn't make

it back to her room." Adrian sighed. "Call Merle and tell him . . ."

"Not to touch anything?" Lisa finished for him. She grinned. "We may not get much action here, but I watch *CSI*, *Blue Bloods*, and *Law & Order*. I know about preserving a crime scene."

"Seems we need some training," Adrian said. "Not sure watching TV is the proper way for my staff to learn about protecting evidence."

Lisa laughed. "I'm just teasing you, boss. You've done a great job training your people. And Tim has been a real asset. I'm sure he'll be careful with the scene. Hopefully, he'll find something that will help. Although, I hear that author you took to look at our victim had some helpful insights."

Adrian frowned at her. "I just left there. How can you possibly know what happened just . . ." He looked at his watch, "an hour ago? And don't tell me that news travels fast in a small town. That may be true, but nothing moves this fast."

Lisa's face flushed and she began to fiddle with a file on her desk. Adrian didn't move, just continued to watch her. Finally, she sighed loudly and looked up.

"Doc Gibson's nurse and I are good friends. He called her from the scene to let her know when he'd get back to the office. Seems he wasn't too thrilled about that Delaney woman being there."

"You need to be careful listening to gossip. It's usually not completely accurate. And Joyce isn't the most reliable person. You know that, right?"

Lisa didn't say anything. She just stared at the file in front of her as if it was the most interesting thing she'd ever seen.

"You'd get more out of that file if it wasn't upside down."

"Oh, for crying out loud," Lisa said. "I need to know what's going on in Sanctuary. I answer the phone. How would it look if all I ever said was 'I have no information about that,' the way you told me to?"

"They would probably think that you don't have any information about whatever it is they want to know. They would also be glad to know that the Sanctuary PD doesn't spread idle gossip."

Lisa leaned back in her chair and pressed her lips together tightly, obviously trying to keep from smiling. Then she shook her head. "I hear you, boss. I'm sorry. I just get . . . curious, you know?"

He grinned at her. Time to let her off the hook. He honestly had no idea what he'd do without her. Lisa kept the station on track. She might be a little nosy, but she was outstanding at her job.

"Yes, I know. I'll try to do better at keeping you updated. But I need you to try hard not to spread things that might not be true. Or information I don't want out there yet." He frowned and then glanced around him. There were several officers at their desks. To avoid being overheard, Adrian nodded toward his office door. "Let's go into my office. I'll fill you in on what I can, but it's important you don't share what I tell you. I'll brief everyone else when I'm certain who our victim is. I'm only telling you this now because of the calls you might get this afternoon." He lowered his voice. "We may have a very serious situation on our hands, and we need to keep it quiet. When we're done, I've got to get over to the resort and check out the missing woman's room."

"You could send someone else," Lisa said.

"I know, but just in case it's the woman we found this morning, I want to be there."

Lisa nodded and stood up. She followed him into his office and shut the door behind her. Adrian sat on the edge of his desk and motioned to Lisa to sit down in one of the nearby chairs. He quickly filled her in on the scene and what they'd learned.

"That Delaney woman thinks we have a serial killer?" Lisa's mouth gaped open. "We've never had a serial killer in Sanctuary."

"That may be true, "Adrian said, "but Sanctuary began with a death. Let's hope its legacy isn't continuing." He pointed at her to emphasize his next words. "We're still not sure someone else will die, so you absolutely cannot repeat what I told you. If you get any phone calls about this case, all you know is that we found a body in Watcher Woods. There's no more information right now. When we identify her, we can share that, but only that. Do you understand?"

He realized his tone was firm, but he'd seen in Chicago what could happen when cases got out of hand and stories were spread that contained false information or half-truths. Convictions could be overturned and trials moved out of the area because of overblown media attention. He wasn't going to let that happen. It would only impede the investigation. He trusted Lisa to keep a lid on things until more facts could be released.

If there really was a serial killer in Sanctuary, Adrian was determined to stop him and make sure he paid fully for the evil he'd brought here.

TEN

They'd found his sacrifice. It made him feel powerful, excited. He hated God and the angels He'd dispatched to take away his mother. Thankfully, he'd found another god. One who filled him with revulsion for human beings and promised him dominance over the whims of a being who had robbed him of the only thing he'd ever loved. He had more to do. Much more. And when it was done, he'd continue to hide in plain sight. No one suspected who he really was. No one ever had. When he was young, the principal at his grade school had told his grandparents that he was destructive. Troubled. The principal recommended a *therapist*. This ridiculous person had prescribed some kind of pills. Supposedly, they would make him *normal*. Whatever that was.

He tried them, but they made him feel dead inside. Powerless. That's when his new god, the one who really cared about him, taught him how to play the game. To pretend that he was like everyone else. That he cared about other people. It wasn't true. To him, people were nonexistent. Just pieces of meat that moved around and said things. Stupid, useless beings. In his world, the one his god had created for him, he was the only person who mattered. Who was truly alive. His god was helping him to become the person he was created to be. A ruler. A judge. A king. In bed at night, he'd laugh at everyone. His grandparents, his teachers, the principal he'd thought about killing. When he became quiet, he could hear the whispers. *You can do whatever you want. You can make the angels cry.* His god began to show him what he needed to do so he could fulfill his true destiny. First, he killed his grandparents. No one knew he'd done it. It was easy. Supposedly, his grandfather had fallen into the creek, hit his head, and drowned. According to the local ME, anyway. The truth was, he'd hit him on the head and held him under the water. Then he went home and helped his grandmother clean the house. No one suspected him, of course, and he acted sad when he heard the news. Then, a year later, when he was eighteen, his grandmother accidentally took too much of her heart medication. Some people wondered if she'd done it on purpose, but no one even considered that he was involved. After all, he was the good grandson. "He's turned into such a good boy" people would say. Even the principal who had originally suggested that he needed therapy was convinced he was cured. He had become a new creation. Someone people liked and respected. They had no idea how much he despised them. Eventually, he quit seeing the therapist. He was pretty sure he'd convinced the charlatan that he was okay, but from time to time, he'd seen a look in the doctor's eyes that made him wonder. Eventually, the therapist moved away. Good thing for him. If he hadn't, he might have had to die too.

After selling his grandparents' farm, he went to college. There he received additional training. Became someone who could easily find a position in Sanctuary. One that would make it simple for him to fulfill the vow he'd made. People accepted him here. Those who remembered his troubled childhood were gone. Now the area was full of tourists. It was a great hunting ground, and he was ready to strike again . . .

And again.

And again.

Erin nibbled on some of the fresh fruit she'd found in the refrigerator. She'd decided to wait for lunch until Kaely arrived. She probably hadn't had a chance to eat.

Erin sat in the living room, her body nestled into the soft leather couch that faced the massive stone fireplace. Her mind was in overdrive, bouncing from the body found in the woods to meeting Kaely face-to-face. Kaely was so easy to talk to. She knew what Kaely looked like and had spent hours and hours on the phone and online with her. So why was she so nervous about spending time with her in person? How could it be any different? She knew Kaely, and Kaely knew her. So why couldn't she keep her legs still? They kept tapping out a beat on the wooden planked floor. Every time she tried to quiet them, they'd start again a few minutes later. True, she hadn't been around a lot of people after . . . that night . . . but she'd been a police officer for several years. She'd spent a lot of time around people. Friends had tried to support her after the shooting, but one by one she'd pushed them away. She needed time to process, she'd told them. But here she was two years later, still not past what had happened. Although she'd written her book as a way to heal, in the end, it had become more of a burden than a blessing. She almost wished she'd never written it. But it had brought Kaely into her life. And money. Enough money that she didn't have to find another job right now—which would have been torture. What could she possibly do? Become a security guard? That's what some of the other cops who'd quit had done, but she just couldn't see herself protecting buildings instead of people. She knew her attitude was wrong, but there it was. Writing the book had seemed like a perfect escape, but she hadn't counted on the kind of success she'd experienced. Now it seemed that everyone wanted to be in her life—something she absolutely didn't want. Kaely was the only person who seemed to understand. In a sudden flash of self-awareness, she realized she was afraid Kaely wouldn't like her. And for the first time in a long time, it mattered.

She forced her thoughts back to the crime scene she'd witnessed earlier, wondering if she'd missed anything. As she replayed the scene in her mind, she suddenly heard a car door slam. Kaely. Erin swallowed hard and got to her feet, butterflies racing around in her gut like crazed bees, and went to the door. She waited for the knock she knew was coming, took a deep breath, and swung the door open. Kaely's curly auburn hair was pulled back from her face with hair clips, and her dark eyes were fastened on Erin's. But the thing that stood out in that moment was her wide smile. It chased away any nervousness she'd been feeling.

"Hi, Erin!"

Before she could stop to think, Erin stepped forward and wrapped her arms around the only real friend she had now. She only felt joy that Kaely was here. She knew Kaely. And

Kaely knew her—and accepted her. She had to blink away the tears that filled her eyes before she let Kaely go.

"I'm so glad you found the cabin," Erin said, holding the door wide so Kaely could come inside with her large duffle bag. "Can I help you get the rest of your luggage out of the car?" she asked.

Kaely laughed. "When you've worked for the FBI, you learn how to pack lightly. Believe it or not, I've got everything I need in here."

"You'll have to teach me that trick," Erin said.

Kaely smiled. "I'd be happy to. The trick is packing outfits with interchangeable pieces." She waved her hand toward Erin. "Let's save that for later. Show me around?"

"Sure, but as soon as possible, we need to talk."

Kaely frowned. "Uh, oh. Is something wrong with the cabin?"

Erin sighed. "Not sure how to answer that. Would you like me to start with the ghost that's been roaming the woods for decades or the dead body just discovered this morning?"

ELEVEN

"Wow," was all Kaely could say by the time Erin finished telling her about her morning. "I thought this kind of stuff only happened to me."

Erin grinned. "If I wasn't convinced you were an honest person, I wouldn't have believed all the stories you told me when we were working on the book. I think I'm going to have to blame you for this one too."

Kaely laughed. They'd just finished ham and cheese sandwiches with fruit and ice cream. She was impressed with the cabin and all the food Steve had left for them. He and Noah hadn't seen each other in years, so she hadn't expected this kind of welcome. At least they wouldn't have to worry about shopping for a lot of supplies. That would give them more time to talk. Kaely was here to listen—something Erin needed right now to help her deal with the tragedy she'd endured. Kaely also hoped to get her out a few times to have some fun. Shutting herself up in her apartment for the past two years wasn't healthy. Kaely had seen some cute shops and a few restaurants in Sanctuary. Hopefully, she could talk Erin into visiting the town while they were here.

For now, though, they could both just kick back and relax. Well, anyway that was the plan before Erin told her about the body found in the woods.

Kaely scooted off the bar stool next to the breakfast bar and gathered their dishes. She took them over to the sink, rinsed them off, and stacked them up. Might as well wait for tonight before running the dishwasher. When she turned around, she caught Erin frowning at her. Although Kaely felt as if they were already friends, being together face-to-face was different. A little awkwardness was normal.

"You said you took some pictures?" she asked.

"Yeah." Erin picked up her phone from the counter and clicked a few buttons.

Kaely sat down next to her and waited.

"I probably went overboard," she said. "I just wanted to make sure you saw everything." She handed the phone to Kaely, who took it and began scrolling through the photos.

"Tell me again what you told the chief," she said as she studied each one.

Erin began to repeat her observations while Kaely nodded.

"So can you do that thing?" Erin asked.

"Not sure what *thing* you mean."

Kaely knew what Erin was referring to. She'd shared her profiling technique with her, and Erin had incorporated a modified version of it into her book. But in reality, Kaely hadn't used it in a while. After Noah was transferred to the Behavioral Analysis Unit at Quantico, she'd quietly worked a few profiles with him without his supervisors knowing. It still worked well for her, but she avoided teaching it to others. A few years earlier, she'd shared it with someone else and the results had been a little disturbing. It had reminded her that there were two forces at work in the world. One good—and one decidedly evil. She had authority over evil through her relationship with Christ, but not everyone else knew about that power or were trained to use it.

"Let me get settled in," she said. "Then we can talk about that. So, about this ghost . . ."

"I'm sure you don't believe in that type of thing," Erin said. "But I'm not so sure. I've heard some weird stories."

It was true that Kaely didn't believe in the kind of ghosts Erin was talking about, but she knew that demons were real. However, that wasn't a conversation she could have with Erin now. It wouldn't make any sense to her. Kaely smiled. "Why do you think I don't believe in ghosts?"

Erin frowned. "Do you? I mean, I know you're a Christian."

"Maybe I don't, but it's clear to me something odd happened to you. My guess is that some kind of animal made the noise you heard. But I have to tell you, it would have spooked me too. I may be a Christian, but I'm still human."

Erin laughed nervously. "I'm sorry. I didn't mean to imply that you weren't."

"It's okay. I really don't get offended easily. I'm the same person you've talked to on the phone for the past couple of years. Just relax, okay?"

Erin nodded. "Thank you. I guess I am a little tense. One of the officers who worked out of my station was a Christian. She was pretty hard to get to know, and I always got the feeling she was judging me—and everyone else."

"Like I said, Christians are still people. Some are better than others at showing who God is." She shrugged. "That's why it's important to follow Christ—not Christians. I'm sorry she made you feel that way. I hope I never do. If it should ever happen, I give you permission to put salt in my coffee."

Erin grinned. "I'd say that's not a very harsh reprimand, but I know how much you love your coffee."

Kaely laughed. "Now, if you'll show me to my room, I'll unpack."

"There are three bedrooms upstairs. I slept in one of them last night, but if you want it, I'll gladly move."

"I'm not very particular," Kaely said. "I care more about a soft bed than I do about the room's decor."

"Okay. I'll lead the way."

Kaely followed Erin upstairs and chose the bedroom at the other end of the hall. The bed was soft, and there was an electric blanket underneath the soft, down comforter. It had a fireplace, just like Erin's, and a bathroom attached. The walls were painted a dusty blue and the comforter was cream colored with blue and cream accent pillows. It was restful and inviting. Besides spending time with Erin, Kaely wanted to relax—get a break from the treatments and the worries about getting pregnant. Although she was distressed to learn that a young woman had been murdered, the idea of profiling an UNSUB actually appealed to her. Although her first goal was to start a family, she missed working for the FBI. She'd spent several years working for the St. Louis field office after being transferred out of the BAU because of her father, a notorious serial killer. She missed her friends there, especially her boss, Special Agent in Charge Solomon Slattery. They stayed in touch by phone and online, but it wasn't the same. She and Noah were making friends in Virginia, and that helped. They'd found a great church with wonderful people. It would take some time, but she could tell that she and Noah were going to be happy there.

But for now, she not only had a chance to help Erin, she could also work a profile for the local police. Creating the profile of an unknown subject was like putting together a puzzle. The stakes were life and death, and the reward came when your profile helped authorities locate and arrest a criminal. It was incredibly satisfying. Of course, there was a downside. A terrible price that had to be paid if you chose to pursue a career in law enforcement. Only those on the inside truly understood what it was like to view horrific photos of victims and hear stories that couldn't be repeated anywhere else. Most serial killings had a sexual aspect that the public never heard about.

At this point, Kaely was pretty sure the woman found in the woods hadn't been molested by her killer. The white dress suggested purity. This wasn't a sexual sadist. This killer would never molest someone he treated so carefully. Kaely felt that the angel figurine had something to do with his reason for killing. His anger wasn't directed toward the woman. So, what did it mean? Did he think the angels were telling him to kill? That didn't quite feel right. This crime scene was different. Kaely suspected that writing a profile wasn't going to be easy. There was something odd about the scene and the message the killer had sent.

She'd just unpacked when she heard the doorbell ring downstairs. She checked out her reflection in the bathroom mirror and then headed down to where Erin waited. She was certain that dealing with the local police was a strain for Erin. She would most likely need a buffer. Kaely suspected Erin had developed agoraphobia. She barely ventured out of her apartment, so this trip was a great step in the right direction. She was convinced that the trust they'd built between them was the reason Erin was willing to meet her here—someplace out of her comfort zone.

"Are you expecting anyone?" she asked Erin when she joined her near the front door.

Erin shook her head. "Didn't expect anyone earlier either. Now what?"

Kaely stayed close to Erin as she opened the door. A tall man with dark hair and striking hazel eyes stood there. It was clear by his expression that he was upset. His body language made it clear he was uptight and very uncomfortable. Why?

"Chief Nightingale," Erin said, "this is my friend Kaely Quinn-Hunter."

"Nice to meet you, Chief," Kaely said, trying to fill the awkward silence.

The chief nodded at her. "I . . . I don't quite know how to tell you this," he said, after clearing his throat. "But there are more. . . . Bodies, that is. So far, we've found three of them."

TWELVE

Erin looked at Kaely, who stared at the chief with her mouth open. Erin was pretty sure she knew what Kaely was thinking. *Here we go again.*

"Can you tell how long they've been there, Chief?" she asked.

"These are older," he said slowly. "At least one is. All of them buried not far from the body we found this morning. But maybe they're not connected."

"Of course they're connected," Erin said sharply.

Kaely reached out and touched her friend's arm.

"I . . . I'm sorry," Erin said. "I shouldn't have snapped at you. I didn't mind helping you with the body this morning, but seriously? I was really hoping for time to relax. Not . . . this."

"I'm sorry," the chief said. "This isn't your situation to worry about. I shouldn't have bothered you."

"No, you were right to come here," Kaely said gently. She crossed her arms over her chest. "Let me ask you a question, Chief. How long have you lived in this area?"

Chief Nightengale frowned. "A long time. Why?"

"Have you ever found bodies in the woods before?"

He frowned and shook his head. "No. Never."

"So, you find one body lying on top of the ground and then uncover three more buried near the same location. What are the chances they're not related?"

"I see your point. But why leave one body exposed and the others under the ground?"

Erin glanced at Kaely. She was pretty sure she knew the answer, but she wanted to hear it from Kaely.

"The other bodies were practice," she said, echoing Erin's suspicions. "He buried them because they weren't right. Weren't what he wanted. The one you found was perfect in his estimation. There will be more."

The chief's face turned pale. "I was afraid you were going to say that." He shifted back and forth on his feet. "Look, I want to call the FBI in on this, but the mayor and the council won't go for it. They're not convinced the bodies we just discovered have anything to do with the woman we found this morning. They're also afraid a large FBI presence would hurt the tourist trade. It's stupid. This isn't our busy season."

"But if it gets out to the media, it could definitely impact the area for a while," Kaely said. "Not that I agree with them. I don't. I'm just trying to explain their reasoning."

"Well, if they won't change their minds, I could really use your help."

Erin had learned a lot about the FBI from Kaely. The chief was right. Unless local authorities invited them, they wouldn't interfere in a local investigation. That would only change if this was a federal crime. Which, of course, it wasn't.

"I understand," Erin said. "I'm certain Kaely can help you." She looked at Kaely, who stared at the ground. What was she thinking? Had Erin just offered Kaely's assistance without her permission? But why wouldn't she want to help?

Before she could say anything else, Kaely said, "Chief Nightengale, I'd be happy to write a profile for you. It should help you narrow your search. Profiles aren't always right, but they're usually helpful. But first, I need to ask you some questions."

"I've got to get back to the scene," he said. "Can you come with me?"

Kaely looked at Erin. "Is that okay with you?"

Erin nodded. "Of course. It's your decision."

Kaely nodded and then turned her head and met the chief's gaze. "Before we leave, I need to ask how you found the other bodies."

The chief frowned. "Our dogs. We have two of them. They used to work as cadaver dogs in Knoxville. When Mutt and Jeff were retired, my administrative assistant, Lisa, adopted them. One of my officers let them out after Miss Delaney left, just to see if they could pick up any kind of a trail. They went nuts. Ran to a spot about twenty yards from the body we found this morning. Started pawing at the ground. My officers dug around and found the first body. After that, they just followed the dogs. They alerted two more times. After the other two bodies were dug up, they quieted down. And yes, my officers wondered if there were more, so they allowed them free rein. They just went back to the car. If there's anything else out there, they didn't alert to it."

Kaely nodded. "Your UNSUB either lives in the area or he comes here regularly. We need to narrow down TOD for each victim."

"The doc is looking them over now and should be able

to give us an estimated time of death sometime today. If I had to guess, I'd say at least one of them has been there over a year. But I'll let Dr. Gibson give you a more definitive time frame."

"Okay," Kaely said. "We'll get our jackets and join you shortly."

"Thanks. I'll wait out here for you. And by the way," he said, addressing Erin. "The body you saw this morning was identified as a woman who went missing from our local resort. I thought you'd want to know." The chief turned and walked down the steps, headed for his car.

"I'm sorry about this," Erin said after closing the door. "I'm sure this isn't what you were expecting."

"Actually, I should have known," Kaely said with a sigh. "I swear, it's like this kind of thing follows me wherever I go."

"I may not believe in God," Erin said, "but if I did, I might think that maybe this happens because it's supposed to. Because it's your calling. God is using you to help people."

Kaely's eyebrows shot up. "For someone who doesn't believe in God, that was pretty intuitive. You could be right." She shook her head. "I have to admit that part of me has missed this. Just helping to bring justice to victims and their families." She grinned at Erin. "Not the people dying thing."

In spite of herself, Erin laughed. "That's awful."

"Don't point your finger at me," Kaely said, smiling. "You write about this kind of stuff."

"Okay, we're both terrible human beings," Erin said, grinning. "Let's grab our coats and get in the car."

Kaely saluted her. "Yes, ma'am."

As Erin got her coat and pulled it on, she realized that, even though she'd been worried about going out in public, away from her safe space, for the first time since she'd arrived in Sanctuary, she wasn't afraid.

They'd taken the bait. He hadn't been certain about displaying his first offering until he found out the famous author and her FBI friend were coming here. After three imperfect attempts, he'd felt confident enough to share this gift with the world. It showed his brilliance, and he was proud of it. They would never connect it to him. He would beat them at their own game. And he would never stop. He'd studied their methods and knew how they thought. He intended to contradict every one of their suppositions.

He would not only break them. He would break the angels.

He heard his god sigh with pleasure, and it made him smile.

THIRTEEN

Kaely was silent as the chief drove them to the crime scene. She'd made the comment about death following her in a cavalier manner, not expecting Erin to take it seriously. But there could be some truth in it. Although she'd come here for her friend, she felt the need to disconnect as well. She needed some time to stop thinking about having a baby. She'd planned to do that by concentrating on Erin. Helping someone else was the best way to get your mind off yourself. But now, here she was again. Dead bodies. A serial killer. She knew that there were a lot more serial killers in the world than people realized. The truth was, most of them never made the news. Some killers knew how to cover their tracks. And a lot of deaths were attributed to something else. Accidents. Undetermined deaths. However, one of the traits that led to capture was a psychopath's desire for fame. Then, there were the killers who murdered for the single desire to take a life. They were the most dangerous. Even trained behavioral analysts like Kaely couldn't contribute to their capture. At least this guy was taunting them. Daring them to catch him. That would make it easier to apprehend him.

She'd told Erin that, in some ways, she'd missed this. That was true as well. She'd said perhaps God led her to situations where her help was needed. Erin might not be a Christian, but sometimes God could speak through others. She fought back a smile as the thought *even donkeys* popped into her mind. Not sure Erin would want to be compared to Baalam's donkey. Or Baalam for that matter.

"Hold on," the chief said. "The road is pretty rough here."

Kaely, who was sitting in the backseat, clutched the grab handle. Noah liked to call it *the chicken handle.* Sure enough, the car began to bounce. It was obvious the chief was trying to keep the car as steady as possible, but the road here was dirt and full of holes. Kaely loved the Smoky Mountains, but a lot of the area was rather wild. That was the part she adored the most. If she had her way, she and Noah would retire here someday. For now, they were happy in Virginia. Even though they lived in a more suburban-type neighborhood, they didn't have to drive far to find forests and gorgeous scenery. It wasn't that Kaely was unhappy with the life they had. She just wanted something different someday. Far away from the FBI and Noah's job. She knew how the job could drain you. Change you. She could see the haunted look in his eyes during particularly tough cases. But he felt strongly he was where he was supposed to be. And now, here she was. Was she doing what she was called to do too? Was God telling her she would never be a mother? That this was what He had for her? If so, why did her heart cry out to hold a child? Sometimes in church, watching a mother cradle a baby overwhelmed her emotions so strongly she couldn't stop the tears that spilled unbidden from her eyes.

"Here we are," the chief said suddenly, the wild ride coming to an end. Two police cars and a dark blue truck were parked nearby. "We'll need to walk the rest of the way."

He got out, and they followed him through the woods until they finally reached a clearing. Yellow crime-scene tape protected a rather wide area. Kaely looked around to see if there was another area roped off. Sure enough, about twenty yards away there was another area framed with the same yellow tape—the place where they found the woman this morning. She glanced at Erin. She seemed calm, engaged, interested. She would have made a great analyst. Kaely wondered if she'd actually been diagnosed with PTSD. If so, that would complicate her ability to join the BAU. For now, the best thing for Erin was to take time healing. She had a lot to overcome. The death of the young girl accidentally killed by Erin's wayward bullet. Watching her partner die. Not only her partner, but a man she'd loved—until he cheated on her. Their relationship was tense, and Erin had been nursing a broken heart. She'd admitted to Kaely that she'd been unkind. Refused to forgive him—even requested a new partner. Now, she not only had to deal with his loss, but she was left to wonder if she should have given him another chance. He'd died after she'd rejected his pleas for forgiveness. It had taken Erin a long time to share this part of her story. She was carrying a lot of guilt. The kind that can crush the spirit.

Kaely noticed an older man kneeling on the ground. She was startled to see that the three covered objects next to him were concealed under plastic tarps. They should have been covered by sterile body sheets. It could be worse. Plastic tarps generally wouldn't carry as many hairs and fibers as cloth sheets. And with bodies this old, holding them together was important. The stronger plastic tarp would do a good job of not only covering them but also being placed underneath so that the bodies could be successfully moved from this spot.

The man stood up and looked at the chief. Then he nodded at Erin. She'd mentioned that the local doctor acting as the ME hadn't been very friendly at their last encounter. Kaely noticed that the doctor's resistance to Erin—and to her—was muted. He'd probably realized he was in over his head with this kind of crime scene.

"Are you ready to look at these bodies?" the chief asked.

"Certainly, if your ME doesn't object," Kaely said loudly enough for the older man to hear. *A little honey to soothe the ego.*

She watched as the man squared his shoulders, some of his dignity restored. "Not at all," he said, waving his hand toward the covered corpses.

The chief held up the crime-scene tape, and Erin and Kaely stepped inside the boundaries. In another setting, it would have been important to cover their shoes with booties, but these deaths happened so long ago, there was very little chance any evidence remained on the ground surrounding the burial site.

The man held out his hand when Kaely approached. "Dr. Gibson," he said.

Kaely shook his hand. "Nice to meet you, Doctor. I'm Kaely Hunter. Thank you for allowing me into your crime scene. I used to work for the FBI and would like to write a profile for the chief. Anything you've observed would help me immensely."

Erin glanced sideways at her, the sides of Erin's mouth twitching slightly. Kaely wasn't trying to be disingenuous. She didn't know Gibson and felt she owed him respect for the position he held. However, Kaely suspected Erin thought she was just trying to *handle* the doctor.

Gibson slowly pulled back the first tarp. This must be the body the chief thought could be over a year old. The problem was, to determine TOD a lot of things came into play. Temperatures in the area, the makeup of the soil, along with animal and insect activity. Still, she felt the chief was pretty close in his estimation.

"It's female," the doctor said. "She was buried in some kinda garment, although it's degraded quite a bit. There are shoes and she's wearin' a necklace. Can't quite tell what it really looks like. Once I get her back to the office, I can clean that up. Other than that, there's not much I can tell you."

"Her right leg was broken at some point," Erin said. "I can see where the bone knit together."

"Yeah, I noticed that," Gibson said, his voice low. Obviously, he was still a little irritated with Erin. "That's a detail the chief will get once I finish my autopsy."

"Do you mind if I take some pictures?" Kaely asked. She nudged Erin in an attempt to encourage her to wait on any other comments for now. They'd go over the photos when they got back to the cabin. Erin looked at her and nodded slightly. She understood.

"Nah, you go ahead," Gibson said.

"Why don't I take the pictures while you look at the other bodies," Erin offered.

"Thanks. Good idea," Kaely replied. Maybe Gibson would relax a bit if Erin wasn't with them.

Gibson led the way to the next tarp. This body had more flesh left. It was pretty disturbing, but Kaely had seen worse.

She hoped it wouldn't upset Erin and wondered if she should take the pictures herself. She looked it over while Gibson told her what he'd seen. He was actually pretty good at pointing out what was important.

"The rib has been nicked here," he said, pointing toward the ribcage.

"You're right," Kaely said. "I didn't notice that on the other body."

Gibson nodded. "People don't realize that most killers who stab their victims miss the heart unless they know what they're doin'. Missin' the ribs isn't easy."

Surprised, Kaely looked up at him. "You're absolutely right. I see that all the time in TV shows and movies. And the other thing is . . ."

"Bright red blood after several hours?" Gibson interjected.

"Exactly. Drives me up the wall."

"Me too. I suspect Ms. Delaney got her facts right because she had you to help her."

Erin had told her that the doctor didn't seem to know who she was. Obviously, that was wrong. He'd read her book.

"Well, she also used to be a police officer, you know," Kaely said, "and as far as the rest of it, she was a quick learner." She smiled at him. "The chief is very fortunate to have someone like you here."

If Gibson was a rooster, he probably would have puffed his chest out and crowed. "I'm grateful you're around to help," he said. He pointed toward a tall man with glasses and dark blond hair talking to a police officer a few yards away.

"That's Detective Johnson. He's got a lot of training in forensics. To be honest, with you two here, me, and the detective,

I think we can handle this thing." He pointed toward the last corpse. "You ready to look at the next one?"

She nodded. As she followed the doctor toward the last blue tarp, she felt a chill. It really was getting colder. She couldn't help but shiver.

"We gotta snowstorm headed our way tomorrow night," the doctor said, noticing her discomfort. "The temps are dropping fast. That doesn't bode well."

"It's only November," Kaely said. "Isn't that a little early for this area?"

"Not really," he replied. "But this one may be a doozy. Worse than we've had for a while."

Kaely thought back to the last time she'd had to deal with a snowstorm and a serial killer. She really wasn't looking forward to reliving that.

She stopped when they reached the last body. The doctor pulled back the tarp, and Kaely gasped. The girl couldn't have died more than three months ago. She would have been considered well preserved if it weren't for the viciousness of the attack she'd endured. Instinct told her that the killer hadn't been happy with his results and had taken it out on this poor woman. They were dealing with someone who was cold, calculated, organized . . . and full of the kind of rage that wouldn't be contained.

She waited for Erin, who turned white as a sheet when she approached the last body. Kaely reached out to grab her arm when she noticed that she swayed a little. Erin pulled her arm away, took the pictures, and then hurried back to where the chief had parked the Jeep. Kaely followed behind her. She was clearly upset, and Kaely was worried. Maybe this was too much for Erin right now. It was then that she noticed the tall man, the one Gibson had said was the forensic specialist, watching them out of the corner of his eye. He smiled at her, and she returned his smile, but not before she noticed that his right hand was bandaged. Although she could be wrong, it almost seemed as if he tried to hide it from her.

FOURTEEN

Erin carried two cups of hot chocolate over to the coffee table. Kaely had started a fire in the massive fireplace. Although she'd seen many horrific scenes as a police officer in St. Louis, the savagery of the last body she'd witnessed in the woods had shaken her to her core. She tried to keep her hands steady but was pretty sure Kaely noticed her trembling fingers.

She sat down in the overstuffed leather chair next to the couch. "You said you were surprised by the third body they uncovered."

Kaely nodded. "You know that serial killers are angry. But with an organized killer, that anger is usually displayed in certain ways. Posing the body in a way to humiliate the victim, removing their clothes . . . and there are other things. But the rage displayed in the last body we saw this afternoon . . ." She shook her head. "Normally, I would say that she was the main target, but I don't believe that's true. The way he posed the woman found this morning, the one you saw? He's finally got it right. The other three bodies were failures. The savagery we saw on the third body? His anger was because he was frustrated with his lack of success."

"That's chilling," Erin said.

"Yeah, it is. And my guess? He's killed before this. Not in the same way. This is special. His mission. But many times, we find that serial killers have taken lives when they were young. People they knew and hated. Most of the time the deaths were made to look like accidents. Sometimes they're caught, but many times they get away with it."

"We should go over the photos," Erin said. "I think it took him several tries to learn how to miss the ribs and hit the heart."

Kaely nodded. "I tend to agree with you. Look, we came here so you could relax and we could talk. This isn't exactly working out the way we'd planned."

Erin was grateful that Kaely cared about her, but she was a little embarrassed that she'd reacted so strongly to the crime scene. She'd tried to hide it, but Kaely had noticed. This wasn't her first body. Her first murder. Far from it. Why had the third buried body upset her so much?

"I'm fine. Really. I think it's because of that . . . that night. As a police officer, I became hardened to most of it. But watching Scott die and seeing that little girl . . ."

"It's personal now," Kaely said gently. "It's taken over your nightmares."

"Yeah."

Kaely's voice held no hint of pity. She was just stating fact. Her understanding of Erin's struggle was the reason she'd been able to share what she was going through with Kaely. No one else seemed to be able to help her. Strengthen her. Her close friends on the force hadn't been able to give her what she needed. What she craved. Although several of them tried, to be honest, Erin felt that most of them were embarrassed by her emotional state. Many times, those in law enforcement were only able to face the job if they could build a wall around themselves. If the wall should ever crack, their world would crumble. Empathizing with her was too dangerous. It would make them vulnerable in a way they couldn't handle. But Kaely was different. Erin was certain it was because she'd had to face her own demons and knew what it was like.

"Okay, so here's the deal," Kaely said. "We'll talk about the case tonight, but tomorrow, we go into town and do some shopping. Then we come back here and talk about . . . other things."

Erin felt a stab of fear that made it hard to breathe. "What . . . what are we shopping for? Food? We have a lot. More than we could possibly eat."

Kaely's eyebrows shot up. "Well, we might need a few things. Remember that Dr. Gibson said a snowstorm could be headed our way. But the shopping I'm talking about has nothing to do with necessary supplies. I noticed a lot of cute stores on my way in. We're going shopping for fun." She paused and stared at Erin a moment before saying, "I know you've had trouble getting out of your apartment, Erin. But you can't lock yourself away forever. You know it's not a reasonable fear, right?"

Erin took a deep breath, trying to quell the anxiety that threatened to overwhelm her. The words *I can't do that* almost slipped out of her mouth. But then she remembered when she actually used to love spending an afternoon shopping for cute clothes or gifts for her friends. Now they were all gone. She'd cut everyone out of her life. She really was alone. She didn't even have any family left. Her parents were both dead, and her sister had disappeared years ago. She had no idea where she was. Maybe Kaely was right. Maybe trying to enjoy herself the way she used to would help.

"I'll be with you," Kaely said. "And anytime you want to come back here, we'll leave. Okay?"

"All right," she said, trying to keep her voice from shaking. "Some of those shops really did look interesting. I guess if I was able to get into a car and drive all the way here, I should be able to spend some time in Sanctuary." She offered Kaely a small smile. "I still say you picked this place because of the name."

Kaely laughed. "I wish I was that clever. When I called Steve for suggestions of places to stay in the area, he told me he'd recently bought and restored this cabin. It just happened to be in this town. I promise I had nothing to do with it." She stood up. "Let me see what I can find us for supper. Then we'll look at the photos. Can you put them on the TV so we can see them better?"

"I think so. I'll work on it while you rustle up some grub."

Kaely laughed. "The cowgirl in you coming out?"

"Well, we are in the wilderness."

"At least we're driving cars instead of riding horses. It's getting really chilly out there. Hope this storm doesn't knock out the electricity. Not sure even this fireplace can heat the whole place."

"Steve told me there's an automatic generator in case anything happens."

"Suddenly, I love Steve," Kaely said.

"Yeah, I'm growing fonder of him too. I just wish he'd

told us before we arrived that a storm was on the way. We could have postponed our trip until things settled down." Erin frowned. "You don't need to know how to read people to see that Steve was acting a little weird about the cabin."

"I'm pretty sure it's too cold even for the ghost tonight." Kaely stood up and turned around. "You know, I never thought of Steve like that. Believing something so silly, I mean."

"I don't know," Erin said. "He spooked me." At Kaely's expression, she waved her hand dismissively. "I know you don't believe it, but I've seen some strange things."

"Okay, how's this? I'll protect you from ghosts if you get those photos from your phone onto the TV."

Erin smiled at her. "Deal."

While Kaely continued to rummage through the refrigerator, Erin set up the TV settings and cast the photos from her phone onto the screen. Now they could gaze at larger images of death. Not a very wholesome collection to view while eating supper—at least for some people. Except for the last body they'd viewed today, she found the photos very interesting.

As she clicked through them, she became so involved, she didn't notice when Kaely came back into the room. When she spoke, Erin jumped.

"Sorry," she said. "I find this fascinating."

"It is. Maybe we should eat first before we go through them?"

Erin shrugged. "Doesn't bother me, but if you want to, we can wait."

Kaely shook her head. "I'm good. I agree with you that this UNSUB is really remarkable. He isn't staying true to what I'd expect to see. The savagery of the body we saw this afternoon compared to the way he dressed the victim from this morning. Dressing her in white. Closing her eyes. The statue in her hands. That killing was careful. Controlled. So different."

Kaely put a plate and utensils down in front of Erin. Blackened salmon, garlic mashed potatoes, and roasted asparagus. These premade meals were incredible. They smelled great.

Kaely was right. The bodies that were buried were handled differently than the one found in the woods this morning. They were assuming that his anger was because he was learning—but could there be something they were missing? To stop him, they'd need to understand something that was beyond reason. Something vicious and malevolent.

FIFTEEN

"Have you encountered an UNSUB like this before?" Erin asked Kaely before she took another bite of her salmon.

She shook her head. "I've encountered killers who practiced first. More than once. But changing his MO as much as he has? No, not really. Not like this."

"Do you think he's perfected his method of killing?"

Kaely sighed. "Yes, but one thing to remember. Many times, it's that very mindset that makes it easier to catch them."

Erin frowned. "How do you mean?"

"It actually makes them more predictable. If we're right, and he's figured out how to kill the way he feels compelled to, we can begin to predict his next movements. It helps us to understand his signature. The thing that drives him."

"And if we're wrong?"

Kaely shrugged. "Then things will become much harder. Let's hope he sticks to his plan." She sighed and shook her head. "I know how cold that sounds, but hopefully you understand what I mean."

"He's only started, hasn't he?"

"Yeah," Kaely said. "I'm afraid that's true."

Erin frowned. "Care to share your prediction for his next attempt?"

Kaely was quiet for a moment. "You know, I don't think our UNSUB will move too far out of the area. The forest is huge. It's easier for him to stay here—in a place where he can hide so easily. I also suspect that this area is important to him. I think he started killing here."

"Will he stab her?"

"Sure. He's worked hard to perfect his method of killing. He enjoys the kill. He may want to throw us off, but I don't think he'll be able to end a life without experiencing it up close and personal. That way he can watch the life drain from her eyes." She frowned. "The angel will be there."

"Do you have enough to write a profile?" Erin asked.

"After we go through these photos, I can give it a try. I've written them with less to go on."

As they ate, Erin clicked through the photos. From time to time, Kaely would ask her to stop, and she would write something in her notebook. When viewing the first body, a thought popped into Erin's mind.

"Why the angel?" she asked Kaely. "Is it a religious symbol? Maybe the killer is a religious nut?"

Kaely was quiet for a moment as she considered Erin's question. "I do believe there's some kind of religious significance to the placement of the angel—and the white dress. But this guy doesn't love religion. He hates it."

"Why do you say that?"

"If this woman were a prostitute, then yes, he could be trying to punish her for her supposed sins. But from looking at her, I see what you saw. Good teeth. Excellent grooming.

Perfect hair." She held up her hand when Erin started to say something. "Yes, I know. There are some high-dollar prostitutes who would pay this kind of attention to their hair, teeth, and nails. But here? Really? It just doesn't work. I could be wrong. She may be a lady-of-the-night on vacation. But my gut tells me this isn't the case. I have no idea who the other bodies belong to, but I'm going to guess that they'll match missing person reports from this area. And they won't be prostitutes either. Remember, he was trying to kill them in a certain way. If he'd succeeded, he would have left them on display instead of covering them up. As far as the woman from this morning—the white dress, the angel statue... I feel like he's focusing on angels. He's actually trying to kill angels. The real reason for the white dress. He thinks angels wear white."

"But why would anyone hate angels?" Erin asked, confused. "Even if they existed, why would anyone want to... kill them?"

Kaely smiled at her. "Well, many people do believe angels exist. This guy believes it. He wouldn't show so much anger toward something he didn't believe was real. That tells me he's had some kind of religious upbringing, and he specifically blames angels for something he thinks they did. My guess is a parent who focused a lot of his or her religious beliefs on angels."

"People do that?"

Kaely nodded. "Angels appear in several different religions. Christianity, Judaism, and even Islam."

"Islam?" Erin was surprised.

Kaely nodded. "Add an obsession or some kind of mental problems associated with the concept of angels. It's a perfect storm for someone with anger issues to strike out against beings they can't see."

"Kind of like aliens?"

Kaely smiled. "Careful. I believe in angels. However, I don't worship them, and I certainly don't blame them for anything that's gone wrong in my life. There are a lot of erroneous beliefs out there about angels—and God. Like someone saying God *took someone away*. As if God suddenly decided to give someone a dreaded disease as a way to bring them to heaven."

"You don't believe that?"

Kaely's eyes widened. "No. God is a good God. A loving Father. He doesn't visit death and disease on His children."

"But in the Old Testament . . ."

Kaely smiled at Erin. "What people call the *Old Testament* is a collection of writings during a time before Christ. Things were different then. Not sure where some of the bad things came from. If you read Job, you'll see that the evil he went through actually came from Satan. Still, some of the writings make it sound as if God doled out judgment. I won't argue that with you. The important thing is that when Jesus came, things changed. We see who God really is in the form of His Son, Jesus. He brought healing, love, and forgiveness. This is what we live under now."

"Aren't there also fallen angels?"

Kaely nodded. "There's not a lot about them in the Bible. It talks about how they were thrown out of heaven for conspiring with Lucifer, an angel that God loved and anointed. There's a passage that says they're actually in chains, awaiting the day of judgment. Some people believe they're the demons that roam the earth. I don't know. To be honest, I try to focus on my relationship with God. I don't concentrate on demons or fallen angels, but believe it or not, we faced the idea of angels several times when I was at the FBI. Criminals . . . serial killers . . . who were brought up to believe that their god or angels wanted them to kill. Maybe our guy is coming at it from the other side. I have to wonder if he blames the angels for taking away someone he loves. Now he wants to hurt them. I can't think of any other reason for painting tears on the figurines. I haven't seen anything like this before."

Erin thought about what she'd said. "But if he believes angels are evil and that they did something that hurt him . . . why is he taking it out on women?"

"I realize it doesn't make any sense. This killer is clearly delusional. I think in his mind, if he can't strike back at an angel, he can put a woman in a white dress and kill her. I wonder if he thinks he's challenging the angels by ending lives they hadn't planned to take." Kaely sighed. "Even the most organized and intelligent serial killers have a hard time with reality. We saw that a lot. Like you said, if the angels are evil, why would they care if he hurts people? It's not logical, but rage never is. Hate never is."

"Well, it's nuts, but it fits the statues. Unless he's really angry at people who make angel figurines." She smiled at Kaely who laughed lightly.

"Now that would be an interesting twist. I never thought of that."

Just then, Erin's phone rang. She picked it up. "I think it's Chief Nightengale." She'd given him her phone number this morning after finding the first body in the woods.

Sure enough, when she answered, it was the chief. Erin motioned to Kaely for something to write with. Kaely flipped over to a new page in her notebook and then pushed it, and a pen, over to where Erin could reach it. She quickly wrote down what the chief said. When he said good-bye, she disconnected the call.

"Well, the ME says we were right about everything. The first girl they found this morning was stabbed in the heart and the body was moved to where it was found. He's still working on the other bodies, but the woman this morning and the buried body killed most recently have both been identified. The name of the woman missing from the resort is Chloe Banner. And the newest body that was uncovered this afternoon is a missing person, reported six weeks ago. Terri Rupp. She was supposed to be visiting a friend about ten miles from Sanctuary. Her car was found a few miles away, abandoned."

"Well, at least their families will have closure," Kaely said. "Although, I've never thought closure was everything it's cracked up to be."

"I agree." Erin stood up. "Let me take our plates into the kitchen. Then we'll talk a little more about the photos." She paused for a moment before saying, "I'm hoping you'll do your . . . thing. You know, your way of profiling. The one you told me about?"

"Maybe not tonight. I want to go through what we have first. And, I'd like to know more about these victims. After I get that information, I'll show it to you. Just remember that this really isn't the way FBI behavioral analysts do their job. It's a procedure I came up with on my own."

"I understand. I'm just really interested in seeing . . ." Erin stopped talking when she heard a noise coming from outside. It wasn't loud, but it was clear enough.

It was the sound of a woman sobbing.

SIXTEEN

Adrian thew away the cartons of Chinese food from his supper. He'd eaten while going over his notes about the events of the morning. As he walked away from the trash can and headed back to the living room to look for something—anything—that made sense about the murders, he suddenly realized that if anyone had asked him what he had for dinner, he couldn't have told them. He wanted nothing more than to find the person behind the killings and to bring them to justice. Adrian felt intense pressure to prove he wasn't just some small-town police chief who didn't know what he was doing. His decision to come back to Sanctuary had been right. He was happy here, even though he was still single and hadn't found the woman he was waiting for. He felt confident God had someone for him, although he sometimes wished He would hurry up.

He sighed loudly, causing his dog, Jake, to raise his head and stare at him.

"Sorry, pal. Go back to sleep."

These murders . . . He saw them as an attack against the town he loved. A threat to the peace and strength he'd found here. This mystery had to be solved. The town and its citizens were counting on him. He had no intention of letting them down.

He poured another cup of coffee and had just sat down again when the phone rang. Erin. When he answered, she sounded somber but concerned.

"What can I do for you, Miss Delaney?" he said.

"Sorry to bother you again, Chief," she said. "I know we just spoke a few minutes ago. . . . This might sound a little nuts, but there's something in the woods. I-I've heard it twice. At first, I thought I was imagining it. But tonight, Kaely heard it too. And we both saw something."

"You heard and saw something in the woods?" he repeated slowly. "I'm not sure what you mean. You know we have all kinds of animals out here, right? Including bears?"

There was silence on the other end of the phone until he heard Erin clear her throat. "It's not a bear. Look, last night and tonight I heard something that sounded like a woman crying. It was loud enough for us to hear it from inside the cabin. Tonight, Kaely and I both looked outside. There was someone . . . someone standing near the tree line in front of the cabin. We couldn't tell if it was a man or a woman. The person wore something like a long, dark cloak. But it . . . it glowed. Kaely wanted to go outside to check it out, but I stopped her. I was afraid it might be dangerous. Maybe connected to the killings. That's why I'm calling you. Just in case."

Adrian felt a flash of irritation. Did they think this was funny? Two sophisticated women jerking the chain of the local police chief? But as soon as the thought entered his head, he dismissed it. The women he'd met today wouldn't do anything like that. They were both serious and professional.

"I don't know what you saw," he said. "If you think you've seen the Woman in Watcher Woods, I can guarantee you that you're mistaken. There's no such thing. It's a stupid story concocted a long time ago, based on a terrible tragedy."

"We realize that," Erin said sharply. "I mean, I'm not sure if ghosts are real, but I seriously doubt that they stand around outside, trying to get attention. My first reaction was that someone is playing a joke on us. But with what happened not far from here, it's certainly not funny, and there's a slight possibility it could be something more serious. As I said, that's why I called you."

Although Adrian rather doubted that what they'd seen and heard had anything to do with the serial killer, if it was someone playing a joke, it needed to stop.

"Is this . . . person still there?" he asked.

"Not the last time we looked. We were watching her when she suddenly disappeared." She sighed dramatically. "Yes, I know how that sounds too, but that's what happened. Could you please send someone out here? See if they can find anything in the woods that proves somebody was out there? Kaely and I came here for rest and relaxation. Not to be the victims of some kind of practical joke."

Adrian had no intention of sending one of his officers out in the cold this late to follow up on a *ghost sighting*. "I'll come and check things out. To be honest, any sightings we've had of the Woman in Watcher Woods have been from teenagers having fun or tourists who have had too much to drink."

"I can assure you that Kaely and I haven't been drinking," Erin snapped. "If we hadn't actually seen someone out there, we wouldn't have called."

"I understand," Adrian said. "I didn't mean to imply anything. If you say you saw something, I believe you. And you're right. After finding a body in the woods, it pays to be careful. Don't leave your cabin. I'll be there soon. Please make sure all your doors are locked and don't open them for anyone except me. Okay?"

"All right," Erin said, her voice shaking slightly.

Instantly, Adrian felt guilty. She really was nervous. He said good-bye and hung up. Then he got his gun, put it in his holster, and grabbed his jacket. Jake whined and cocked his head to one side, making it clear he wanted to come with him. At first, Adrian started to say no, but Jake had spent a lot of time alone today. A ride in the car would do him good.

"Okay, you can come, boy," he said.

Jake's ears straightened up, and he rewarded Adrian with a wide smile. His fluffy golden retriever's tail thumped loudly on the floor. Adrian smiled at him.

"Wanna find a ghost?" he asked.

He might as well have asked him if he wanted a thick, juicy steak. Jake's joy was just as exuberant. On his next day off, Adrian vowed to spend some quality time with his best friend. It had been a while since they'd gone for a hike or even a long car ride into Edgewood where his friend Martin lived. Martin's dog, Fancy, and Jake were great pals, and he hadn't seen her in a couple of months. He'd call Martin tomorrow and set something up.

Adrian opened the front door, and Jake bounded out, headed straight for the Jeep. Adrian locked up, opened the car door for Jake, and then got inside himself. While his furry friend reveled in the prospect of a car ride, Adrian wasn't as eager. A murder this morning and three other bodies found in the woods. Now, here he was, chasing a ghost? Really?

SEVENTEEN

"He thinks we're imagining things," Erin said when she disconnected her call to Adrian. "You should have heard him. I mean, he was polite and everything, but I could tell he doesn't believe us."

Kaely took a sip from her mug and then set it down. "So, he's coming? Even if he thinks we're somewhat unbalanced?"

Erin sighed. "Yeah. I feel so silly about this. I mean, I know you don't believe in ghosts, but what we saw tonight . . ." She frowned at Kaely. "I'm just glad you not only heard it, but you saw something too. So, Miss I-Don't-Believe-It's-a-Ghost, what do you think now?"

"Let's not make that my nickname, okay? It's too long and just . . . weird." Kaely shook her head. She'd been asking herself the same question. The sound of a woman sobbing was loud enough for them to hear it inside the cabin. To be honest, at this point, she wasn't certain exactly what she'd heard. It was more like a wail. A cry of pain. She'd definitely heard something, and then Erin had told her what she thought it was. Had she made herself believe it was a woman crying because Erin put it in her head? It was entirely possible, but regardless, she could understand why Erin believed it was someone sobbing loudly. Yet when they looked outside and saw . . . What did they see? Someone tall, wrapped in some kind of cloak, an odd light emanating from them. Of course, that was impossible, right? It had to be light from somewhere else, illuminating the figure in the woods. The moon? It wasn't that late, but it was possible. Perhaps it was an outside light from the cabin? Was there a motion sensor light out front? Maybe that was it.

Kaely realized that Erin was talking. "I'm sorry, what did you say?"

"I was just wondering, if we didn't see an actual ghost, why would someone want to pull a prank like this on us?"

They were sitting in the living room, waiting for the chief to show up. Kaely was parked in the overstuffed leather chair, and Erin was on the couch. Kaely leaned forward and picked up her cup. She'd brewed some Earl Grey tea and realized it was probably getting cold. As she took a sip, she thought about Erin's question. It was a good one.

"I'm not sure. No matter the reason behind it, doing it now means taking a rather big risk. I realize that the murders didn't happen close to the cabin, but if I wanted to play a practical joke, it wouldn't be right now. Not only is there a murderer roaming around, but I'd also wonder if the police might be patrolling the area."

"You're right," Erin said, frowning. "So, you think people know about the murders?"

"I'd bet in a town this small, word spread rather quickly. The police were trying to identify the woman. I'm guessing they were asking around in town. Then there's the police officers, the ME, and the people working at the resort. Trust me, people know."

"I don't see how the figure in the woods could be connected to the killing . . . or killings," Erin said. "Why would they want to do something that would bring attention to themselves?"

"You said this figure is called the Woman in Watcher Woods." Kaely frowned and thought back to some of the cases she'd worked. There was something familiar about this situation. It was then that she remembered one case she and Noah had worked. The killer believed himself to be the ghost of a renowned serial killer. He would dress up like John Wayne Gacy and kill young men. She shivered involuntarily.

"Okay, I saw that. What was that about?" Erin asked.

"Trust me, you don't want to know. It's not impossible that the killer thinks he's a ghost, but from the lovely poem you recited to me, it seems that except for using a knife, William Watcher killed his wife in a different way. Besides, where does the angel figurine come in? It has nothing to do with the Woman in Watcher Woods. From my experience, I'd agree that these two things aren't related."

"So glad you said that," Erin said, breathing an audible sigh of relief.

"It's just an educated guess," Kaely said. "Don't take it as gospel. Frankly, I'm itching to write that profile. I need to get a handle on this killer."

"Kaely, are you sure we should be here?"

Kaely heard the nervousness in Erin's voice. Was this too much for her? She'd come here to get away from murder. From death. And here it was again. She prayed silently, asking

God if they should leave, but she didn't get an answer—or a warning. She quietly formulated a measured response.

"I think that if you want to leave, we should go," Kaely said. "But in my opinion, if we're on our guard, we'll be fine. If we were closer to where the bodies were found, I'd be a bit more concerned. Also, the woman who was killed was alone. There are two of us, and we're ex-law enforcement. I don't care who this guy is, if he has a brain, we're the last people he would want to target. But again, I want to do whatever you feel is best for you. If this situation is adding any stress to you, let's go home. Or somewhere else. This isn't the only town in the Smokies, you know."

Erin stared at her for a moment before saying, "Well, with the snowstorm coming, I doubt our killer will venture out once it hits. Besides . . ." She shook her head. "I really thought I needed a break from murder and mayhem. But to be honest, since we've been here, I've felt strangely exuberant. A little nervous, yes, but not so much that I want to leave." Her eyes widened. "Don't get me wrong. I'm not excited because someone died. I just . . ."

"You miss using your talent to combat evil?" Kaely smiled at her. "Trust me, I understand that, Erin. I know why you felt you had to leave the police department. I made the same decision when I left the FBI. But that fire inside doesn't just fade away. In your case, you had to write a book to let it out. And here I am, itching to write a profile. Wanting to understand the UNSUB behind these horrific crimes."

"Why is that? What's wrong with us?"

Kaely leaned forward in her chair and took another sip of her tea. She had to be wise in how she answered Erin's question. Finally, she took a deep breath and said, "You've asked me a question. I'm going to respond with what I believe the answer is. You might not like it, but I have to be honest. I believe that God creates us with special gifts and abilities. We feel pulled toward them because of that."

Erin snorted. "He creates people that like to be around death and destruction? To have to deal with the worst that mankind can produce?"

"Erin, answer this question for me. If there weren't people like you and me, what kind of shape would the world really be in? No one willing to confront evil? No one who cared about the innocent victims of crime? No one to protect people?"

Erin just stared at her, but she blinked several times, telling Kaely that she was thinking. It was a good question. One that she'd had to ask herself more than once down through the years. She was surprised when Erin's eyes suddenly filled with tears.

"So, you think God made me like this?" she asked, her voice trembling.

Kaely smiled. "I think He made you a warrior. Someone to hold criminals accountable and to protect those who need defending."

A tear slid down Erin's cheek, and she quickly wiped it away. Kaely knew about Erin's background. Her parents died in a car accident when she was young, and she had a sister who was a drug addict and disappeared after her parents' deaths. She was raised by an aunt who only took Erin because she thought it was her duty. The only man Erin had ever loved had betrayed her, and she'd watched him die in front of her. Yet here she was. Still fighting. A woman who would defend the underdog at the drop of a hat. Kaely had taken a chance, bringing up God. But she felt that Erin was touched by the idea that God saw her as unique. Someone with special gifts.

Erin opened her mouth to say something, but before she could get the words out, someone knocked on the door, causing both of them to jump.

EIGHTEEN

Erin looked through the peephole. Chief Nightengale. She swung the door open, and Kaely stood behind her as backup. Or so it felt.

"Thank you for coming, Chief," she said, still a little embarrassed for calling him.

"I looked around outside," he said. "Everything seems to be okay. If there was anyone out there, they're gone now."

Erin noticed that he'd said, "*If* there was anyone out there . . ." but she decided not to mention it. "Thank you, Chief." The sound of a dog barking startled her. She glanced toward the chief's Jeep. A large golden retriever peered through the passenger side window and barked at them.

"Is that your dog?" she asked. *What a stupid question. Do you think the dog unlocked the car door and jumped inside when the chief wasn't looking?*

"Yes, that's Jake. And he's fine in the car. He's just trying to get you to feel sorry for him."

"His name is Jake?" Erin asked.

The chief nodded. "Yeah, just like the guy in your book. I don't think they look much alike though."

Erin could barely believe it. The chief looked like Jake and his dog's name was Jake? Strange.

"I love dogs," Erin said. "Can he come in? I'd love to meet him." She turned around and looked at Kaely. "Is that okay with you?"

"Of course. Noah and I don't have a dog," she said to the chief, "but we have a cat with a lot of personality. Mr. Hoover seems to think he owns our house." She smiled. "If you don't let him out, we'll probably keep bothering you until you do."

Chief Nightingale shrugged and went back down the steps. When he opened the car door, the dog jumped out and bounded up to the front door, his big fluffy tail wagging so fast it was hard to see.

"Jake!" the chief yelled. "Calm down."

The dog completely ignored him and, to Erin's delight, jumped up on her. She laughed as he licked her face.

"Jake!" the chief said again, his voice stern. "Get down."

This time Jake obeyed, but it looked to Erin as if compliance was almost painful.

"I don't mind, Chief," she said. "He's so beautiful."

"He's a pill. He's not quite a year old, and he has his own mind. He only listens to me when he wants to."

Erin smiled. "I think he's trying." She waved them both inside. Jake followed her into the living room. When Erin and Kaely sat down on the couch, Jake jumped up and wiggled in between them, causing both women to laugh. It was amazing how much better she felt now, after only spending a few minutes with the chief's beautiful dog. Erin had thought about getting a dog after she left the department, but the responsibility felt like too much for her at the time. Maybe after she went home, she'd go to a shelter and find a dog that needed a home as much as she needed a furry best friend.

"Jake, get down from the couch," the chief said, his face pink from either embarrassment or the cold.

"Oh, please let him stay," Kaely said. "Unless it will cause you a problem with his training."

Chief Nightengale plopped down into the chair as if he'd given up his last ounce of willpower. "It's up to you. I probably shouldn't have brought him, but he loves riding in the car."

"Well, he's welcome here any time," Erin said. She smiled at the chief and then realized that her comment could have been misconstrued. "And you are as well, Chief." It was her turn to feel embarrassed. She felt her cheeks grow hot.

Suddenly, Kaely burst out laughing, and Chief Nightingale joined in. Although she was still somewhat self-conscious, she was relieved that the chief had found her comment humorous. The tension in the room had lessened considerably. Leave it to a dog to lighten up the atmosphere.

"Can I get you something to drink, Chief Nightengale?" Kaely asked the chief. "There's a one cup-coffeemaker in the kitchen. We've got coffee, hot chocolate, cappuccino . . ."

"Normally, I would say no," the chief said. "But a cup of hot chocolate sounds perfect. I'm chilled to the bone. And please, call me Adrian. I think we've been through enough together that you can drop the title. And to be honest, only the tourists call me Chief Nightengale."

"Chief . . . I mean, Adrian," Erin said, "why didn't you ask one of your other officers to come out? You didn't need to drive out here yourself. I'm sure you have other things to think about right now."

"I actually live closer than anyone else. Besides, I was wondering if you'd come to any conclusions yet."

"We're just going through the photos now," Kaely said. "I'd like to complete that before I write the profile. I'll try to do all I can tonight. We're going into town tomorrow to do some shopping. Can I bring what I have by your office?"

"Certainly. I'd appreciate that." He sighed. "We have other, larger departments reaching out, offering to help. That means they want to take over. When I tell them we have your help, I hope it will give us some breathing room. A chance to solve this thing ourselves."

After petting Jake, Kaely stood up. "I'll get your hot chocolate. Then we can talk about what happened tonight."

Erin noticed Adrian's jaw tighten. Seems he wasn't as happy to respond to her phone call as he'd said. "So how long have you been the police chief here, Adrian?" she asked, hoping to keep the mood cordial. It was an obvious conversation starter, but it was the best she could come up with.

"I've been chief for five years now."

"You look pretty young to be in such a position of authority. I noticed that your officers seem to respect you. Not so sure about Dr. Gibson though. I got the impression that he doesn't have much use for anyone else."

Adrian's tight expression relaxed some, and he smiled. "You're very perceptive. I'm blessed to work with great officers. They might be looked down on some by people who see Sanctuary as a small town with small-town attributes, but I truly believe they could compete with any police department in any city."

"I used to work in St. Louis, a huge town with a lot of

crime, and I was impressed by what I saw this morning. You're also fortunate to have an officer trained in forensics."

"Yes, I am. Timothy could get a job at almost any large police department, but he was born here and loves it, just like I do. Like me, he doesn't have any living relatives. The department and the people in Sanctuary are our family."

"With the strange story I heard about the man who originally built this place," Erin said, "I find the name of the town rather odd."

Just then, Kaely came into the room carrying two cups. She put one down on the coffee table near Adrian and then handed Erin the other one. "I know your tea is cold. I made you another cup."

"How nice, but you didn't need to do that," Erin said, surprised. "I could have taken care of it."

Kaely wrinkled her nose at Erin and smiled. "I know that, but I think you need someone to pamper you once in a while."

Erin took a sip. Perfect. Kaely must have watched her make her original cup of tea. It was a small thing, but it meant a lot to her.

"I heard you mention Timothy," Kaely said. "I noticed that his hand was bandaged this morning. Is he all right?"

"Yeah. He's a brilliant officer, but he's a little clumsy. Cut his hand chopping carrots for a salad. Nothing work related. He'll be fine."

"You were talking about the name of the town," Kaely said after sitting down on the couch again. "I'd love to hear how that came about."

"You'll probably find the answer surprising," he responded. "William Watcher was actually the man who settled and named Sanctuary. He'd left New York City because he felt it was growing too quickly and he wanted some place quieter and more peaceful. He bought land and built his home here. It was in town. Victorian, palatial, and impressive. As the first settler in this area, he named it Sanctuary. It was his idea of heaven on earth. But he eventually wanted a place where he could go to be alone. To get away from his wife. He actually built a cabin on this property. Other men would come with him on hunting parties, or getaways, so they could play poker and drink. Of course, the original cabin didn't resemble this. Steve actually tore down most of the previous structure and rebuilt it." Adrian pointed at the wall on one side of the living room. "That's an actual wall from the first cabin. And many of the bricks in the fireplace are original as well."

"I'm sure his wife wasn't too thrilled about this place," Kaely said.

Erin felt something and looked down to see that Jake had put his head on her lap and was looking up at her adoringly. She stroked his soft head.

"You could say that," Adrian said. "In fact, accounts I've read say that she was miserable. It seems that Mr. Watcher was raised in a family known for keeping a tight watch on their wives. The Watcher men weren't known for their kindness. Wives were created to serve their husbands, and a disobedient wife was beaten if she wasn't as submissive as her husband expected her to be."

"Hmmm," Erin said. "So I take it Mrs. Watcher disobeyed, and her husband dealt with it severely?"

"Yes, unfortunately. He eventually killed her."

"I hope he went to prison for it," Kaely said.

Adrian shook his head. "He did not. An inquiry resulted in the judge deciding that he'd been pushed past the point of his endurance by a willful and sinful wife. I have no idea exactly what her sins were, but the judge felt she deserved to have her throat cut. Hard to believe, I know. But back then, people saw things much differently than they do today."

"So, what happened to the murderous Mr. Watcher?" Erin asked.

"I guess it proves that no sin really goes unpunished," Adrian said. "William started telling people that the ghost of his wife was haunting him. That she wouldn't leave him alone. Reports say he became gaunt and nervous, jumping at everything. Eventually, he took his own life. Here, in this cabin."

"Here?" Kaely said.

Adrian nodded. "Well, in the cabin that used to be here."

"I thought you said she hated the cabin, and that Mr. Watcher came here because he knew she wouldn't join him," Erin said. "I guess she changed her mind?"

Adrian chuckled. "At his inquest, William said that she had decided to follow him every time he came here. She intended to take away the pleasure the cabin gave him."

"Whoops," Kaely said. "Guess he shouldn't have upset her."

"I guess so."

"You seem to know a lot about William Watcher and his wife" Erin said. "Mind if I ask why?"

Adrian turned red and coughed. "It's not something I share with many people, but I discovered I'm indirectly related to William Watcher. I'd appreciate it if this didn't go any further. People around here take the story about Watcher Woods very seriously."

"So why did Steve Tremont act so weird about this place the first day I arrived?" Erin asked. "I mean, this stuff happened so long ago."

"Even though the ghost is said to roam the woods since the incident," he replied, "no one ever said they saw it except a few children trying to frighten people. But recently, according to some of our citizens, it's been seen several times. Steve sunk a lot of money into this place, hoping to make money on it by renting it out to tourists. Now, he's terrified that people won't want to come if they think a ghost is haunting the place."

Erin's stomach tightened. Although she didn't say it, she completely understood. At that moment, she wasn't thrilled about being stuck in an isolated cabin in the woods with a serial killer on the loose and a frightening specter hiding behind the trees that surrounded them like prison guards, determined they would never leave this place alive.

NINETEEN

Adrian noticed the look in Erin's eyes. She was spooked. Kaely seemed okay, though. More focused on the murders than on the ghostly apparition supposedly haunting Watcher Woods. She was the one who made him believe they'd actually seen something. Erin was smart, yet he sensed some instability. Not that she was weak. She wasn't. He was convinced that the haunted look in her eyes came from something more personal. Her pain was deep and not as easily vanquished as a mere ghost. He might have suspected that the murders in the woods were too much for her if he hadn't noticed that she seemed calmer and more focused when her concentration was directed toward helping him find the person responsible. She was a hunter, intent on capturing her prey, and she had no plans to back down before the quest was at an end.

"So, describe to me what you saw." He nodded at Kaely, wanting to hear her version of their sighting first.

"We heard someone wailing," she said."

"Miss Delaney said she heard *crying*,"

"Kaely's right," Erin interjected. "It was more of a wail."

"We both heard it," Kaely said. "It was loud enough for us

to pick it up from inside. At first, I wasn't certain what it was, but as we moved closer to the window, I could hear it more clearly. I'm certain it wasn't an animal. It was human. That's when we saw it." She took a deep breath and met Adrian's eyes. "The person was tall and hidden beneath a dark cloak or covering of some kind. I couldn't see it very well."

"Then how could you tell that he was tall and that he wore a cloak?"

"There are lights outside, in the front," Kaely said. "They illuminated him enough that we could make him out. But then we noticed an eerie glow coming from the figure. As if the light were inside the cloak." She shook her head. "I'm sorry. It's the only way I can describe it."

"Did you see a face?"

"No," Erin said. She looked at Kaely. "Anyway, I didn't. Did you?"

Kaely shook her head. "I specifically looked. The face was either covered by the cloak or . . . something else. It was just black . . . or, I should say it was dark. In that kind of lighting, I can't definitively tell you what color it was."

Adrian paused for a moment before asking, "Did the . . . figure make any sound while you were looking at it?"

Both women nodded at the same time. "Yes, it let out a really loud moan."

"You keep referring to the figure as him, yet you hinted that the sound you heard was female?"

"Yes," Erin said quickly, but Kaely didn't look as convinced.

"I'm not sure. I think we're referring to the person we saw as 'he' because we're not certain if it was a man or a woman," she said. She looked at Erin. "Couldn't a man have made that sound? I mean, if he was trying to sound like a woman?"

Erin's confident expression slipped a little. She looked down at the floor for a few seconds, but then shook her head. "Maybe, but I don't think so. It definitely sounded like a woman to me."

"Did this . . . person notice you?" Adrian asked. He was trying to sound professional, but the truth was, he was dog-tired and stressed out. This felt silly and unnecessary, yet even a small chance that what these women saw had something to do with the bodies in the woods made it important for him to take them seriously.

"She was looking right at us," Erin said.

"But after he—or she—made that . . . noise," Kaely said, "she kind of . . . disappeared." She blushed slightly. "Look, Chief—Adrian—again, I know how this sounds, but every word of it is true. I spent several years in the FBI. I'm not prone to fantasies or high imaginations. We definitely saw something, and we're describing it as succinctly as we can. I'm certainly not telling you it was a real ghost. I don't believe it was. But it was . . . something."

Adrian leaned back in the chair and rubbed his eyes. "If you see it again, call me right away. But for now, there's not much I can do. I don't see how it could be connected to the bodies in the woods, but at this point, I can't be certain of anything. I don't want to take any chances. Please don't go outside if you see anything suspicious."

"Like I would do that," Erin said under her breath.

"I'm going to work on a profile for you tonight," Kaely said. "I know this sounds awful, but if there was more than one recent body, it would be easier. I can't be sure whether or not the killer has a certain type of victim, and that can shape a profile quite a bit."

Just then his phone rang. "Excuse me," Adrian said. "This could be important."

"Of course," Kaely said.

Adrian answered and listened to the voice on the other end. After asking a couple of questions, he disconnected the call.

"God must be listening," he said as he put his phone back in his pocket. "Another body has just been identified. The woman murdered before Terri. Her name is Ann Squires. Annie, as she was called by those close to her, was reported missing by her parents when she didn't come home from college on break. Some of her friends thought she'd run away with her boyfriend. He was interviewed by the police and was able to prove he hadn't seen her. He thought she might have decided to visit her aunt in Taylor, a small town just a few miles to the north of Sanctuary. The aunt said she hadn't contacted her, but she did have a habit of just showing up unannounced. They were really close."

"Has the evidence revealed anything yet?" Kaely asked.

"Detective Sergeant Johnson went over the dress and the shoes and couldn't find anything that would help us," Adrian said. "Locard's exchange principle appears to have failed us this time. Gibson didn't add much, but he did establish TOD at around four to six hours before we found the body. So between one and three in the morning. It could have been earlier because it was so cold last night. He feels pretty confident about his estimation though. He agreed with your assessments, Erin. The dress was put on her. Her undergarments were her own. She wasn't sexually violated either. The killer knew exactly where to stab her. That doesn't happen very often. The other two bodies didn't show the same kind of skill. The ribs were nicked, and he saw something odd in the second oldest body. The hyoid bone in her neck was broken."

"She was strangled," Kaely said. "He didn't hit the heart when he tried to kill her, and she fought back. He had to strangle her to get her to die."

Adrian nodded. "Exactly what Gibson thought."

"Anything on the oldest body?" Erin asked.

"Not yet," Adrian said. "Although two of her ribs are broken. Doc can't tell us how that happened though. Was there a struggle? Did it happen when he buried her? We just don't know."

"None of the buried bodies wore dresses, blue ribbons, or had a figurine," Kaely said softly. "We believe he was waiting for the perfect kill. She was the only one who deserved his attention. The dress, the blue ribbon, and the figurine are his signature. They're what's important to him."

"I think that's right."

"Do you know where the killer crossed paths with the victims?" Erin asked.

Adrian shook his head. "You do remember that we only discovered the first body this morning, right? I think we're doing pretty good here. Of course, being able to access records of missing persons helped." He sighed. "Identifying the first body might take a while. She's obviously been missing a long time, and there's very little to go on." He downed the rest of his hot chocolate and stood. "I'll let you know if we find anything in the morning. For tonight, please keep your doors locked. I'm more than willing to send one of my officers out here to keep an eye on things, if you'd like, but I have a feeling that my offer wouldn't be accepted."

"And you'd be right," Erin said. "We're both trained and armed. We can take care of ourselves."

"I have no doubt of that."

Adrian couldn't think of anything else to say and made a clicking noise with his tongue. Jake jumped down from the couch. He took a look back at Erin and Kaely as if hoping Adrian would change his mind and stay a little longer. It appeared that Jake had made some new friends. "I should be in the office pretty early tomorrow. I appreciate your offer of a profile. Anything I can learn that will help me to know where to look or who I'm searching for is appreciated more than I can say." He sighed. "I was certain that working in Sanctuary would give me a quiet life. Just goes to show how wrong you can be."

"I'm sure you have your challenges, even without trying to find a serial killer," Kaely said with a smile.

"It's true. But nothing like I faced in Chicago. I know you've both encountered the same things." He shook his head. "This is a nice community. Good people. This kind of thing shouldn't happen here."

"Unfortunately, evil doesn't seem to have borders, Adrian," Erin said.

"Sadly, that seems to be true, Miss Delaney." He nodded at them. "Call me any time. I'll get back to you as soon as I can."

Erin smiled at him. "If you want me to call you Adrian, you must call me Erin."

"Sorry, Erin. Habit learned from dealing with the public." He headed for the front door, with Jake following behind him, his nails clicking on the wooden floor. When Adrian had arrived, he hadn't really been concerned about the so-called ghost in the woods. But after talking to Kaely and Erin, he was worried. They'd seen something. But what? Were the women in danger? Although they seemed confident they could take care of themselves, he wasn't convinced. Something terrible was happening in Sanctuary, and he wasn't sure that anyone was safe.

TWENTY

"So, what do you think?" Erin asked after Adrian left.

"He believes us."

"How can you tell?"

Kaely smiled. "Body language. When someone is being honest, they lean toward you. Adrian's legs were relaxed, and he met our eyes. Remember when he first sat down, he leaned back in his chair and seemed rather jumpy?"

Erin *had* noticed, but she'd concentrated more on what he'd said. Kaely was right. In fact, when he changed his body language, she'd felt more relaxed. Must have been an innate understanding that his attitude had changed.

"Okay, I get it," she said. "I learned to read body language when I was on the force, but only the more obvious reactions. We had to anticipate someone's actions in case they were getting ready to pull a gun or a knife. But we weren't taught the more subtle signs."

"While we're together, I'll try to teach you more about it," Kaely said. "I'm sure you could use it in your books."

Erin shook her head. "Not sure there will be any other books."

"You still haven't decided what you want to do?

"No. My agent keeps calling, and my editor has left several messages. The publisher has even offered a larger advance and an increased royalty percentage. It's a great offer. I just don't know if this is what I want to do with my life."

"You enjoyed writing the first book, right?"

"Yeah, I did," Erin said. "But like I told you, it was a way for me to live out my dream." She shrugged. "That dream was to be a behavioral analyst for the FBI. Not to be an author."

"You told me that writing the book helped you."

"In some ways, yes. I had nothing else to do. I needed something to fill my days. Working on the book accomplished that. But it wasn't everything I'd hoped it would be."

Kaely stared at her for a moment, making Erin feel a little uncomfortable.

"Can you explain that? I'm not sure I understand."

Erin frowned at her. "Did they train you how to interrogate suspects in the FBI?"

Rather than look offended, Kaely laughed. "Actually, we didn't do that at the BAU. About the only interrogation we administered was to each other. Sometimes it helped us to write a profile if we picked each other's brains."

Erin was sorry that she'd snapped at Kaely and grateful that she didn't seem upset. It wasn't Kaely's fault that she had certain sore spots.

"Like I said, working on the book helped me in several ways," she said. "But it also made me realize that I had no chance of ever living out the life I was writing about. That made it harder."

"You know, it's true that leaving the police department

could hurt your chances of joining the FBI—and becoming part of the BAU. It depends on whether or not you received counseling. If you required heavy meds. A doctor would probably have to provide a written assessment stating that your symptoms were minimal. You might even have to pass a psych evaluation administered by a Bureau psychiatrist."

"So simply being a coward isn't a problem," Erin snapped, unable to keep the bitterness out of her voice.

"You're not a coward, Erin," Kaely said gently. "You went through something horrific. I don't know anyone who wouldn't have been affected by what you experienced that night. I've known agents with the Bureau who took their own lives because of the pressure of the job and the things they saw. You're still here. And you've become a bestselling author. These aren't the attributes of a coward."

Erin bit her lip. They'd just ventured into dangerous territory. She felt closer to Kaely than to anyone she'd ever known, but she wasn't ready to talk about the locked box she'd been keeping in the closet at home. The box that was now upstairs in the bedroom. Although part of her wanted to tell the truth, she just couldn't do it. Kaely told Adrian they were both armed, but it wasn't really true. She'd told Kaely she'd brought her gun, but she hadn't told her that she hadn't picked it up since that night. Or that it was locked away because she was afraid she might use it on herself. She may not ever be able to ever share that shameful truth with anyone. Not even Kaely.

"Thanks, but I barely leave my house. I jump every time the phone rings or someone knocks on my door. I think you're giving me too much credit."

"I'll say one other thing, and then I'll leave this alone,"

Kaely said. "I'm certain there are a lot of police and former military who have applied to the academy and who have dealt with PTSD. There's a process for evaluating the severity of their symptoms and determining whether it would interfere with decision-making and job performance. If you want, I can check it out. Find out if you'd be a viable candidate."

Erin shook her head. "No. At least not for now, anyway. I was in pretty bad shape when I quit the department. I'm fairly certain the FBI wouldn't be interested in taking a chance on me when there are so many other qualified people who apply to the academy."

"Well, let's table that conversation for now," Kaely said. "But you didn't answer my other question. Was writing that book so unsatisfying that you have no desire to do it again?"

Erin sighed. "No, it was satisfying. In fact, I actually enjoyed it. Especially the research. I loved that part. I enjoy learning, and you were so helpful. I truly couldn't have written the book without you. And making up stories? It can be exciting. But I learned that *writing* the book is the easy part. After that comes the editing . . . again . . . and again. But that's still not the worst part."

Kaely grinned. "The worst part was all the money you made?"

Erin grunted. "No, the promotion. For crying out loud. I hoped people would read the book and just . . . like it. Tell other people about it. But it was this interview and that podcast and a book-signing tour—which I refused to do, by the way. I'm a very private person, Kaely. I don't want to . . ."

"To let people get to know you? To realize that your book meant something to your readers, that they want to connect with you?"

Erin clasped her hands together. "Look, being a police officer is one of the toughest jobs in the world. Over the last several years, we've seen more and more distrust and animosity toward the police—the people out there putting their lives on the line to protect others. The police should be heroes—not villains. Trust me, no one in uniform hates the bad apples more than the officers who work with them. But to many people, one abusive officer means they are all like that. It didn't matter that most of them face danger, death, and the destruction human beings can visit on each other in an effort to keep them safe. I'm only bringing this up to emphasize the difference between being a police officer and a writer. The men and women I worked with should get accolades for what they do. But for the most part, they don't. And that's fine. That's the job. But I write a book, and suddenly I'm in the spotlight? It doesn't make any sense to me. It's like I'm suddenly on display. Not just my story, but *me*." She sighed. "I'm not saying this right."

"You said it just fine," Kaely said with a smile. "I get it. As a police officer, everything was focused on your job. You were a public servant. As a writer, you feel exposed. Vulnerable."

Erin shook her head. "I take it back. You do get it." She shrugged. "I'm not used to it, Kaely. I just hate the attention. Don't get me wrong. I like people . . ."

"Are you sure about that?"

Shocked, Erin could only stare at her.

"Don't misunderstand me," Kaely said softly. "Did you have any friends besides your fellow officers?"

Erin's mind drifted back to her previous life. It seemed so long ago. She had no family except for a sister who was probably dead. The police department had definitely become

132

her family. And now, that was gone. Several of her former friends on the force had tried to stay in touch, but one by one she'd pushed them away. Once she was published, it seemed as if they'd given up.

"I guess not," she said finally.

"So the only human beings you were around, outside of your fellow officers, were criminals. I'm sure there were people who appreciated you, Erin, but like you said, many didn't. You had to deal with people who hated the police. But those who want to connect with you on social media or who come to a book signing don't hate you. They're not criminals nor are they the people who don't trust the police. They love your books, and they love your characters. Law enforcement characters. Do you understand?"

"You're saying I think everyone out there is against me, right?"

"Is it true?"

"You know, if you keep answering my questions with other questions, I might start getting a little irritated," Erin said.

"No, you're not." Kaely grinned at her.

"Okay, I'm not. And I get it." She took a deep breath and let it out. "I enjoyed writing the book, okay? And I guess I could get used to the rest of it, but goodness. Why can't I just write books and still have a personal life?"

"I'm sure you can. But why not just give it a chance? Who knows? You might find out you like people after all. I mean, you like me."

"Let's not get carried away, okay?"

"Very funny," Kaely said.

Erin smiled at her. "Now, if you're through giving me the third degree, can we get to your profile?"

"Sounds good. I told Adrian I'd have something ready for him by tomorrow. I wouldn't normally rush this, but my main priority is spending time with you. And with a possible storm coming in, I think getting it done tonight would be best."

Erin nodded and brought the pictures up on the TV again while Kaely gathered their notes together. As she clicked through the photos, Erin tried to concentrate on what she was seeing. But her mind was full of the questions Kaely had asked and the answers she wasn't certain she was willing to accept.

TWENTY-ONE

He watched through the window. The women sat in the living room. They seemed to be concentrating on something. Suddenly, pictures appeared on the large screen television on the wall. He recognized them. His work. His offerings. He felt excitement explode in him like dynamite. His god whispered something in his ear, and he laughed. Yes, he knew what was coming. He was scouting now. Looking for the next one. It had to be just right. Would they figure it out? He was sending them a message, but so far, they hadn't understood it. Clearly, they weren't as smart as he was. No one was. His god would make sure the killing continued. It was his will.

He backed away and left them to it. As he walked toward the trees, he smiled up at them. Watcher Woods. A spirit of death existed here. The wind whipped up suddenly, and the forest whispered his name. In the glow of moonlight, he laughed and planned for his next sacrifice.

"Okay, let's go over this together," Kaely said. She was impressed by Erin's natural ability to read a crime scene.

Although Kaely had helped with her book, much of what she'd written hadn't come from her. It was Erin's own innate ability to see things others couldn't.

She picked up the notebook that held Erin's observations at the scene. "You were right about the victim being a tourist. Seems this isn't part of our UNSUB's MO though. The other two victims that have been identified weren't tourists." She read through the notes. "You saw the hair on her shoes and decided she has a cat." She looked at Erin. "What made you think that these were her shoes? I agree with you, but I'm just curious."

"The shoes fit her perfectly. They weren't new . . . like the dress. There were scuff marks on the soles, so I felt they were probably hers. Also, her lipstick matched her shoes. If the lipstick had been a shade that didn't go with her shoes, I would have gone another way. Also, the dress was pristine—except for the dirt and leaves beneath her. And the wound where she was stabbed. He dressed her carefully, yet the shoes were muddy. The shoes weren't important to him, but the dress was."

"Exactly right," Kaely said. "Very good."

Erin's slight smile told Kaely that her praise was important. Good to know. It would help her learn.

"I also agree with you that our UNSUB put something under the body when he transported her," Kaely said. "Something that didn't leave any trace evidence. Or if it was there, it was lost in the dirt and the leaves where he put her. I'm wondering if he has knowledge of forensics. Did he purposely pick something that wouldn't leave any evidence for the police to find?"

Erin frowned. "Isn't it possible they missed something? This isn't St. Louis—or Quantico."

"It's always possible, but I get the feeling Adrian runs a pretty tight ship. And Detective Johnson has excellent training."

"Not so sure about Doctor Gibson," Erin said.

Kaely understood Erin's reservations, but there really wasn't anything they could do. They had to trust that Gibson was doing his job the best he could.

"I also agree with you that Chloe was getting ready to go out before she was killed," Kaely said. "Her makeup was perfect. I don't think our UNSUB put it on her. If he had, it would have been messy." Kaely frowned. "But there aren't any signs that he tried. Nor did he remove her shoes. High heels. Hot pink. They don't really match the style of the dress."

"Maybe shoes and her makeup weren't important to him. Or their jewelry. He's focused on something else," Erin said. "But why the white dress? Is he trying to make her like the angels? And what about the blue ribbon?"

"My guess?" Kaely said. "The dress is important, as is the ribbon. The shoes and makeup don't bother him because . . . maybe his mother wore makeup and fancy shoes? Maybe unlike some serial killers, he actually loved his mother."

"Could she have been a sacrifice? You know, to the angels? He tried to make her seem more virginal as a way to . . ." She shook her head. "I started to say maybe he was trying to appease the angels, but that doesn't fit, does it? He desecrated the figurine." She met Kaely's gaze. "We touched on this before. That maybe he's actually angry with the angels. Or with God."

"I think that's very perceptive," Kaely said. "And from

these pictures, I also agree with you that if, as the owner of the resort said . . . What was his name?"

"Hubbard," Erin said. "Merle Hubbard."

Kaely grinned. "I started to say Merle Haggard, but I was pretty sure that was wrong." Kaely found his name in the notebook. "Yeah, that's right. Mr. Hubbard said she was going to the Grits and Grains event, but he didn't see her leave the resort with anyone. So, either she planned to meet someone there, or she was hoping to meet people at the event. Either way, it would explain why she was so dressed up."

"That's true," Erin said. "How far away was this event again?"

"About twenty miles, it says in your notes."

"Wait a minute. Where's her car?"

"That's a good question," Kaely asked. "If it was at the festival, she probably met her killer there."

"But if it's still at the resort . . ." Erin said.

"Then she never left on her own," Kaely finished for her. "So that means the killer probably lives in Sanctuary. He's been killing for a while, so he's not a visitor."

"Unless he comes here just to kill," Erin said slowly.

"Either way, he has ties here. Whether he lives here, or he travels here to kill, this place is important to him. Sanctuary is important to him. Remember that most serial killers have comfort zones. I'm guessing that he lives here."

Erin looked at her and nodded. "Do you need to call Adrian and ask about her car?"

Kaely turned Erin's question over in her mind. Finally, she said, "Yes. It could tell us if he purposely tried to avoid being seen at the resort."

"So, it's possible Mr. Hubbard might recognize him?"

Kaely nodded. "I'd like to know if she ever made it to the event. It's entirely possible that he asked her to pick him up somewhere along the way."

"Then her car could be anywhere."

"That's possible," Kaely said. "If I had to guess, I think she met him there. But I doubt they ever went inside. Too risky. If I was the killer, I would have met her near the event. Then I would have gotten her into my car."

"Would he have stabbed her there?"

"No. He wouldn't taint his own property. He's smarter than that."

Erin sighed. "I'd bring up chloroform, but you taught me that people don't instantly go unconscious when it's used."

"It's possible that if a large enough amount of chloroform was used, the victim would become unconscious quickly, but they would fight back. Besides, the amount needed could kill them."

"So, what did he do?" Erin asked.

"I don't know. He could have choked her, but I didn't see any bruises on her neck. Maybe he hit her."

Erin frowned. "No one said anything about her being hit on the head, and I didn't notice blood in her hair."

Kaely picked up her phone. Adrian probably hadn't gotten home yet. She clicked on his number. He picked up on the second ring.

"Sorry to bother you," Kaely said, "but we have a couple of questions. I need to know everything I can to write you a profile that will help you."

"Sure, I understand."

He sounded drained. This was a huge case for a small-town police force. Kaely felt guilty, but she was being honest about needing his help. She wanted to give him a profile that would help him find this killer before anyone else died.

"Where did you find Chloe's car?"

"What makes you ask that?" he said.

"It has to do with where the UNSUB took her and why. Did he try to stay away from everyone because someone in this area might recognize him?"

"Interestingly enough, we haven't found her car yet. Merle said she drove away in it, and that she was alone. But that was the last time he saw it."

"Okay. My other question is this: It's possible he stabbed her immediately. If that happened, there might be blood in her car. I just wanted to find out if he did anything else. Did Gibson find any other wounds? Was she hit on the head? In the pictures, there's no bruising around her neck."

"There's no indication of any other kind of trauma to the body except for the knife wound. Maybe Gibson missed something. I'll check with him, but it will have to wait until the morning. He doesn't take kindly to being bothered this time of night."

"Whereas you don't mind at all?"

Adrian chuckled. "It's fine. I'm just tired. It's been a long day."

"I understand," Kaely said. "One last question. Has the tox screen come back?"

"No. We had to send the results to Knoxville. We won't have anything back until sometime tomorrow. Why? What are you thinking?"

"Just trying to find out how he got her into a situation where he was able to stab her. I don't see any defensive wounds on her body."

"You're right. There weren't any that Gibson could find. You think he drugged her?"

"I don't know," Kaely said, "but I'd like to. Will you let me know as soon as possible if you find out anything helpful from the tox screen?"

"Yeah. I will. Hopefully, I'll have something for you by the time you get here tomorrow."

"Thanks," Kaely said. "Appreciate it."

"Not a problem. I'm grateful for all your help. See you tomorrow."

Kaely said good-bye and disconnected the call. She looked over at Erin and shrugged. This UNSUB was unusual, and she hadn't written a profile by herself in quite a while. Was she up to it, or would a serial killer claim another victim because she couldn't help Adrian find him in time?

TWENTY-TWO

After telling Erin what Adrian had said, the women went back to the photos. Erin couldn't shake the feeling that she didn't belong here—trying to help Kaely. She hadn't worked for the FBI, and she'd never received the kind of training Kaely had.

"You're pretty quiet," Kaely said after a few minutes. "Anything wrong?"

"I'm just thinking that you'd do better if you had someone else to help you. Someone who actually knows what they're doing. Not a clueless author who's only parroting the information you've given me."

To her surprise, Kaely laughed. When she saw the look on Erin's face, Kaely reached over and took her hand. "You know, I've worked with several analysts at the FBI. They were great. But my interaction with you matches or exceeds anything I ever experienced on the job."

Erin started to protest, but Kaely waved her comment away. "I've taught you a lot, but you soaked all of it up like a sponge. And some of the things you noticed on the body? I didn't teach you that. It was instinct. You're a natural. Not only as a cop, but as an analyst. I realize a lot of that comes from working on the streets of St. Louis. But when we're working together, it's like our minds are in sync. That doesn't happen very often. I think you're extraordinary. Forgive me for saying this, but I wish you wouldn't give up on your dream of joining the Bureau and applying to the BAU. In the end, it's your decision. And you might be right. It's possible that the FBI might not see you as an acceptable candidate. But I'm willing to go to bat for you, if you ever change your mind."

Erin sighed. "I know you're trying to help, and I appreciate it. Let me think about it. I'm not sure what I want. Do I want to try for the FBI and fail? Or even win? Or do I want to keep writing? I know it's frustrating, but I just need some time. I never expected this book to take off the way it did. Like I told you, I had a couple of novels published by a small press when I was in college. People seemed to enjoy them, but I didn't sell a lot."

"Are they still available?" Kaely asked.

"Yeah. After they went out of print, I published them myself. They're only available online as ebooks."

"Have they been selling?" Kaely asked.

"No, not really. I haven't done anything to promote them in a long time."

Kaely frowned. "I don't understand. With the sales of *Dark Matters*, I'd think they should be selling like hot cakes."

Erin smiled. "I published them under a different name. I didn't want my college friends to make fun of me."

Kaely's mouth dropped open. "Erin, don't you realize that a lot of people would buy those books if they knew you wrote them?"

"I'm not sure how good they are."

Kaely shook her head. "Oh, my dear friend. You have such a natural talent. I'm certain they're wonderful."

"Well, I'm not so sure of that."

"Why don't you let me read them? If they're good, I'm sure your publisher would be thrilled to release them under your real name. You could make a lot of money."

Erin shook her head. "I have a lot of money, and it hasn't made me happy. Until I've decided what I want to do with my life, I'd like to keep those books a secret."

"Okay, if that's what you want," Kaely said. "But it won't hurt to let me read them, will it? You should know me well enough by now to be confident that I'll be honest with you."

Erin hesitated. She wasn't sure if she wanted anyone to read her other books. But if she had to pick the one person she trusted the most, it would be Kaely.

"All right. They're under the name A.J. Waide."

"Did you make that up?" Kaely asked.

Erin shook her head. "No, it was my mother's maiden name."

"Well, let's go through the rest of these photos. Then I need to finish that profile. To be honest, I'm tired. It's been a long day. I want to give Adrian my best, so I need to get to work as soon as possible."

Kaely brought up the photos of the other bodies. After Chloe, there was Terri and then Annie. Erin and Kaely looked them over carefully. Erin didn't see anything she hadn't noticed earlier. The other bodies weren't wearing white dresses or blue ribbons, although it's possible the ribbon had disintegrated on the oldest one.

"Why didn't he remove the jewelry?" Erin said. "Don't serial killers like to collect trophies?"

Kaely nodded. "Many do, but not all of them. We might ask Dr. Gibson if they're missing any hair."

"You mean, maybe the killer cut some of it off and kept it?"

"Yeah."

"I didn't notice anything like that on Chloe," Erin said.

"Me either." Kaely sighed. "This guy really is different. He isn't offended by jewelry, makeup, or fancy shoes. He dresses them in virginal white dresses, but he adds a blue ribbon."

Kaely spoke slowly. Erin realized she wasn't asking a question. She was thinking, repeating information they'd already discussed. Erin stayed quiet. Finally, Kaely straightened up and looked at Erin. "The white dress has nothing to do with purity. He thinks angels wear white. He's angry with them. You said something about it earlier. I think you're right. He blames the angels for something."

"But he thinks angels wear makeup, jewelry and fancy shoes?"

Kaely shook her head. "No. I think he's killing for someone who wore those things—or wanted to."

"It's hard to believe this guy is angry at angels. That's so...twisted."

"Of course it is," Kaely said. "Serial killers aren't rational people. If you can't understand that they aren't mentally sound, you can't figure them out at all. That's why the study of psychopathy is so important."

"So, he's a psychopath? Because he's organized and carefully plans his kills, right? A sociopath is more impulsive. Erratic."

"Exactly. But trust me, there's a method to this guy's

madness. We just need to find it. Understand it. That way we can help Adrian catch him."

"I hope you're right about the local police department being up to the challenge," Erin said.

"We better pray they are." Kaely rubbed her temples as if she had a headache.

"You okay?"

"Yeah, I will be. I just need to get this profile right."

"Are you going to . . . you know . . ."

Kaely met Erin's gaze. "Yes, I am. And yes, you can watch."

"Great. I think it's fascinating. But why won't you let me write about it?"

"Because it isn't standard practice. The analysts at the BAU don't use it, and I don't want to anyone to think it's a valid procedure."

Erin nodded her assent, but she still couldn't understand Kaely's reluctance to allow her way of profiling to be included in a novel. The stories in novels weren't real. Everyone knew that. But, if it was what she wanted, Erin wouldn't go against her wishes.

She was excited to finally be able to watch this unique way of profiling.

And to be honest, just a little bit frightened.

TWENTY-THREE

After he got home, Adrian changed clothes and made himself a cup of decaf caramel cappuccino. He'd purchased a one-cup coffeemaker for Christmas and had been experimenting with different flavored coffee pods until he found these at a large discount store in Knoxville. They were much better than some of the more expensive types of coffees and cappuccinos. He sat down on the couch and turned on the TV. Jake jumped up next to him and put his head on Adrian's lap.

"Yeah, you love me until you get the chance to flirt with a couple of pretty women," he said, stroking Jake's head. "I can't believe how fickle you are."

Jake made a low moaning sound, and Adrian laughed. "Sorry. You're not getting away with your disloyalty that easy."

Jake's head went up and he placed a paw on Adrian's leg. He sighed dramatically. "Okay, okay. You're forgiven."

As if he understood, Jake put his head back down, closed his eyes, and went to sleep. Adrian kept the TV on for a while, but he wasn't really watching it. As he sipped his cappuccino, he kept going over the case in his mind. He felt uneasy, but he wasn't sure why. Of course, he was bothered by the murders, but there was something else. Something he couldn't seem to remember. As he clicked through everything in his mind that he'd seen, and all of the facts they'd accumulated, it was as if there was a voice whispering to him, trying to get him to listen.

His grandmother used to tell him that if he learned to listen to the Holy Spirit, he would always have access to everything he ever needed.

"The Holy Spirit will guide you along your way, boy," she'd said. "Just learn to listen with your heart."

Problem was, his heart didn't seem to be paying much attention lately. Although he had to act confident in front of his officers in their ability to solve these murders, he couldn't help but wonder if they should contact the FBI—or get Knoxville involved. Were they really up to this? The only reason he was willing to wait was because of Kaely Hunter and Erin Delaney. If his heart *was* telling him anything, it was that he had some of the best resources available to anyone through the training and talent of these two remarkable women.

He felt himself begin to nod off in front of the TV. As he drifted off, the brilliant green eyes of Erin Delaney seemed to look deeply into his. And it made him smile.

If she didn't know better, Erin would have been worried that Kaely could actually hear her heart beating. It seemed loud to her, but she knew that wasn't actually possible. Ever since Kaely had told her about her "process," she'd wanted to watch it. She would never tell Kaely that she'd tried it herself, but that it hadn't worked. In fact, she'd felt silly. While working on her book, she'd asked several questions about Kaely's method, but her responses had been a little strange. At one point she said that there was a spiritual side to her method that Erin wouldn't understand. Kaely was right. She didn't understand. Kaely was good about not bringing up God very often in their conversations. Erin had made it clear from the beginning that she wasn't interested. When Kaely read parts of her novel that contained profanity or graphic violence, Kaely hadn't said a word. That had surprised her. Erin had wondered if she might back out of the project— tell her she couldn't lower herself to work with someone who wrote things that went against her Christian principles. Funny thing was, Erin didn't use profanity when she talked to Kaely on the phone—or now that they were together. It wasn't that she thought Kaely would judge her. She honestly didn't want to make her friend uncomfortable. Kaely wasn't one of those judgmental, critical Christians. Instead, she was sweet and understanding. She'd been a better friend to her than the people she'd worked with for several years. Although she had no intention of asking questions about God, if she ever changed her mind, Kaely would be the person she'd turn to.

Now they were sitting at the kitchen table, Kaely on one side, and Erin in a chair a few feet away. The chair across from Kaely was empty. Kaely had her phone set to record and had left it on the table in front of her. She had Erin's phone next to her with the crime photos pulled up on the screen. She'd asked Erin not to say anything until she was finished. Why was she so nervous? It was more than excitement. It was as if there was something in the room. A kind of energy. She had no idea what it was—but she was certain it wasn't her imagination.

"Before I start," Kaely said, "I need to explain that I used to actually eat dinner with the UNSUB." Kaely laughed at Erin's expression. "No, the UNSUB didn't actually eat. When I originally got the idea of trying to *see* the person I was profiling, it came about while studying what people eat and why. For example, someone with bad table manners might have been raised in a certain type of home. Those who ate certain foods could also be profiled because of their choices. Eventually, I dropped that part of the profile. I still think looking at what people eat and how they eat can be really helpful. I've just moved beyond it." She stared at Erin for a moment before saying, "As I told you, there's a spiritual aspect to this. At one point, there were some problems with . . . well, with the wrong spirits becoming involved. I've learned how to take authority over that, but if for any reason, you should become uncomfortable, just leave the room. I'll understand. But like I said, please don't say anything. I need to complete the profile. Do you understand?"

Erin nodded and tried to look nonchalant about what was getting ready to happen. She tried to dismiss her feelings, but they wouldn't be easily vanquished.

Kaely spread out their notes in front of her. Then she closed her eyes and lowered her head. She'd explained to Erin that she always prayed before she started. This was one time when she didn't seem to be concerned with how Erin would react. She didn't *ask* if it was okay. She simply informed her that this was the way it was going to be.

After she lifted her head, she rifled through the notes,

clicked through the photos, and then she started to speak. She looked at the chair across from her as if someone was there.

"You're angry," she said in a matter-of-fact voice. "You've been angry a long time. Ever since you were a child. Something happened to make you this way. You've been planning to pay someone back for a while. Not long ago, you started practicing. Practicing for vengeance. Against God. Against the angels."

Kaely frowned as she looked at the chair. "You're in your late twenties, early thirties. Maybe even your late thirties. You're nice looking, but not so handsome that you are considered unattainable by your victims."

Although they hadn't discussed this before, Erin realized immediately that this was true. Chloe had obviously been attracted to him at some point. Either before she went to meet him or after she arrived at her destination. She didn't have defensive wounds, so she'd apparently gotten in the car with him. Yet Erin understood that if he was exceptionally good-looking, it wouldn't work in his favor. If he was just nice looking, he could attract almost anyone regardless of age.

Kaely glanced down at the papers on the table again. "You don't like women, although your anger isn't really directed at them. They're only a means to an end." She paused. "The most important thing isn't the woman—it's the figurine you force them to hold." She paused again for a moment. "You're uncomfortable touching them. You have no physical attraction to them. You want to kill them in a certain way. You practiced it several times before you killed Chloe. However, what you did to the first three wasn't perfect, so you buried them. But you got it right with Chloe. That's why you displayed her. She was perfection." She frowned and stared at the chair again.

Erin gulped. She'd never experienced anything like this before.

"I don't see any connection between the women," Kaely continued. "We're not going to find you that way, are we? You're not actually killing *them*. You're killing because of someone else." She was quiet for a moment. "Okay, let's move on. You don't mind the makeup, their shoes, or their jewelry. Why? Is it because you're uncomfortable with touching them that way?" She stopped again. "No, that's not it." She shook her head. "You don't know anything about angels. If you did, you'd know that as far as we know, they're all male. That tells me you don't read the Bible. My guess is that if anyone ever tried to get you to go to church or read the Bible, you rejected it." Suddenly she smiled. "That's it, isn't it? Someone tried to force the Bible on you, but you didn't want anything to do with it. You hated them for trying to make you into what they wanted you to be. Did you kill them too?" Pause. "I think you did. What was it that set you off? What did they do to you? And how do the angels tie into it? Did they blame the angels for something? Did they tell you the angels . . ." She stopped, gazing at the empty chair as if she could actually see someone there. Her expression relaxed and she smiled. "They told you the angels took someone away that you loved, didn't they? Like your mother, maybe? And that's why you dress these women up as angels and put that figurine in their hands. You think you're paying the angels back for what they took from you. You don't remove their makeup, jewelry, or their shoes because the only thing you believe about angels is that they are female and wear white robes." She stopped suddenly and a look of surprise changed her expression. "No, that's not it. You don't take off their makeup, jewelry, or their shoes because your mother wore makeup, liked jewelry and high heels. You can't remove them because it would betray her in some way. My guess is whoever told you that the angels took her away also believed your mother shouldn't wear those things. That's it, isn't it?" She quickly clicked through the photos. Even though she didn't say what she was looking for, instinctively, Erin knew. Although they couldn't tell if the other women were wearing makeup, she wanted to know if they were wearing high heels or jewelry. Kaely didn't say anything, but she nodded. "Two of these women wore heels. One didn't. Two of them are still wearing jewelry."

Kaely sighed and leaned back in her chair. Then she stared at the chair across from her and frowned. "You're very dangerous, aren't you? The women are picked at random. You'll go after anyone who is available. Anyone who dresses the way you want. Like I said, I can't profile you by studying the women. They're only the vessel for your angel figurine, the white dress, and the blue ribbon that you add. My guess is that you might have been willing to add shoes and jewelry to the corpses, but that could leave evidence behind. We could find out where those things were purchased. But tracking down blue ribbon is nearly impossible."

Erin wished she had her notebook so she could write down what Kaely was saying, but it was on the table, and Erin didn't want to disturb her process.

"So, you live in this area. You're in your late twenties to

late thirties, you're nice looking . . ." Kaely almost whispered this. She was repeating the observations she'd already made. She seemed frustrated. Was she going to stop? As Kaely rubbed her forehead, Erin wanted to ask her, but again, she knew she had to stay silent.

"You have a good job," Kaely said suddenly. "One that makes you seem appealing to the women you killed. Or . . . one that made you seem safe."

A thought popped into Erin's head that made her feel sick to her stomach. A job that made the victims feel safe? Like someone in law enforcement? No, it couldn't be. She pushed the thought out of her mind. Her research had shown her that many serial killers posed as police officers. But surely no one on the Sanctuary police force could do these terrible things, right?

She heard Kaely speaking but missed part of it.

"I can see you now," she was saying. "Young, attractive, strong, and working a job that demands respect."

Erin was startled when Kaely stared at the chair and smiled as if she actually saw someone sitting there. Did she?

"Women are not afraid of you because of the job you have," Kaely continued. "You live in Sanctuary, and you have a past. My guess is that your mother is dead, and you blame the angels for her passing. Someone told you this when you were young, and now, you're visiting vengeance on God. You may be focused on angels, but your real hatred is for Him. We're going to find you, you know. We've narrowed down the search, and you will make a mistake. In fact, you may have done so already. We're coming for you."

There was a silence as Kaely continued to stare at the empty chair. Then she smiled again. And for just a few seconds, Erin was convinced she saw a figure in the chair herself. She put her hand over her mouth to keep from crying out. It was impossible. Had to be her imagination. But a brief glimpse of a man sitting in that chair rocked her to her core.

TWENTY-FOUR

Kaely worked quickly on the profile. She could see the UNSUB clearly. Not his face, but *him*. His soul, his essence. The evil that emanated from the chair across from her was almost overwhelming. This had happened to her before. Sometimes it made her feel physically ill. She wanted to catch this guy. He had to be stopped. This was the only part about being a behavioral analyst that she didn't like. Walking away after the profile was done. She wanted to put her hands on the man who had killed those women. She wanted to make him pay. She knew it wasn't godly, and it made her feel ashamed. One of the reasons she'd left the FBI was because of the toll it took on her soul. Yet, she missed it. And she didn't want to.

She glanced over at Erin. She seemed rather shaken. Kaely knew this way of profiling was strange and that some people didn't understand it. After she was finished, she smiled at Erin.

"Do you have any questions?"

Erin looked away for a moment. "I . . . I don't know. I mean, I've never seen anything like that before." She frowned at Kaely. "When you do that, do you . . . I mean, do you actually *see* someone sitting in the chair?"

"Yes, sometimes I do. In fact, there was one instance where I could clearly see him. The murders happened in another city. As I worked the profile, I began to see an actual person. It was a witness who'd talked to the police. My boss called the police chief and told him to arrest the witness. Sure enough, it was him."

"That's amazing. I really, really wish you would let me write about this."

Kaely grinned at her. "Wait a minute, I thought you weren't sure you wanted to write anymore."

"I'm . . . I'm not."

"Well, you certainly jumped at the chance to write about my process," Kaely said.

"So, will you let me?"

"Again, I have to say no . . . for now. Let me think about it." Kaely sighed. "What behavioral analysts do is incredible. The basis of what I do comes from that training. I just create a profile a little differently. I would never want anyone to think that what I do is a better way of profiling. It isn't."

"It's up to you," Erin said, "but I think it's fascinating."

"I'm glad you think so," Kaely said with a smile. "But some of the people I've worked with might not."

"What about Noah?"

"He knows about it, of course," Kaely said, "but I'm pretty sure he'd have a problem if a lot of people read about what I do."

Erin looked surprised. For just a moment, Kaely wondered if she'd made a mistake. Should she have kept her process to herself? Was Erin a true friend—or just an acquaintance that she'd worked with? Could she really trust her? Kaely's gut told her she could, but she couldn't worry about it now. She needed to get this profile written up. She'd email it to Adrian tonight, but she wanted to take a hard copy with her to the police station and go over it with him tomorrow. It was important to make certain he understood it.

"How do you feel about being here?" Kaely asked. "It never occurred to me that you'd come face-to-face with a serial killer." She shook her head. "I'm sorry. I really am. This was supposed to be a time for you to relax and talk about how you've been feeling."

Erin shrugged. "Well, I wanted to get my mind off of . . . that night. This should certainly do it."

"That might be true, but I can think of lots of other ways to distract you."

"Look," Erin said, "I'm going to bed. You need to write up your profile, and I don't want to interfere. Unless there's something I can do to help?"

"No, there really isn't. You go ahead. I'll get this done and then turn in myself." She pointed at Erin. "Tomorrow we'll spend some time shopping in town. It will be fun. And even though the idea of a winter storm is a little worrisome, getting snowed in will give us time to talk. I've found that most serial killers stay home during bad weather."

Erin stared at her for a moment before she burst out laughing. "I'm so sorry," she said, gasping for air. "For some reason that just struck me wrong. Serial killers are afraid of bad weather? Who knew?"

Kaely had to laugh with her. Her comment was based on statistics, but it really was a little funny.

"There was that one case I told you about," Kaely said.

"The killer who called himself the Snowman? Now he wasn't afraid of a good snowstorm."

Erin's eyes widened, and her mouth quivered. This time it was Kaely who laughed.

"Okay, this has been a very odd day, and I think we're both tired," Kaely said. "Before we disgrace ourselves any further, why don't you get some sleep?"

Erin stood up. "I think that's a good idea. And let's promise each other that we'll never tell anyone that we got the giggles talking about serial killers, okay?"

"You have my word. I would never live it down."

"I know you think going into town tomorrow will help me, but . . ."

Kaely nodded. "I realize it will take some courage, Erin, but you know you can't keep hiding from the world, right?"

Erin started to respond, but Kaely interrupted her. "Look, I showed you something very few people have seen. I did so because I trust you. Now, I want you to trust me. You're strong enough to do this, and I'll be right there with you. I won't leave you alone."

"I know my fear seems ridiculous," Erin said, "but it feels real."

"I never doubted that for a moment, but it's because you're afraid of giving up control. That's what agoraphobia is. But the truth is, you've given fear control. What you're fighting against is what you've actually given into." Kaely shook her head. "You can do this. Like I said, I'll be with you—and so will God. Trust me? Maybe give Him a chance?"

Erin stared at something past Kaely for several seconds, then she met Kaely's eyes. "Okay. I really don't want to give into this anymore. Maybe this is the day I finally get free of it."

"It might take a little longer, but still, one day at a time."
She smiled at Erin who nodded back. Then she said good-
night, picked up her cup and took it to the kitchen. After
that, she headed up the stairs to her bedroom.

Once Kaely heard the bedroom door close, she spoke
softly to God. "Help me to help her, God," she said. "She's
hurting, and I need Your wisdom. I came here because I believe You told me to. So I have to trust that You've prepared
her heart and that You'll use me. And please help me write
this profile. Here I am, tracking a serial killer again. Did I
leave the Bureau too soon? Maybe it wasn't Your will for me
to walk away." She sighed. "I've got to put this in Your hands.
Right now, I have to concentrate on Erin. I trust You to heal
her and show her how much she needs You. Thanks, Lord."

She felt better. Carrying the weight of her time with Erin
was too much to bear. She could see how much Erin needed
God, but she had to be very careful. If she pushed her too
much, it could cause her to shut down.

Kaely sighed and picked up her phone. Then she started
listening to the recording of her session. As her own voice
played back, she made notes and began writing the profile.
She glanced at the clock on the wall. It was almost eleven,
and it would take her at least a couple of hours to write
this the way it needed to be done. She felt as if she could
sleep for twenty-four hours and still not get enough rest.
But right now, tracking a serial killer was important. Lives
were at stake. He had to be caught before she and Erin left.
She couldn't leave knowing he was still around, stalking and
killing women.

When Erin got to her room, she closed the door, started a fire in the fireplace, and then sat down on an overstuffed chair in the corner. Did Kaely think she was nuts? She hadn't planned to laugh like that. It seemed so . . . insensitive. It was just nerves. She'd needed this. Getting out of her apartment and spending time with someone besides herself. No, she hadn't planned on a serial killer, but somehow it had energized her. Kaely was right. Law enforcement was in her blood. Part of her. Writing about it had helped. A lot. But working with Kaely and Adrian had made her feel useful again. As if something had awakened inside her. The part of her that led her to join the department all those years ago. Right now, there were two voices in her head. One actually wanted to write another book. The other one felt she should try to get into the FBI. However, she was certain the Bureau wouldn't accept her. Kaely had mentioned that it would probably depend on her diagnosis, which had been severe PTSD. She'd been on rather strong medication for a while, and she hadn't kept up with her therapy. Talking to doctors had made her feel weak, and she hated thinking of herself that way. Yet the truth was, she *was* weak. The thoughts of suicide were still in her head. She hadn't felt like herself until . . . until Adrian showed up that first morning and asked for her help. It wasn't the murder that she'd needed—it was his belief that she was able to assist him. That she wasn't worthless.

She got up and started getting ready for bed. Tomorrow she and Kaely would go into town. She wasn't sure how well she would do. She felt safe back in her apartment, and she felt safe here with Kaely. But being someplace new. Out in open spaces. Someplace she'd never been. Around people. She swallowed the sour bile that forced its way into her throat. Fear was her enemy. She hated being afraid, but she was. She didn't want to look like a wimp in front of Kaely. The last thing she wanted was pity.

Her fingers trembled as she pulled a sweatshirt over her head. Where had she gone? Erin Delaney had disappeared somewhere and left behind this pitiful creature whom she hated with every fiber of her being. If she fell apart tomorrow . . . She walked over to the dresser. The metal box with her gun was in there. If she . . . No. She couldn't do that to Kaely. No matter what happened while she was here, she wouldn't do that until she went home. She'd send a message first, letting one of her old friends at the station know what was happening. Then she'd unlock the front door so they could get inside. She'd already made out a will. She'd left everything to a nonprofit organization called BackStoppers out of St. Louis. They raised money to support first responders and their families when there was a loss of life or a catastrophic injury that occurred in the line of duty. She couldn't think of a better way to use the money she made from the book. They'd stepped in to help Scott's family when he died.

Scott. His face flashed in her mind. The look on his face—as if he couldn't believe he'd been shot. He wanted her to help him, but she couldn't. By the time she reached him, he was gone.

She pushed back the image. Would she ever be free from it? Would she ever stop blaming herself for not protecting him? And for . . .

"Stop it. Just stop it," she whispered under her breath. How long was she supposed to live like this? If there was a God, where was He? She blinked away the tears that filled her eyes. No. She wasn't buying into the whole *God* thing. She liked Kaely. In fact, she'd changed the way she'd seen all Christians because of her. Kaely was smart and strong. Capable. She'd helped Erin when no one else could. Kaely believed in a God because she had to. Because she had to believe there was good in the universe.

But Erin would never believe that.

Never.

TWENTY-FIVE

Kaely finally finished the profile. She emailed it to Adrian and printed out two copies. One to take with her to the station. And one to keep.

She didn't really want to look at the clock, but when she did, she was sorry she'd done it. A little after two in the morning. She sighed loudly. Time to get some sleep. She realized that she'd never talked to Erin about what time they needed to leave.

She found a pad of paper and a pen in the kitchen and wrote out a quick note. Then she put it next to the coffeemaker. If Erin was anything like her, that would be the first place she'd head when she got out of bed.

After doing a quick cleanup in the kitchen, she turned off some of the lights, leaving a couple on for security, and then checked the front and back doors, making sure they were locked.

A sound caught her attention, and she hurried to the living room and looked out front. Someone was driving away. A dark colored truck. Should she be concerned? It hadn't stopped. Maybe it was someone who was lost—or who lived nearby. She also scanned the woods.

"Don't be silly," she said to herself. "There's no ghost." Thankfully, everything was quiet.

She hurried upstairs, took a quick shower, and climbed into bed. She'd just fallen asleep when a loud wailing made her sit straight up in bed. Without thinking, she glanced at the clock on the nightstand. 3:33 a.m. *Erin.*

Kaely jumped out of bed and hurried down the hallway to Erin's room. When she swung the door open, she found Erin sitting up in her bed. Her eyes were wide, and her face was wet with tears.

She approached her carefully, not wanting to frighten her in case she was still entrenched in the nightmare that had plagued her for so long. Erin turned to look at her. Then she reached both arms out. Kaely sat down and held her while she wept. Her body trembled.

"It's okay," she said softly, many times over, until the sound of crying stopped and Erin let her go.

"I . . . I'm sorry. I didn't mean . . ."

"Erin, don't be silly. We've talked many times after one of these episodes. You don't need to apologize. I'm actually glad I'm here with you instead of feeling so helpless talking to you on the phone."

"I know you were up late," Erin said. "You need your sleep."

"I'm just fine. Truly. Do you want me to make you some tea? I brought some chamomile. It will help you sleep."

Erin stared at her for a moment before saying, "If you're certain it's not too much trouble."

"I'm certain. I'll make us both a cup. I'll be right back, okay?"

Erin nodded. "Thank you."

Kaely got up and hurried downstairs. It only took a couple of minutes to make the tea. She took it upstairs, handed a cup to Erin, and sat down in the chair in the corner with her own cup.

"Can we sleep in a little later in the morning?" Erin asked after taking a sip of her tea. "I'm so tired."

Kaely smiled at her. "Funny you should say that. I left you a note downstairs asking you the same question."

Erin offered her a tremulous smile in return, but it didn't mask the pain in her eyes. Kaely so wanted to pray with her. Let her know how much God wanted to help her, but there was a check in her spirit, and until she was released, she'd wait. The Holy Spirit was the only One who knew when the soil of Erin's heart was prepared for Him.

"How about we sleep until nine?" Kaely said. "We can grab a quick, light breakfast, go into town, and then have a late lunch. Will that work?"

"Sounds perfect." Erin took another sip of her tea and then set it down on the nightstand. "I'm feeling sleepy. Do you mind?"

"Of course not." Kaely stood up and walked toward the door. But before she left, she had a question to ask Erin. "Erin, do you remember what time it was that night . . . when Scott died?"

She shook her head. "No, I wasn't looking at my watch when it happened."

"What about when you had to leave his side and go inside the apartment to find the little girl had been shot?"

Erin frowned at her. "Why are you bringing this up now? What does it matter what time it was?"

"Just be patient with me a moment. When you were in that apartment, did you happen to see the time?" Kaely silently prayed that she wasn't making a mistake. But she had a feeling . . .

"Of course not. It wasn't really important, you know."

Her voice was sharp, and Kaely could see that she was getting upset. She suddenly regretted that she'd brought this up. She started to apologize when suddenly, Erin's face grew pale.

"Wait a minute. I . . . there was a clock on the living room wall. I happened to glance at it. I'd forgotten all about it." She shook her head. "How could I have forgotten? I don't understand."

She looked at Kaely with an expression that almost ripped her heart in two. She was right.

"It was 3:33," she said in a whisper. "Why didn't I . . . I should have . . ." She shook her head as tears streamed down her cheeks. "The clock was behind the little girl's father. I was looking at him. I . . . I didn't look at it on purpose, but I did see it." She turned her tear-stained face toward Kaely. "How could I have forgotten?" she asked again.

Kaely put her cup down and went back to Erin's bed where she sat down next to the distraught young woman.

"You've been trying so hard to protect yourself from those terrible images," she said. "The time on that clock just got mixed up with everything else. But your mind remembered. And your body reacted. This isn't the first time I've seen this. I had a friend at the Bureau who used to wake up almost every morning at the exact time her mother passed away."

"It seems impossible," Erin said, wiping her face with the back of her hand.

Kaely got up and walked over to a tissue box on the edge of the dresser. She pulled out a couple of tissues and took them over to Erin.

"You've proven that it isn't," Kaely said gently.

Erin reached up for the tissues. "Thank you," she said. After she wiped her face she asked, "Do you think I'll stop waking up now that I know what caused it?"

"I'm not sure, Erin. But I do believe that the pain you have on the inside has to be addressed for you to feel better. You didn't like seeing the therapist the police department sent you to?"

She shook her head and made a face. "There were several. The last one was the worst. She was weird. Kept talking about my *feelings* and asking me what I thought I should do. If I knew what to do, why did I need her?" Erin sniffed and wiped her nose. "When she asked me 'how's that working for you?' I knew it was over. I can watch Dr. Phil on TV. I don't need her."

Although Kaely tended to agree with her, Erin definitely needed some kind of support. She wanted to ask her about speaking to a minister, but once again, she got a check. It was so frustrating to know what Erin needed and not be able to say anything about it. Why did it seem that people who need God the most appeared to be the ones who rebelled against Him so violently? Probably the enemy battling to keep them. Even Christians went through this. It was heartbreaking. But at least when their struggle was over, they were with the One who loved them the most. Their Comforter and Savior. The Lover of their souls.

"Why don't you try to get some sleep?" Kaely said. "Just remember that I'm just down the hall if you need me."

"Thanks again, Kaely. I'm really glad I came. I needed this more than I can say."

Kaely nodded at her and closed the door. She waited in the hall for a moment before heading back to her room. Erin needed much more than she'd received tonight, but if—and when—she was ready to listen . . . that moment was in God's loving hands.

TWENTY-SIX

Adrian was in his office early. He read through Kaely's profile slowly, trying to digest it. He was amazed by how detailed it was. However, if she'd given him a name, he would have been happier. He knew he was being watched carefully. The mayor and the town council were wondering if he was up to the task of catching what was likely a serial killer. So far, he hadn't confirmed to them that there was one. Although he was pretty certain about it, he had no plans to state it publicly for a while. Not until he had to.

He'd been at his desk for a little over an hour when his phone rang. Dr. Gibson.

"Hi, Doc," he said. "What have you got?"

As he listened to Gibson give him the news he was waiting for, he swallowed hard. Things had just gotten much more dangerous, in his opinion. The person who killed Chloe Banner knew what he was doing. He thanked Gibson and hung up. Then he went back to the profile. There it was. Kaely suspected that Chloe had been incapacitated by some kind of drug. She qualified that conjecture by stating that she hadn't witnessed any defensive wounds and that autopsy results could alter her opinion.

Gibson had discovered flunitrazepam, also called the date-rape drug. There was also alcohol in her system. Not a lot, but mixed with flunitrazepam, it wouldn't have taken long for Chloe to lose consciousness. Gibson had promised the complete autopsy results, but when the fax machine began to growl and spit out the first page, Adrian jumped.

"Keep it together," he said to himself as he pulled each paper from the machine. Once everything was in front of him, he went through the report carefully. No sexual assault. One knife wound to the heart. Chloe died about four to six hours before she was found. Gibson agreed that she hadn't died where she'd been found and that her clothes had been changed. He was a little confused by the stomach contents. She'd consumed alcohol, but no food. If she'd gone to the Grits and Grain event, there should have been food and even more alcohol. Besides, the timeline told him that she must not have made it to the event at all. What did that mean? She consumed the drug-laced drink somewhere else?

He began pulling up the names and addresses of every bar or restaurant in the area. Was it possible someone saw them? Would remember them? This was a resort area. There were too many possibilities. If they could just find her car. . . . Of course, that didn't necessarily mean anything. He might have taken her somewhere in his own car.

Adrian wrote down the time of death and the location where the body was found. He sighed in frustration. The two-hour time-of-death window made the area they'd need to search too large. He wasn't getting anywhere with the facts he had right now.

Lisa poked her head inside his office. "Just made coffee. You want some?"

Adrian was surprised. He thought he'd made it. In fact, he thought he'd already had some. Boy, this case was messing with his mind.

"I would love that. Sorry, I meant to start it when I got here. I totally forgot."

Lisa grinned at him. "I never thought I'd see the day when you forgot about coffee." She walked over and picked up his empty cup. "I'll get you some before your head explodes." She smiled at Jake. "I have some of those treats you like, Mr. Jake. How about one?"

Jake's tail thumped loudly against the floor, signaling his reaction to her offer. Adrian smiled. Jake and Lisa went through the same routine every morning. She was so good with Mutt and Jeff—and her ability with dogs translated easily to Jake, who not only loved her but loved her dogs. If only Adrian could get that enthusiastic about things in his own life. Until these murders, he'd fallen into a slump. He loved his job and this town, but calls from tourists asking for directions and neighbors having petty disagreements had started to wear him down. Sure, there was their fair share of shoplifting and even domestic squabbles—but all in all, nothing very stimulating ever happened in Sanctuary—until now. Although, this current situation had brought with it some concerns. He was grateful for Kaely and Erin, but would he be able to use their information to find this killer before someone else died? And if they found another body—would it be his fault?

"Here you go."

Lisa placed his cup of coffee on the desk and then removed

a dog treat from her pocket. Jake sat up and put out his paw, which always made Lisa laugh. She tossed the treat up in the air, right above his head, and Jake snapped it up as it reached his nose.

"Thanks, Lisa," he said.

She looked down at his desk, "Autopsy in? Anything new?"

"Yeah. Why don't you grab your own coffee and come in. I'd love your opinion."

"You got it, boss."

Adrian had encouraged Lisa more than once to apply to join their small force, but she always turned him down.

"I like what I do now," she'd told him every time he brought it up. "Seems silly to trade a job I love for something I *might* like. If that ever changes, I'll let you know."

A few minutes later, she was back, her coffee cup in one hand and a small paper plate in the other. "Tim brought doughnuts. I'll bet you didn't eat either." She looked over at Jake, who was now lying on his dog bed in the corner. "I hope you at least fed Jake."

"Do you really think I could get out of the house without feeding him? He wouldn't allow it," he said, grinning.

"No, I suppose he wouldn't."

Lisa put the cup and the doughnuts on Adrian's desk. Then she pulled up a chair. "So, did you learn anything interesting from the autopsy?"

Adrian brought her up to date. "My question is, where were they when Chloe was roofied?"

"Why don't you let me work on that? Her family is supposed to be in town today sometime. They're going to stop by here first. I asked them for a current photo. Once we have it, I can send it to bars and restaurants in the area."

"You heard from the family already?"

She nodded. "Lonzine and Dale found their contact information in Chloe's room when they searched it."

"What time are they coming in?"

"Should be here around one." Lisa watched him for a moment before saying, "Do you want me to talk to them?"

Adrian shook his head. "I feel like this is something I should do, although I'm pretty sure you'd be better at it."

Lisa took a bite of her doughnut, chewed, and swallowed. "I think you're wrong."

Adrian frowned at her. "How can you say that? You saw how I fell apart when I had to tell Susan Simmons that Rod was gone."

He still got choked up when he thought about it. Rod Simmons had managed the local hardware store. He'd had a sudden heart attack and was gone before the ambulance arrived. Rod and Susan were such a great couple. Everyone in Sanctuary loved them. They hosted Christmas parties in the winter and held a huge BBQ every summer in their large backyard. Going to Susan's house to give her the bad news was one of the worst moments of his life. Rod was the brother he'd never had. He cried so much, Susan had to comfort *him*. It was embarrassing.

"Boss, that was just what Susan needed that day." Lisa's voice was soft and full of compassion. "You shared her grief. It helped her to know that someone else understood how she felt. If you'd just delivered the news unemotionally, it would have been much worse for her."

"If you say so. I felt totally unprofessional."

"Well, if you're such a failure at your job," Lisa said, "explain to me why every member of your staff would gladly lay down their lives for you."

He glanced over at her, startled. "I . . . I appreciate that, but please don't ever try it. I'll fire you if you die."

Lisa burst out laughing. "Well, so far that hasn't been a problem." She took a deep breath and said, "Okay, so this is the first actual murder . . . well, murders we've ever had since you've been here." She paused a moment. "And we've only had to take down a couple of people who had access to deadly weapons."

Adrian nodded. "Herman Glimscher. He was so drunk he didn't realize what he was doing. Thankfully, that ended okay."

"Thanks to his wife, Rose. Boy, did she read him the riot act. He got rid of that gun and never bought another one."

"Then there was Tillie Perez who tried to run her husband down with her car."

Lisa grinned. "Sorry, not funny, but Louis ran so fast I think his legs caught fire. I hate divorce, but frankly, I was relieved when she left him and moved to Cincinnati."

"Louis was even more relieved." He sighed. "Why don't you make up a list of . . ."

Someone knocked on the door and Adrian called out, "Come in."

Officer Lee stood there. Lonzine Lee was a terrific cop. She was unflappable, someone he depended on. The look of excitement on her face surprised him. Not a look he saw often.

"Just got a call from a state trooper, boss," she said. "They found Chloe Banner's car."

"Where?"

"Pulled off on the side of the road between here and Townsend."

"That doesn't make any sense," he said slowly.

"She had a flat tire," Lonzine said. "Looks like someone slashed it. There were tracks behind it. Pretty sure someone stopped to help her."

Adrian and Lisa looked at each other.

"Our killer," Lisa said.

"So, he cuts her tire and waits for her to pull off the road," Adrian said. "Then he picks her up. But how did he drug her? Wouldn't she have called a tow truck? And why would she have left with him if she didn't know him?"

At that moment, he had more questions than he had answers. But if they were going to stop the killing, that had to change. And fast.

TWENTY-SEVEN

Erin was up before Kaely. She was still thinking about the nightmare she'd had. She finally knew why she was waking up at the same time every night. Now that she understood why it was happening, would it stop?

Although she appreciated Kaely's help, she was a little embarrassed. Talking to Kaely on the phone was different than having her here. Seeing the reaction the nightmare caused in person.

She brewed a cup of coffee and then sat down at the kitchen table. She needed to eat breakfast, but she wasn't really hungry. After downing her coffee, she got up and found a box of cereal. She poured some in a bowl, added milk, and made a second cup of coffee. She was halfway through her cereal when Kaely came into the kitchen. She looked well rested, as if last night hadn't happened. How could that be?

"Good morning," she said.

"Good morning," Erin echoed. "I'm sorry about . . ."

Kaely held up her hand. "Don't you dare apologize again. I'm here to help you, remember? When we get back from town today, we'll talk more about what happened, okay?"

"All right, but . . . it's hard for me."

Kaely smiled. "I know, and that's okay. You can trust me, Erin. I've had my share of hurt and confusion. If there's anyone who understands, it's me."

"I realize that. I appreciate that you've been open with me and shared the difficulties you've had. It helps, it really does." Erin sighed. "I guess that's the one saving grace we have when life has been challenging. It makes us more understanding of others. Still, I think I'd rather be clueless and happy."

Kaely grinned. "Me too."

"At least I know why I've been waking up at the same time in the morning, although I can't understand how my mind knew what time it was when I'm asleep."

Kaely shrugged. "Trust me, I've heard stories stranger than that. Our minds are capable of a lot more than we realize."

"I guess so. I can't believe it's taken this long for me to remember. I go through that night in my mind, again and again, but until last night, I didn't remember seeing the clock. All I could recall was seeing Scott down. I'd just gone to check on him when a man came out of the building next to the street where he lay. He was yelling and screaming about his daughter. I didn't want to leave Scott, but another officer said he'd stay with him, so I followed the man inside. I was actually angry with him. We went into his apartment and into his daughter's bedroom. She was . . . she was lying in her bed, across the room. A bullet had come through the wall and hit her in the head. She was dead. He screamed and yelled at me to help. I called for a bus, but I knew it was too late. The father blamed me. He called me a murderer. Said I killed his daughter. At first, I thought he was wrong.

I was certain it was a bullet from one of the gangs. But later when they examined the bullet . . . I guess I've told you this before." She stared at Kaely.

Kaely reached over and covered Erin's hand with hers. "I'm so sorry. You're going to find a way to deal with this, Erin. It won't go away, but you'll be able to get past it. Tonight, we'll talk about it. I really want to help you."

"Thank you." Erin sighed. "I'm sure you're getting tired of listening to this over and over."

"No, I'm not. We're making progress. The worst thing you can do is to stuff your feelings—and your nightmares—inside yourself. It's like when you cut your finger and someone tells you that leaving it uncovered will help with healing. You've got to uncover the trauma so you can heal." Kaley reached over, tore a paper towel off the nearby spindle, and handed it to Erin. She stared at it, confused. It was then that she realized her cheeks were wet. How does someone cry without realizing it? She thanked Kaely for it and hurried up the stairs to change clothes.

Kaely watched Erin leave. She'd trained as a behavioral analyst and knew that Erin was suffering. She wasn't certain how deep her depression went, but Kaely was definitely afraid for her friend. She really did believe that remembering the clock was a step forward. But what next? She was running out of options. Uncovering the trauma in Erin's mind was one thing. But Kaely truly believed Erin needed what only God could give her. Yet, she wasn't allowed to bring Him into their discussion.

"God," she whispered. "You need to help me. I believe You

have a plan and that You put me in Erin's life for a reason. But I'm not sure what to do next. I'm trusting You to touch her. To bring her to a place of healing. She needs You so much. I'm not capable of doing what You can."

Kaely ate a quick breakfast and checked the weather forecast. Sure enough, a storm was moving their way. It was hard to tell just how many inches of snow to expect. Down through the years, Kaely had learned how imprecise forecasts could be. Major storms turned out to be nothing, and light snow ended up a foot deep. It was hard to know how this one would end up, but the winds were certainly a concern. In an area like this, the wind was blocked some by the trees. But it could still wreak havoc when it was as strong as predicted.

She was grateful they had time to go into town today and that Erin had agreed to come with her. She needed to get out among people. Eat at a restaurant. Act normal. Buy stuff. There were so many cute shops in Sanctuary, Kaely was hopeful it would help her get her mind off of the night that had caused her so much pain—and the requests from her agent and publisher for more books. She'd heard Erin's phone vibrate quite a bit since she'd joined her in the cabin. Erin never answered it. Kaely caught her checking her phone a couple of times, but she'd never seen her call anyone back.

Last night had been disturbing. When she was awakened by Erin's screams, she'd run into her room and found her sobbing and shaking, disoriented and breathing so quickly that Kaely was afraid she was going to pass out. She was hopeful that the nightmares would stop now that she'd remembered the clock in the girl's apartment. But the underlying trauma was still there. It seemed to Kaely that Erin still had a lot to deal with. All Kaely could do was follow the

Holy Spirit and let him guide her. He was the Healer, and He was the only One who could set Erin free.

Kaely finished her breakfast, and then got up and headed upstairs to her room, praying quietly that God would order her steps and give her wisdom during the rest of their time together. From the things Kaely had noticed in Erin, it was possible that her life hung in the balance. And that made Kaely cling to God as hard as she could. This was a fight that must be won.

TWENTY-EIGHT

Mr. and Mrs. Banner had just left his office when Lisa knocked on Adrian's door.

"How was it?" she asked after he told her to come in.

"About how you'd expect," he said. "I got the feeling they blamed me somehow. That if our department was larger, Chloe wouldn't have died."

"I'm sure they don't think that."

Adrian shrugged. "Not consciously, but there was an . . . undercurrent. Of course, they were extremely upset after identifying their daughter's body at the morgue. That made it worse. But I'm sure some of it was because I couldn't give them much information. I can't bring up the other bodies because we're not sure they're connected to Chloe's death. I know what Erin and Kaely think, and I agree with them, but there's no proof yet. Nothing to tie them together. For now, all these poor parents know is that their daughter came here on vacation and now she's dead."

"Why *did* Chloe come here?" Lisa asked. "A woman alone, who doesn't seem to know anyone? Doesn't make much sense to me."

"Seems she had a friend who vacationed here last year. Went on and on about it. Chloe had been going through a stressful time in her life. She broke up with her long-term boyfriend, and her job had been taking a lot of her time. She wanted to get away and have some fun."

"She just called the resort out of the blue?" Lisa asked.

"No, actually, the friend referred her to Steve Tremont."

"The guy who owns the Watcher cabin?"

Adrian nodded. "He mentioned the resort. That's all I know about it." He frowned. "I've known Steve a long time. We're acquaintances, not friends, but I can't see him mixed up in this. Might be best though . . ."

"To find out where he was Saturday night?"

"Yeah."

Lisa had a knack for finishing his sentences. It didn't irritate him though. They'd just worked together for so long they knew what the other one was thinking.

"Where are the Banners staying?"

"At the resort. Merle gave them a free room. Told them to stay as long as they needed to."

"Merle? That's surprising."

Merle Hubbard wasn't known for his benevolence. Of course, he was in business to make money, not friends. Merle had never had a guest murdered, though. Something like that could make anyone compassionate. Even Merle.

"I agree." He shook his head. "I think the Banners were in shock. I wish I could have said something to help them, but I couldn't find anything comforting." It would be a long time before Adrian would be able to get the look in Mrs. Banner's eyes out of his mind. They were dead. As if her daughter's murder had stolen her life as well. Mr. Banner was more aggressive. Trying to take charge. Probably for his wife's sake. But Adrian noticed his hand tremble when he reached out to shake hands with Adrian. The man was suffering. "Oh, here's the picture they brought. I promised we'd copy it and get it back to them." He handed Lisa the photo. It was weird, looking at Chloe when she was alive after seeing her body. It was hard to believe they were the same person. The fire of life changed someone's features. Her pale face had color in the photo. Her eyes sparkled, and her smile made her look like someone else. Someone who hadn't suffered at the hands of a depraved human being who had no respect for the living.

Talking to the Banners left him feeling drained. He wanted nothing more than to go home and sleep. Try to forget the past few days. The quiet bodies, the lifeless eyes of the living and the dead. His past had come back to haunt him, and he hated it. He came to Sanctuary to start again. To be a law enforcement officer in a place that wouldn't exact such a terrible toll. But the horror of murder and destruction had found him again.

"Hello?" Lisa said.

"Sorry. Just . . ."

"I know. I feel the same way."

Adrian sighed. "Go ahead and start sending the photo out to bars and restaurants in the area. If you get any nibbles, send Lonzine and Dale out to talk to them. We've got to have more information. Check for video surveillance. I'd like to see who she was with, although I have a feeling he's too smart to get caught on camera."

"Sure, boss. I'll get right on it."

Lisa had only been gone a few minutes when she swung

the door open again. "Boss, Erin Delaney and Kaely Hunter are here to see you."

"Thanks, Lisa. Send them in."

Adrian stood to his feet and waited. When they entered his office, he waved them toward the chairs facing his desk.

"Good to see you," he said.

"You too, Adrian," Erin said. "Anything new on your end?"

After they were seated, he sat down too. "Yeah, the autopsy results. Something interesting there."

"Care to share?" Kaely asked.

"Chloe had been given flunitrazepam prior to her death," he said. "With alcohol. It would have rendered her unconscious."

Kaely frowned. "So, he took her to that event . . . what was it called?"

"Grits and Grains?" He shook his head. "I doubt it. There wasn't any food in her stomach. Oh, and we found her car. One of its back tires had been slashed. It went flat, and she pulled it off on the side of the road between the resort and Townsend."

"I don't understand," Erin said.

"My officers found tire tracks behind her car. It looks like someone pulled up behind her. My guess is that it was the killer."

"This isn't the first abandoned car connected to these deaths," Erin said.

Adrian nodded. "Terri Rupp's car was also found abandoned. However, further checking reveals that there was a problem with the engine. There wasn't any sign that it had been tampered with. Not sure we can connect the two cars."

"Back to Chloe," Kaely said. "So, was the killer the person she dressed up to meet?" Kaely asked.

"Possibly. Whoever it was, she must have gotten in his car," Adrian said. "So she had some level of trust in him. And it seems she was comfortable enough to get a drink with him. Somewhere."

Erin looked at him like he had three heads. "None of that makes sense. She was dressed to the nines. She wasn't planning on *having a drink* with this guy. She was going to that festival. Probably planned to meet him there. And if there wasn't any food in her stomach, then she was prepared to eat. So, even if it was her date and he just *happened* to find her on the road, why didn't they call a tow truck and then go on to the festival?"

"And if he didn't pick her up, I'd guess that he lived close to the event," Kaely said slowly. "Otherwise, wouldn't he have offered to drive?"

"I'd think so," Adrian replied, "but that's a lot of speculation. Maybe she wanted to go somewhere afterward. Or maybe she didn't feel she knew him well enough to let him drive her there and back."

"You could be right," Erin said. "But it appears she went somewhere with him to get a drink. Odd that there wasn't any food in her stomach. Bars always have some kind of food to snack on."

Adrian sighed loudly. "It's frustrating. I agree that it doesn't seem to make sense, but there might be an explanation we haven't thought of."

"You need to look at bars near the place where they found her car," Erin said. She looked at Adrian. "Could you ask the detectives if there was a spare tire in her car?"

He nodded and picked up his phone. Lisa answered. "Lisa, either Lonzine or Dale here?"

"Dale's out, but Lonzine is still here."

"Have her come to my office, will you?" he said.

"Sure, boss."

He hung up the phone. "I think I know where you're going with this," he said, directing his comment to Erin.

There was a knock on his door, and he called out, "Come in."

Lonzine stepped into his office. He introduced her to Erin and Kaely before saying, "Was there a spare tire in Chloe Banner's car when you found it?"

"No, boss. I looked because I wondered why she didn't change her tire. Most women know how to do it. Especially single women."

"Thanks, Lonzine."

After she closed the door, Adrian nodded at Erin. "Tell me why you asked that question, but I think I know."

"Why didn't she change the tire?" Erin said. "Or, why didn't the person who pulled off the road help her change the tire? Because there wasn't a spare. I think the man who stopped to supposedly help her knew that. He could have told her he knew someone who could assist her. Either he could bring a tire that would fit her car, or else they could have her car towed to a garage where she could get her tire changed the next morning. If that happened, it would explain why they went for a drink. She was waiting for something."

"And that's also why there wasn't any food in her stomach," Kaely said. "She was still planning to go to the festival."

Adrian stared at her for a moment before saying, "That makes sense. So we need to find someplace nearby where she could get a drink, and close enough so she could get back to her car when help arrived."

"Help that never came," Erin said softly. "He lied to her. He didn't want to go to that festival. Too many eyes. Too much of a chance they would be noticed. So he roofied her drink, and then when she couldn't fight back, he took her back out to his car and completed his plan to kill her."

He picked up the phone again and asked Lisa to limit her search to bars or restaurants close to the place where they'd discovered Chloe's car. He could only pray that they would find a place where someone would remember Chloe . . . and the man who took her life.

TWENTY-NINE

"So, have you had time to read the profile I sent you? Do you have any questions?" Kaely asked. She wanted to go over it with him, but at the same time, she didn't want him to think she didn't respect his acumen as a law enforcement officer. She did. Adrian was sharp. Smarter and more intuitive than most police officers she'd worked with in the past.

"No. It makes sense. I realize it's an educated guess, but it feels right to me. He's in his late twenties or thirties. Fairly attractive. Probably has a respectable job." He frowned. "It looks like he picked her up, so wouldn't you say he had a nice car?"

"I think so," Kaely said. "That goes with his persona. He wouldn't be seen in something that didn't make him feel important."

"Can you tell by the tracks what kind of car or truck he drives?" Erin asked.

"Not really. We can narrow down the kind of tires and then check to see what vehicles use them, but to be honest, there are a lot of cars and trucks out there that use a variety of different tires. Now if there's something wrong with a tire, that could help us match it to a specific vehicle. We're working on that now. If we get anything that helps, we'll add it to our search." Adrian frowned. "He's not a tourist, is he?"

Kaely shook her head. "I'd say no for two reasons. Number one, he would have to come in and out of town to hunt. Usually, killers like this guy like to scout things out ahead of time. And they stay in areas they know. The other reason? Whatever their trigger is, it probably happened here. In Sanctuary. He's trying to strike back at whatever it was—or whoever it was—that hurt him."

"You believe there's a spiritual side to this?" Adrian asked.

"Yes. The angels are important. Like we said, he's angry at God, but he's taking vengeance out specifically on angels. I'd look for someone brought up in a dysfunctional religious home. Maybe with parents or guardians who blamed angels for everything bad that happened to them. Or to him. These people wouldn't be well versed in the Bible since he's using the figurine of a female angel, although male figurines might be hard to find."

Adrian nodded. "So, I'm looking for an attractive man in his twenties or thirties who probably grew up here, in a dysfunctional family. Who has a nice car and probably a good job. So, forget eighty-year-old hillbillies with skin conditions?"

Kaely couldn't help but laugh. "Yeah, I think you can ignore them . . . for now."

"Shouldn't the police look for the angel figurines?" Erin asked. "Even the material the dresses are made from . . . and the blue ribbon?"

"Sure," Kaely said to Adrian. "You have to try to track those things down, but I don't think you'll be able to. The dress looks homemade, but not well-made. I think he sewed it, by hand, himself. It's not hemmed, and it's not cut correctly. My guess is that he's already made several of them. And it's almost impossible to trace blue ribbon. Too much of it out there. The figurines? Maybe. But again, they're plain. I believe he bought them online." Kaely leaned down and reached into her bag. She took out a folded piece of paper and handed it to Adrian. "I found those on Amazon last night. As you can see, there are hundreds of reviews. My guess is they sold thousands of them. And not just through this site. I'm sure they're available from a lot of different online stores, as well as in brick-and-mortar retailers. Tracking down our killer that way is nearly impossible."

"That looks like the figurine," Adrian said. "Amazon works with law enforcement, but I'd need a subpoena or a court order for them to open up customer records. And I can't fish. I'd need someone's name. So, until I have a suspect, this won't help me. And like you said, Amazon is probably not the only seller." He frowned. "Wouldn't hurt to look around town, just in case. I'll have one of my officers check it out."

"Even if they were," Erin said, "this guy would have covered his tracks. He's smart." She shrugged. "Too smart to be caught this way. But he's also crazy, so that should help."

Kaely smiled at her. "We try not to call UNSUBs *crazy*, but you have a good point. If you understand the killer's psychopathy, it will help you narrow down your search."

"Can you define that a little more for me?" Adrian asked.

"Normally, I'd tell you to look for someone with a lack of empathy and remorse. A man with a grandiose sense of self-worth. He's manipulative and deceitful. Impulsive and reckless. He has poor impulse control. He seems callous and unemotional. He had early behavioral problems. Poor relationships. He may also have exhibited some early criminal behavior. The thing to understand, though, is that he's hiding. Psychopaths can learn to copy others. Pretend to have empathy. Make you think he's humble and caring. It's harder for him to hide his childhood, but the adults in his life may have already done that for him." Kaely paused a moment. "If I were searching for this guy, I'd look first for someone who helps others. Like I said, he's hiding. But many times, these men will go too far in trying to make you think they would never take a life."

"Let me get this straight," Adrian said. "You want me to look for someone who couldn't possibly be our killer? Seriously?"

Kaely laughed. "I know, it sounds ridiculous, but there were several times when I was with the FBI, that we found our UNSUB by looking for the person it couldn't be."

"Or you could just yawn around him," Kaely added, grinning.

"Yawn around him?" Adrian looked confused. "Not sure if while I'm facing down a murderous psychopath, my first reaction would be to yawn. Can you explain that a little more?"

"She means that a psychopath won't yawn after you do," Erin said, grinning. "Remember? No empathy?"

"Unless he's learned to do it because it's normal behavior," Kaely added. She pointed at the profile. "There's much more in there. But don't forget, as you said, it's an educated guess. However, most of what we profiled when I was in the BAU was on target."

"She's being modest," Erin said. "Most of the profiles *she* wrote were on target. In fact, while writing one profile in particular, she was actually able to name the killer."

"I'd appreciate it if you could do that now," Adrian said. "It would make my job much easier."

Kaely appreciated Erin's enthusiasm, but it also embarrassed her. "There were much more experienced analysts at the FBI. I learned from them, and trust me, without their help, our profiles wouldn't have been so accurate."

"Thank you for this," Adrian said. "I know you didn't do it to get paid, but while you're here, maybe you'd let me take you both to dinner? With the insight you've provided, I feel we have a shot at catching this guy."

Kaely looked at Erin, who nodded. She smiled at Adrian. "We'd like that. I guess we need to get past this storm first."

"You're right. Today is going to be busy. How about the first day the roads are open again?"

"You think the roads will be closed?" Erin asked.

"If we get the snow amounts that are forecasted, yes. Of course, we might end up with just a dusting and be fine." He frowned. "Your cabin has a generator, right?"

Erin nodded. "Steve said that if we lost our electricity, it would automatically kick on."

"Good. I won't worry about you then. We have other residents who could be in a lot of trouble if their electricity goes out. We'll need to keep an eye on them if things get dicey." He leaned forward in his chair. "Make sure you have all the supplies you need in case you're stuck inside for several days."

"Several days?" Kaely looked over at Erin. "When we stop for lunch, let's make a list of the things we might need from the grocery store. We have a few things in mind, but maybe we should expand our list?"

"You mean if we can't exist on all the food Steve put in the cabin? If you can come up with something, I'll give you money."

Kaely smiled. "I noticed there wasn't much toilet paper in the bathroom cabinets. I take Venmo."

"Just remember I didn't mention how much," Erin said, her eyes wide in an attempt to look innocent.

Adrian laughed. "I have a feeling you two will be fine no matter what happens." He stood up. "Thanks again for the profile. I'll check with you on the other side of the storm for that dinner."

"I know it's not really our business," Erin said, "but is there a way you can keep us updated on your investigation?"

"Sure, not a problem. I'll be in contact soon." He walked over to the door and held it open. "I hope you're going to spend some time in town today. We have lots of great shops. You mentioned groceries. There's a small store three blocks away where you can get most of what you'll need. A larger big-box store is outside town about five miles, but I really think you'll be okay at Grady's. I recommend lunch at Dolly's Diner." He shrugged. "It's Tennessee. Dolly Parton is pretty popular here."

"We do intend to putter around today," Kaely said, getting to her feet. "We'll get back before the storm hits though."

She smiled at him and then walked out the door. As she headed for the front of the station, something inside her seemed to whisper a warning. But about what? The storm? She hadn't been an analyst for a while, but when she was, she would sense things. A warning in her spirit.

And that's exactly what she was feeling now.

THIRTY

Erin and Kaely decided to eat lunch before they checked out the shops in town. Picking up groceries would be last.

They found Dolly's Diner. It was a trip. Erin had never seen anything like it before. But she'd never been to Tennessee, and the one time she'd been to Branson, she hadn't attended Dolly Parton's Stampede. She didn't have anything against Dolly, but there were other things to do. Her friends had been more interested in eating out and shopping than in seeing shows. She felt a stab of pain. She'd learned that emotional pain can hurt as much or more than physical pain. *Her friends.* It was true that she'd cut herself off from people, but not before several of them deserted her after she left the force. Even though she hadn't been charged in the shooting, having your partner die somehow reflected badly on you. As if it were your fault. She'd gone over and over it. There wasn't any way she could have saved him, yet her mind kept trying to find a solution. A way she could have done something. Of course, if she ever did figure out a way she could have helped him—but didn't—it would destroy her.

She and Kaely were shown to a table. Erin couldn't believe her eyes.

"It looks like a giant bottle of Pepto Bismol threw up all over this place," she whispered after the hostess seated them.

The tablecloths were pink. The walls were pink. Even the chairs were pink. There were pictures of Dolly everywhere. Erin picked up the menu the hostess had left at the table. Her mouth dropped open.

"You won't believe this," she whispered to Kaely. "Five to Swine—a shredded pork sandwich. The Best Little Porterhouse in Texas. So-Lean—a grilled chicken breast. My Blue Ridge Mountain Po' Boy. Backwoods BBQ Brisket. First Dog—a hot dog." She shook her head. "I guess some of these are Dolly Parton songs?"

"I have no idea," Kaely said. "This may have been a mistake."

"Don't worry, the food's good."

The voice from behind them made both women jump. They turned to see their waitress, a young woman wearing a big blonde wig and an obviously padded pink sweater with a darker pink polka-dotted skirt, staring at them with a rather bored look.

"I didn't mean . . ." Kaely started to say.

"Yeah, you did, and you're right. This place is ridiculous, but the food is actually delicious." She leaned down closer to the table and glanced around before saying, "I take it you haven't met the owner yet?"

"No," Erin said. "Will I be glad you warned us?"

The waitress grinned. "Dolly Barton. Yeah, that's right. She says it's her real name, but none of us believe her. She tours the dining room every hour. You'll get to meet her. You think the rest of this is weird? Just wait."

She straightened up as another waitress walked past her. "So, what can I get you ladies today?"

"Can you give us a couple of minutes?" Kaely asked. "We're not sure yet."

The waitress nodded and walked away.

"It's not too late," Erin said, trying not to laugh. "We can still make a run for it."

"Not in a million years," Kaely said, hiding her mouth behind her hand. "This is a first. I want to see it through."

"You're braver than I am."

After perusing the menu, Erin settled on the Blue Smoke Burger while Kaely decided to try the Smoky Mountain roasted chicken. Erin waved at their waitress when she looked their way. She was just starting to say something to Kaely when a door on one side of the dining room swung open, and a large woman with a wig even bigger than their waitress's came into the room. She wore a pink muumuu with a large white plastic belt, a big pink ribbon in her hair, along with matching lipstick and nail polish. Dangling rhinestone earrings swung back and forth as she sashayed through the dining room.

Erin said a word that Kaely might not approve of, but when she looked over at her friend, she almost lost it.

Don't laugh, Kaely mouthed. Her expression was a mixture of horror and hysterics. That was all it took. Erin covered her burst of laughter with the sound of unrestrained coughing. It was the only tool in her arsenal.

The woman hurried over to her. "Why, darlin', let's get

you somethin' to drink before you choke," she said in a high-pitched Southern drawl.

"Mabel," she hollered to one of the hapless waitresses, although she pronounced it *May-belle*, "will you get this po' woman somethin' quick?"

The waitress hurried away to get *po'* Erin somethin' to drink, while po' Erin tried her best not to actually choke to death in front of everyone.

Kaely looked on, obviously struggling to keep her face void of emotion. It occurred to Erin that Kaely should look more concerned about her possible demise, but before she could spit out any words, *May-belle* ran up to the table with a glass of water. After a couple of sips, Erin was able to catch her breath.

"Thank you," she sputtered. "I appreciate it."

"Trust me," *May-belle* said. "We've had quite a few customers with breathing trouble." She looked at them and rolled her eyes before leaving. Their previous waitress came back to the table to take their order while Dolly Barton fluttered around them, making sure Erin had completely recovered. The woman's cologne was overpowering, and Erin was on the verge of choking again when Dolly finally took a step back from their table.

"Bonnie Sue, whatever these ladies want, it's on the house," she said. "On . . . the . . . house, ya heah?"

"Yes, Miss Dolly," Bonnie Sue said.

Once Dolly was far enough away, Kaely said, "We'll pay for our lunch. That was a nice gesture, but it's not necessary."

"Trust me, she won't take your money."

"Well, maybe we can make it up with our tip," Kaely said.

"That's kind of you. I appreciate it, but it's okay. Miss Dolly pays us very well." She smiled. "I know this place is . . . interesting . . . but you'll love the food. Our cook is exceptional."

"Thanks for telling us that, Bonnie . . . Sue?" Erin said.

"My name is actually Avery, but it didn't fit into Miss Dolly's perfect world. And Mabel's name is actually Karen."

"Your boss is quite a character," Kaely said.

Avery smiled. "Yeah, she is. But if we need something, she's the first in line to help us. I wouldn't want to work anywhere else. I'll be back with your drinks. Your food will be ready soon."

"Well, this is something I won't soon forget," Erin said to Kaely.

"The idea was to get you out and help you get your mind off of things." Kaely grinned. "If this doesn't do it, nothing will."

Erin snorted. "If I thought it was possible, I'd think you set this whole thing up."

"I wish I was that creative."

Erin started to say something about their meeting with Adrian when someone else walked up to the table. It was Steve.

"I had to say hello," he said to Kaely.

"It's been a long time, Steve," she said with a smile. She waved toward the empty pink chair next to her. "Do you have time for a cup of coffee?"

"I-I guess so." Steve sat down, but he seemed nervous and distracted. "This is quite a place, isn't it?"

"I've never seen anything like it," Kaely said. "Do you come here often?"

He nodded. "The food is so good, I'm willing to ignore the decor . . . and Dolly."

"Is her name really Dolly Barton?" Erin asked quietly.

Steve smiled for the first time since he'd approached them. "Believe it or not, it is. I think she had it changed at some point. No one is really sure about that."

Avery came back to the table with their drinks, and Steve ordered a cup of coffee. After Avery left, he nodded at Erin. "So how are you enjoying the cabin?"

Erin sighed. "It's lovely. I just wish it didn't come with its own ghost."

Steve's face drained of color, and he swore under his breath. "You've seen her too?"

THIRTY-ONE

Kaely put her glass down. "You've seen her?"

He nodded. "I'm not the only one who's run across her. She seems to be hanging around the cabin." He gulped. "I planned to rent it out to tourists, but there's no way people will stay there if word of this gets around."

Steve's body language made it clear to Kaely that he was really worried. His body was rigid and his jaw tight. He kept clenching and unclenching his hands. How long had this been going on?

"Why is someone out there, pretending to be a ghost?" Kaely asked him. "What are they trying to accomplish?"

"I have no idea," Steve said. "It doesn't benefit anyone."

"How long has it been going on?" Erin asked.

"Stories about a ghost have circulated ever since Emma Watcher was killed," Steve said. "They died out for a while. Then they started back up during the sixties and seventies. Of course, this is what I've been told. I didn't live here then. After I bought the cabin, the stories started again. I'm afraid it's going to be impossible for me to rent it out."

"I'm not sure you're right," Erin said. "I knew people

who would purposely search for hotels or B&Bs that were rumored to be haunted. If you advertised it as haunted, you could probably keep it rented all year long."

"I know about some of those people," he said, sniffing the air as if he smelled something rancid. "Not the clientele I'm looking for. I wanted the cabin to be a beautiful, restful retreat for the busy executive. The elite." He shook his head. "You know the kind of people I mean."

She knew exactly what he meant. She bit back a sharp retort. This was Noah's friend. She didn't want to offend him.

"Is there anyone in town who is opposed to this idea?" Erin asked. "I mean, the cabin is built on the site where William Watcher's home stood. Maybe it's related to that history?"

Steve nodded. "'William Watcher slew his wife. Slit her throat with his butcher knife. Now she wanders Watcher Woods. A ghastly visage in a cloak and hood. If you should hear her mournful cries . . . you will be the next to die.'"

Although she'd heard the poem before, a chill ran through Kaely. She looked up to see Avery standing next to the table with a coffee cup and a pot. She put the cup down in front of Steve and poured coffee into it. Then she set the pot down on the table.

"Everyone in town has heard the story," Avery said. "But no one I know has ever actually seen her. Even so, you wouldn't catch me anywhere near that cabin." She directed her attention to Steve. "Sorry, but I'm not big on ghostly apparitions haunting the scene of a gruesome murder." She looked around the restaurant, which by this time was almost completely full. "This place is ghastly enough for me." Avery looked at Erin and hesitated a moment. Then she said,

"Look, I really don't want to trouble you, but my copy of *Dark Matters* is in my car. If I bring it in, could you sign it before you leave?"

"Sure, not a problem."

"Thank you." She winked at them and left, checking on a table not far from theirs.

"I really hate that poem," Erin said. "I hated it when I heard it the first time. I hated it when I repeated it to you," she said looking at Kaely then at Steve, "and I hate hearing it now." She leaned forward. "Look, I'm not sure if ghosts exist or not, but the realistic side of me is pretty sure our so-called ghost is someone who doesn't want the cabin to be turned into a rental. Which is weird since there are so many rental properties in this area." She pointed at Kaely. "The next time we see her, I think we should leave the cabin and chase her down. I'd like to have a talk with our ghostly friend."

"I'm in," Kaely said. "And I'm sorry I doubted you the first time you told me about her."

Erin shrugged. "I understand. Just don't do it again." She tried to hold back a smile but failed.

"I won't," Kaely said. "Trust me."

Erin laughed. "Actually, I'm not sure you should trust everything I say."

"Well, you can trust this one," Steve said. "Look, I wouldn't advise going after it. I mean . . . just in case."

Kaely didn't respond. What could she say? Did Steve actually believe the ghost of a woman murdered two hundred years ago was roaming the woods, trying to find someone to kill?

"Thanks, Steve," Erin said. "We'll be careful. But please, see if you can think of someone who might have some kind of grudge against you—or against the idea of you renting that cabin, okay?"

"I will." Steve gulped down the rest of his coffee and got to his feet. "Nice to see you ladies. You have my number if you need anything. And don't worry about the storm that's coming. If it turns out to be anything more than a few inches of snow and you lose your electricity, like I said, the generator will come on. Also, there's a large pile of wood behind the house, although you shouldn't need it. There's quite a bit already inside."

"Thanks, Steve," Kaely said. "We really appreciate it."

"Sure. Tell Noah I said hello." He turned and left.

"Wow," Erin said. "Some great place you picked out for me to take it easy. Murders, ghosts. What else do you have lined up for me?"

"Seriously, this wasn't the plan." Kaely sighed. "I mean, look at the name, Sanctuary. It sounded like such a peaceful place to be." She paused. "How are you doing, by the way? You seem relaxed."

Erin's eyes widened. "I . . . I feel fine. To be honest, I haven't even thought once about being afraid to leave the cabin."

Kaely smiled at her. "Well, that's not surprising." She waved her hand around. "Agoraphobia is neutralized by the color pink. You probably didn't know that."

Erin laughed. "Not sure that's true, but so far, so good." She blinked away tears. "Thanks, Kaely. I feel better now than I have for a long time."

"I'm so glad. Look, after we eat and shop, let's have a nice, comfortable evening indoors, just talking, okay?"

As she said it, Kaely wondered if there was such a thing as a peaceful evening in Sanctuary, Tennessee.

They were in town, snooping around. It didn't matter. They wouldn't find anything. They thought they were smart. But they'd never met anyone like him before. He had already prepared his next offering. If they really were smart, they'd figure it out before he came for them. Well, for one of them, anyway. The other one? She didn't fit into his plan, but couldn't he just excuse her death as collateral damage? He saw no other choice.

Time was ticking away for the famous author and her friend. Before long, they would both be dead.

After a remarkably tasty lunch, Erin and Kaely poked around the small, quaint town. Erin found that love for Dolly wasn't limited to the diner. They stopped by a shop called Wildflowers. The owner, Kathy Flood, introduced herself and explained that she'd loved Dolly Parton ever since she was a child. The shop was named after one of Dolly's songs, which played over and over through the store's speakers. Erin enjoyed it until about the sixth or seventh time. Still, she found herself humming along after a while.

The store was filled with Dolly memorabilia and lots of bling. Most of it wasn't Erin's style, but she found a silver bracelet and a nice quilted throw that she could use on cold winter nights.

Kaely bought some postcards but didn't see anything else she wanted.

By the time they left, they knew that Kathy was divorced and had a son who wouldn't speak to her. Erin wondered if he simply couldn't stand listening to "Wildflowers" one more time.

Kathy only had one employee, a young woman who looked a little frantic. If Erin worked there, she'd be frantic too.

After they left Kathy's shop, they found a couple of other places that were surprisingly Dolly free. A cute boutique named The Little Sparrow. It wasn't until they left that Kaely informed her that "Little Sparrow" was another Dolly Parton tune.

"I feel like I'm trapped in some kind of Dolly Parton nightmare," Erin mumbled as they walked a little farther down the street.

"Just ignore it. We found some cute shirts in the last place. Let's just be thankful for that."

"Sure."

"I'd like to run over to the post office," Kaely said. "I need some stamps."

"Seriously? Ever hear of email? Texting?"

Kaely laughed. "I want to mail the postcards to Noah." She shrugged. "Don't judge me. We haven't had a vacation in years. I'm sending him photos of Sanctuary and the area around it. I intend to write *wish you were here* on them."

"Man, you really are sad," Erin said with a smile.

The post office was only two blocks away, so it didn't take them long to get there. It was housed in a small building with only two clerks. You could fit at least five of Sanctuary's post offices into the one she frequented in St. Louis. Although it wasn't as high tech, it was obvious that the two clerks took their jobs seriously.

"Can I help you?" the man behind the counter said. He looked to be in his thirties, tall, thin, with black glasses that sat on the edge of his nose. His badge read *Allen Dunne*. The woman working beside him was a wisp of a thing with delicate features and large blue eyes. Probably early thirties. Erin glanced at her badge as well. *Olivia Gregson.* A bad habit from her days on the force. When showing up at a crime scene, they would need the names of the people working in any stores or businesses. She checked them out now automatically, without thinking.

"I need some stamps," Kaely said. "A book of twenty?"

"Do you need anything?" Olivia asked Erin.

Erin smiled at her. "No, thank you." Since there wasn't anyone else standing in line, she felt as if she needed to say something else. "So, how long have you worked here?" she asked.

Olivia blinked quickly and for a moment, Erin wasn't certain she was going to answer her.

"I've been here for three years," she replied. Her voice was light and soft. "Allen hired me. He runs things and does all the deliveries. I help him, and I take care of the desk when he's gone."

That was a little more information than she'd expected, but Erin smiled at her.

Olivia reached under the counter and brought out a large spiral notebook with pages that contained pictures of different kinds of stamps.

"Just pick out what you want," she said to Kaely.

"Wow. Lots of great choices," Kaely said. She finally settled on some cute stamps with snow globes.

"Good choice," Olivia said. "They're my favorite."

As she got a page of stamps out and Kaely paid for them, a man came in the front door and headed over to a bulletin board on the far wall. Before he could tack it up, Allen called out to him.

"There's a certain uniformity," he said. He came out from behind the counter and headed toward the board. The man stopped and waited for him to take the piece of paper from his hand.

"I'm sorry. I didn't know," he said.

Allen moved the notices around and then put up the man's flyer. "There. That will work." Then he turned toward the man. "Always check with me first before putting things on this board," he said in a stern tone. "Otherwise, everything will be out of order."

"Again, I apologize." He looked toward Kaely and Erin and rolled his eyes. Erin turned away, trying to hide her smile from Allen.

"A lot of tourists stay here," Erin said to Olivia. Getting mail to them must be a challenge."

"It can be," Allen said brusquely, cutting off Olivia's response. "Most people only stay for a week or two, but some stay all summer. Then they don't tell us when they leave." He returned to his place behind the counter. "We take all the mail to the hotels and resorts. They separate it and give it to their guests. That helps. Of course, the rentals can be confusing. When people like you stay in a rental for a short time and give their address to friends and family, unless the owner notifies us, it can make our jobs harder."

The way he said it was as if she and Kaely were purposely out to get him. She couldn't help but glance at Kaely who raised her eyebrows.

"We'll be staying at Steve's cabin for five more days," Erin said. "But I doubt we'll get any mail."

"No, we shouldn't," Kaely said, frowning. "But I just realized something. With the storm coming, maybe I'd better

fill out a couple of the cards I bought and mail them now."
She looked at Allen. "Is that okay?"

He nodded. "Of course. You can sit there and prepare them if you'd like."

He gestured to a small round table with two chairs near the window. Kaely paid for the stamps she'd selected, and they walked over to the table and sat down. Erin gazed out the window while Kaely quickly filled out two cards. There had been more people walking down the boardwalks when they'd come into the post office. She wondered if the streets were beginning to clear because of the impending snowstorm. She was still amazed at how well she felt about being out, around people. Of course, being with Kaely helped a lot since she felt safe with her. But still, she saw this as a step in the right direction.

Although she and Kaely didn't have far to go, Erin decided to speed things up some.

Kaely got up and took her cards back to the counter. Erin watched Olivia, who kept glancing at Allen. It didn't take much insight to understand that Olivia had a crush on her boss. She found it surprising, since Olivia was lovely, and Allen had almost zero charm and treated all of them as if they were something that had to be dealt with as quickly and with as little effort as possible. He was nice looking, but his manner, the way he looked at everyone, and the unattractive glasses balanced on the edge of his nose made it hard to see anything appealing about him. He barely nodded when she gave him the postcards.

Kaely had turned around and was headed back toward her when Erin noticed Allen picking up the postcards Kaely had handed him and passing them to Olivia as if they were something that needed to be disinfected. He looked over at

Erin and she quickly looked away, but she was pretty sure he knew she'd been watching him.

"Thank you for coming," Olivia called out in her high, sing-song voice.

"It was nice to meet you, Olivia," Erin said, careful to leave Allen's name out.

"Well, that was interesting," Kaely said when they stepped out onto the sidewalk. It felt as if the temperature had dropped several degrees just while they were inside. Erin couldn't wait to get back to the cabin where it was warm.

"I think our friend Allen has quite an ego," she said.

"Actually, my guess is he feels very inadequate," Kaely responded. "That's why people like him have to look down on everyone else."

Erin nodded as she pulled her jacket closer. "That makes a lot of sense. Do you profile everyone you meet?"

Kaely sighed. "Yes. Sorry. Bad habit. I just can't seem to turn it off."

They decided to head for Grady's General Store and get their groceries, but before they could reach their destination, they stopped when they heard someone call out their names. They turned to see Adrian hurrying toward them. From the expression on his face, Erin was pretty sure she knew what he was going to say.

"There's been another one," he said. "Dale and Lonzine found her a few minutes ago. I'm on my way there now. Do you want to come with me?"

There was a part of Erin that wanted to tell him no, but she knew she couldn't. She looked over at Kaely whose expression mirrored her own feelings. Was this ever going to end?

THIRTY-TWO

"We've been patrolling the area constantly," Adrian said. "Of course, we can't cover every square inch twenty-four seven."

"It didn't matter how many people you had out here," Kaely said. "He would have found a way. I'm convinced he's watching you."

Adrian appreciated Kaely's comments but still couldn't help but wonder if he could have done something to prevent this. Maybe if he hadn't been so bullheaded, he would have asked Knoxville for help. And if he'd done that, perhaps this poor girl would still be alive.

Once they reached the site, Adrian led them to the body. They all stared down at her. Curly black hair tied with a blue ribbon. The white dress. Black pumps. She looked like she was sleeping—except for the blood stain on the front of her dress. She was holding a white ceramic angel with a 2 painted on it with red paint. This angel had red tears, just like the other one.

"I don't think she's been dead long," Dale said.

Adrian sighed. "Doc Gibson is on his way. I also called Tim." He looked at Kaely and Erin. "What do you see?"

"Well, the most obvious thing is that this girl is African American," Kaely said slowly. "Older than the others." She shook her head. "I still can't see what connects his victims. They're all different."

"But there has to be something, right?" Erin asked.

Kaely nodded. "There's always a connection, but I have no idea what it is yet. She may have just been convenient."

Erin knelt down, next to the body. She was being careful not to disturb anything. "Same kind of wound. From the bloodstain, I'd say she was stabbed just like Chloe. She was wearing something else and then her clothes were changed." She looked down at the woman's shoes. "My guess is that these are her shoes. Also, she's wearing makeup, but not as much as Chloe." She shook her head and looked up at Kaely. "You're the expert here, but from what you've taught me and from my research, this just doesn't make any sense. Do you see something different than I do?"

"Cheap nail polish, shoes that are supposed to look like Louis Vuitton Archlight pumps . . . but are knockoffs," Kaely said. "Also, her hands look a little dry, and I can see some calluses. This gal wanted to look classy, but she didn't have a lot of money. My guess is she works around here some-where. Maybe as something like a housekeeper? I'd check the hotels and resorts in the area. She wanted to look good for someone. Either it's a boyfriend or someone she recently met. You need to find out who it is, Adrian." She was quiet for a moment before saying. "No defensive wounds that I can see. She didn't see it coming. Whoever this is, he's getting close to them first—before he kills them."

Adrian started to ask Kaely a question when his phone rang. It was Lisa. After speaking to her, he disconnected his phone.

"You said she could be a housekeeper?" he said.

"That's just a guess," Kaely said. "Her dry hands and her calluses make that a possibility. In an area where there are so many hotels and resorts, it made me wonder if that could be the case."

"That was Lisa, from the station. The friend of a local girl who works as a housekeeper in the Brentwood Hotel, a few miles out of Sanctuary, is at the station. She reported her friend missing when she didn't show up for work and wasn't answering her phone. Her name is Hailey Duncan, and she fits the description of our victim."

"Well, that was fast," Erin said.

Adrian called Lonzine over to where they stood. "Would you go back to the station? Interview a gal there who may know this woman. Take a picture and have her confirm her identity."

"Yes, boss," Lonzine said. "I'll let you know what I find out. By the way, we've called every bar and club in Sanctuary and the surrounding area near where Chloe's car was found. No one reported seeing her. If she was all dressed up, it should have made her easy to spot. But some places were really busy and admitted she could have been there and they just didn't notice. We've requested video surveillance tapes from any place that has them. Unfortunately, most of those that have cameras have them trained on the cash registers and the card machines. Not on their customers."

"That's because they want people to feel secure," Adrian said. "Some of them may be there with people they aren't married to." He sighed. "Thanks for trying."

"Lonzine," Kaely said, "ask specifically about anyone Hailey might have been dating. Especially someone brand new."

"You think he could be the UNSUB?" Lonzine asked.

"It's entirely possible," Adrian answered. "Get a description of the guy. We really need one."

Lonzine snapped a picture of the victim and hurried away. Adrian looked back and forth between Erin and Kaely. "Anything else?"

Erin shook her head. "Same MO as the others. Killed somewhere else. Brought here. I doubt you'll find any evidence."

"I agree," Kaely said. "You have an organized psychopath who isn't done." She frowned. "The only thing that surprises me is that you haven't heard from him. Usually, these kinds of killers like to get attention. They crave it. I would have expected at least one letter to the editor of your local paper. Or a phone call to one of the local news channels. Something. His silence is unusual."

"Can you guess why haven't we heard anything?" Adrian asked.

Kaely looked over at Erin. "What do you think?"

"I don't know," she said. "Maybe he's sent a message, but we just haven't recognized it yet."

"If that's true," Kaely said, focusing her gaze on Adrian. "It won't take long before he tries to communicate again, in a much clearer way. It would be much better for everyone if you can keep that from happening. Right now, he feels strong. Empowered. He's bested the police—and us. If he doesn't get the attention he wants soon, he could become angry—and things could get much worse."

THIRTY-THREE

Erin and Kaely hurried back to town and headed toward the small grocery store. There wasn't much they needed, but Erin wanted her favorite breakfast cereal, and Kaely had forgotten to pack her razors. They also needed to stock up on toilet paper. Erin hoped the store hadn't sold out. Toilet paper seemed to be one of the items people thought about when the weather got bad.

"We've also got to have popcorn to eat during the snowstorm," Kaely insisted. "You can't have snow without popcorn. And we need chocolate syrup for hot chocolate. Steve has some instant hot chocolate packets in the pantry, but I want to have the real stuff."

Erin laughed at her. "You have very specific needs when it snows."

"Blame it on Noah," Kaely said, grinning. "He's spoiled me."

They decided to buy another gallon of milk and some bread, but by the time they got to Grady's General Store, there wasn't much left. They settled for a loaf of whole wheat bread and a half gallon of milk that was close to its sell-by date. They also found chocolate syrup and popcorn. Kaely snatched up one of the last remaining packages of toilet paper. Erin noticed some rather angry looks from people who were headed toward the aisles that held some of the items in their cart, but she didn't care. When it came to bad weather, it was every man—or woman—for themselves.

A large man standing behind the only register in the small store gave them a wide smile as they took their place in the line waiting to check out.

"Grady Howard," he said loudly. The people in front of them turned and stared. "You're the author and the FBI agent, right? The whole town's talking about you."

"I guess that's us," Kaely said. "Is this your store?"

His smile widened even more. "Yes, ma'am. Looks like you got some of the last bread and milk before the storm hits. Usually, it's bread, milk, and toilet paper that sell out when the weather gets dicey. I see you were able to grab one of our last packages of toilet paper. I keep extra, but we weren't planning on this storm."

Although announcing to the public about her toilet paper needs wasn't something Erin usually did, she grinned and nodded like some kind of weird bobblehead. She wasn't used to being around this many people, and although she'd been doing just fine, at this point, all she wanted to do was to get back to the cabin and wait for the snow to protect her from the outside world. She'd had enough of people for one day. If she had to come up with one more response to some inane question, she was fairly certain the top of her head would blow off.

"I wish we had some of your books in the store," Grady said, "but I don't have room for much else besides the basics.

Maybe the next time you visit, we can set up a book signing. I know people here would love that."

First of all, she wasn't interested in book signings. And secondly, a book signing in a grocery store? She wasn't a snob, but she felt like asking Grady where the signing would take place. Next to the day-old bread or the frozen chicken livers?

As soon as the thought entered her head, she dismissed it. She wasn't too good to sign books in any venue. The man was attempting to be nice.

"Maybe so, Mr. Howard," she said.

"You just call me Grady," he said. "Wait till I tell my wife I met you. She loved your book."

Was there anyone in this town who hadn't read Dark Matters? "I hope she enjoyed it."

Mercifully, the line moved up several spots, and someone behind them engaged Mr. Howard with a story about how many inches of snow they were expecting tonight. *Twenty or thirty would be nice. Maybe I could get stuck inside until it's time to go home.*

The woman in front of them turned around. "Don't let Grady get on your nerves," she said in a low voice. "He's a nice enough guy, but he's also a busybody. He's into everybody's business. If he hadn't been interrupted, right now he'd be asking all kinds of questions about how long you're going to stay here, why you're here, and how you two know each other. He tells himself it's just polite conversation, but he and his wife, Lola, like to keep tabs on everything and everyone in Sanctuary. If you need to know anything about anyone, just ask them."

Erin wondered what Grady and Lola thought about the

murders. The one thing she'd learned as a police officer was to find the neighborhood's or apartment complex's busybody if you needed information. They could usually provide something helpful. Surely Adrian had already thought of that.

"Thank you," Kaely said. "I'm Kaely Hunter, and this is Erin Delaney."

"Nice to meet you," the woman said. "I'm Bobbi Burke. I run Burke Real Estate right up the street." She smiled. "I'm getting ready for the storm just like everyone else." She pointed to her shopping cart. I should have done my shopping at least a few days ago, but I've been really busy. A lot of people moving into the area."

"Then I'm guessing you know Steve Tremont," Kaely said. "We're staying in his cabin."

"Sure," she said. "I sold it to him a couple of years ago. He bought at a good time. Since then, property values have skyrocketed. And with the improvements he's made, he's got a choice rental property on his hands."

"The area is getting more popular?" Kaely asked.

Bobbi nodded. "A lot of people buying here. Used to be more rentals, but more and more couples have decided to retire in and around our little town. This area is lovely. I'm afraid the larger cities are having crime problems and homelessness. Getting away from urban sprawl has become a goal for a lot of people. I predict that a lot of rentals, like the cabin you're staying in, will be snatched up by former city dwellers in the next couple of years."

"Bobbi, what do you think about this so-called Woman in Watcher Woods?" Erin asked. "Have you ever seen her?"

Bobbi's face turned pink. "No, but I know people who

have. It's best to stay out of those woods at night. Things . . . happen."

She turned to check out the person in front of her, who'd moved up a few feet, before saying, "Well hopefully, we'll be out of here and on the way home soon."

Bobbi pushed her cart up and began talking to an elderly man who didn't seem very interested in the chatty real estate agent.

Erin frowned at Kaely. "That was odd," she said in a low voice. "She really didn't want to talk about the ghost in the woods."

"Seems that way."

"No one likes to talk about that," someone said from behind them.

Erin turned to see the woman who'd spoken to them. She was older and wore a heavy coat and a scarf.

"I would expect everyone would be interested in a ghost roaming the woods," Erin said.

The woman looked around her before saying, "People get really riled up about it. Some say they've seen it, and some say it doesn't exist. But everyone worries about property values declining."

"There are lots of people who enjoy a good ghost story," Kaely said. "I'd think it could help tourism."

"Well, that's what I say, but this is a small town, and without tourists, it could die. People are afraid to take any chances." She smiled and held her hand out to Erin, and then to Kaely. They shook it.

"I'm Brenda Parks. I work at the resort. Night clerk. Merle—he's my boss—he's terrified that this ghost is going to ruin his business." She shrugged. "I think he's nuts, but he won't listen to anyone."

Had she heard about Hailey? Erin had no intention of telling her—or anyone. That was up to Adrian.

"Will you be working tonight when this storm comes in?" Kaely asked.

"Not sure. I'm loading up on groceries in case the roads are too bad for me to get to the resort. If I do make it, Merle will make sure I have food and a room if it comes to that. I live alone—well, except for Percival. My cat. I'll leave lots of food and water for him just in case."

The line moved, and they were finally up to the register where Grady waited. Sure enough, he began asking them all kinds of questions. Frankly, Erin was tired of talking to people about the storm—or anything else. She was ready to get out of the town and back to the cabin. She let Kaely engage in conversation with Grady. He seemed extremely interested in why they were here and how things were going at the cabin.

Grady was probably thirty to thirty-five, blond, with muscles that showed through his shirt, and a wide smile that seemed disingenuous. Erin noticed that a lot of the ladies in line were watching him and throwing him smiles. Grady didn't seem to notice, but Erin was certain he knew. Even though some of the women appeared to want to visit, the long line behind them kept their time with Grady short.

As they started to leave the store, Grady called out to them. "You ladies be careful out there all alone. Don't answer the door to anyone, you hear me? You never know what might be lurking in those woods."

THIRTY-FOUR

Thankfully, a few minutes later they were back in their car and on their way to the cabin. Erin couldn't wait. She was worn out. All she wanted to do was get inside, lock the door, grab a package of Mallomars, and relax. Kaely had mentioned that they had things to talk about tonight. She was nervous about it, but she also knew it was time. She'd failed to make progress with the therapists she'd seen. Kaely might be her last chance. She was confused about what to do next. She knew the way she was living now wasn't healthy. Should she tell Kaely about her gun? She was afraid of her reaction. Afraid Kaely might think badly of her. Afraid she'd try to make her do something she didn't want to do. But she was also afraid that if she didn't talk to someone, she might do something she couldn't take back.

As they got out of the car and carried the groceries inside, the first snowflakes began to fall.

"Boy, we made it just in time," Kaely said as she locked the door behind them.

They'd just started putting the groceries away when they heard a strange noise.

"I think it's coming from the front door," Kaely said.

Erin followed her to the living room. Kaely looked through the peephole. "No one's there," she said.

As soon as she'd said that, they heard scratching and a faint whine. Erin pulled back the drapes next to the door. Sitting on their front porch was a dog. Black and white. She could see it shivering in the cold as the flakes flew around it. Erin turned to look at Kaely.

"It's a dog," she said.

The sound they'd heard before started again, and Erin turned her attention back to the dog. It was pawing at the door.

Kaely stepped up next to Erin and looked through the glass.

"Poor thing," she said. She turned and hurried into the kitchen, coming back with some towels.

"You're going to let it inside?" Erin asked.

Kaely frowned at her. "Sure. It needs help."

"What if it's vicious?"

Kaely stopped and stared at her for a moment. "Are you afraid of dogs? You like Adrian's dog."

"Well, Adrian was with him, so I wasn't worried. But we don't know this dog."

"This poor thing has come to us for help," Kaely said, her voice soothing. "We need to get him out of the cold."

She opened the door, and the dog came inside, wagging its tail.

"Why, hello there," Kaely said, immediately kneeling down and stroking the shivering dog. She began drying him off. "What's your name?"

"If he answers you, I'm out of here," Erin said.

Although Erin knew that bringing the dog in was the right thing to do, she couldn't help but flash back to the night she and Scott had been called to the scene of a domestic disturbance. They were inside, trying to calm a man and a woman who'd been screaming at each other. The man had a gun and was threatening to kill the woman he lived with. Her two children were cowering in a corner, afraid and crying. While Scott tried to calm the man down and get his weapon, Erin went toward the children. She wanted to get them out of the room and to safety. As she approached them, a dog that looked just like this one sprang from the shadows and attacked her. He was obviously trying to protect the kids, but he bit her on the arm. She drew her gun, not wanting to use it, but not seeing any other way. The oldest child grabbed the dog and put himself between her and the frightened animal.

Although she should have called animal control, Erin was afraid the dog would be put down, and the children clearly loved him. After all the trauma they'd been through, Erin just couldn't let that happen. She used their first aid kit to bind her arm and then she checked the dog's collar. The name of the veterinarian was on her tag, so Erin called them. Thankfully, the dog was up to date on her shots.

The funny thing was, once the dog knew the children were safe from her, she calmed down and became very friendly with Erin. She had the strangest feeling the dog was sorry for biting her. She tried to lick her wound, and she put her paw in Erin's lap. At first the children were terrified she was going to have the dog taken away, but once they realized it wasn't going to happen, they quieted down.

Scott wasn't in agreement with not reporting the bite, but

in the end, he gave in. Getting a good report of the dog's health sealed the deal.

The man was the only one removed from the home that night and, because of having an illegal weapon, threatening to kill his girlfriend, and already having two strikes against him, he went away for a long time.

Erin had checked in on the kids from time to time until their mother decided to take them to Colorado Springs where her own mother lived. She seemed to be a stabilizing influence, so the situation had a happy ending. The dog, whose name, surprisingly, was Angel, went with them, and as far as Erin knew, all of their lives changed for the better.

As she stared down at the dog which so closely resembled Angel standing at her feet, she took a deep breath. He wasn't responsible for Angel's actions. This situation was totally different. She bent down to look at the leg he was favoring.

"He's got a cut," she told Kaely. "It doesn't look too bad, but we need to clean it out and bandage it before it gets infected."

"There's a first aid kit under the sink. I'll get it."

A few minutes later, the wound had been cleaned and wrapped with gauze. Erin had dealt with enough scrapes and cuts to feel certain there wasn't any infection, but it would probably hurt for a while. There wasn't anything they could do for that, though.

"Since Steve has just about everything, I don't suppose there's any baby aspirin anywhere?"

"I haven't seen any," Kaely said.

"I've got some willow bark pills upstairs. I'll get him some."

"I'm sorry. Willow bark?"

Erin grinned. "A natural pain reliever. Native Americans used it to help with pain and inflammation."

"And it's okay for animals?"

Erin nodded. "In smaller doses, of course. I'll go grab my bottle and be back."

She hurried upstairs, went through her purse, found her bottle, and brought it back downstairs. Before joining Kaely and the dog in the living room, she looked through the kitchen shelves and found some natural peanut butter. She put a spoonful of peanut butter into a small bowl and then sprinkled some powdered willow bark on that. After mixing it, she carried the bowl back into the living room.

"I think he's really tired," Kaely said.

"I imagine he is, poor thing." Erin held out the bowl to the dog, who hungrily licked up every last morsel of peanut butter.

"Let's take him by the fire."

Erin grabbed a soft throw that was draped over the arm of the couch and put it next to the fireplace. The dog immediately turned around several times and laid down. Within seconds he was asleep.

"He's exhausted," Kaely said. "Must have been out there for quite some time."

"There's a storm coming, and we have nothing to feed him." Erin sighed. "So, what do we do now? He's going to need more than just peanut butter."

"I could run back into town and buy some dog food. It wouldn't take me too long."

"With all the supplies we have," Erin said, "I'm surprised Steve doesn't have some."

"You're right," Kaely said slowly. She walked into the

kitchen and opened the door to the large pantry. Just seconds later, Erin heard her make a noise, and she came out holding a large bag. "He really did set this place up so guests would have every need met." She lifted the bag up and slid it onto the kitchen counter. "Dry dog food. And believe it or not, there are cans of dog food in the pantry too."

"I looked in the pantry when I arrived, but I didn't notice any dog food."

"It was in a large bin with a lid." Kaely grinned. "Good thing I'm so nosy." She came over and sat down on the couch. "For now, I think we need to let him sleep." She picked up her cell phone that was lying on the coffee table. "I'm going to call Adrian. If this dog belongs to someone, they may be worried about him."

Erin was surprised when, for just a second, she found herself hoping the dog was a stray and that no one would come for it. Why would she think that? Dogs were too much trouble, weren't they? Her parents had thought so. They'd never had a dog when she was a kid.

She got up and stirred the fire in the fireplace. When that didn't create the result she wanted, she got two logs from the metal log rack next to the fireplace and added them. Then she sat down, only half listening to Kaely as she spoke to Adrian. Her mind was on what she and Kaely would be talking about. Sure, that's why she'd come—to have someone to listen to what she'd been going through. But now she was getting cold feet. She wasn't used to sharing her feelings. After her parents died and Courtney left, it was just her. Then when she worked for the police department, officers didn't really talk to each other much about what they were going through. They felt the need to look strong and capable of handling whatever awful thing they saw. No one wanted to appear weak.

So, after years of keeping her emotions to herself, she was finally going to pour out her heart and soul to Kaely Quinn-Hunter? A woman who believed in a God Erin was fairly certain didn't exist?

Yet, Kaely had been there early in the mornings, when Erin couldn't sleep. When her nightmares grabbed her by the throat and shook her until she wasn't certain she could continue. When she needed help with the book, Kaely had made herself available. She was one of the only people in the world who knew that Erin had wanted a career with the FBI. And she'd never made her feel silly—or unworthy of the possibility. If she'd ever met anyone in her life that she felt safe around, it was Kaely. She had a strange feeling that it was now—or maybe never. That gun in the box kept whispering her name, and she didn't want to answer.

She realized that Kaely was off the phone and was staring at her.

"Sorry, did you say something?" Erin asked.

"No. You just looked so far away I didn't want to bother you."

"Sorry. Just thinking. What did Adrian say?"

"Before I tell you about the dog," Kaely said, "we have more information about Hailey Duncan. She was married and active in her church. That doesn't mean she wasn't seeing our killer for the wrong reasons, but that might not have been the case after all."

"That's interesting."

"Yeah, it is. And as far as our furry friend, it seems his name is Ozzy, and he's a border collie. He was left behind by a tourist. People in town have been feeding him, and so has the police department. They even built a doghouse for him at the station, and when it's cold or the weather's bad, they bring him inside. They've been looking for him. Adrian said they'd just made the decision to adopt him and let him live at the station. But it seems Ozzy is more of a one-person dog, so Adrian hasn't given up trying to find another home for him."

Erin shook her head. "The owner just left him behind? Some people shouldn't be allowed to have pets. That makes me furious."

"I agree," Kaely said. "Well, at least for now he has us. And the police department will make sure he's safe from here on out, but Adrian asked if we could keep him until the storm passes and the roads are cleaned off. I told him we would."

"Sure, we can do that," Erin said. She frowned. "Ozzy is a terrible name for a dog. Let's call him Chester."

Kaely laughed. "Chester? Any particular reason?"

Erin nodded. "My grandfather's favorite TV show was *Gunsmoke*. There was a character named Chester who had a limp just like this guy. Chester is a much nicer name than Ozzy."

"Then Chester it is. You'd better be careful though, or you may be going home with a lot more than you came here with."

Although Erin didn't respond, the truth was, she wouldn't mind that at all. But first, she'd have to make sure Chester wouldn't find himself without an owner a second time. She had the responsibility to make sure that didn't happen, and she couldn't make that commitment yet.

THIRTY-FIVE

Kaely and Erin worked together to make supper. They settled on trout almondine with new potatoes and roasted carrots—another one of the premade meals in the refrigerator. It was delicious.

The wind and the snow had started to pick up by the time they'd finished eating. Erin added a couple of additional logs to the fire while Kaely cleaned up and started the hot chocolate. She was nervous about talking to Erin. Since Erin wasn't a Christian, Kaely wasn't sure how best to help her. Should she mention God or keep His name out of their conversation completely? She prayed silently for wisdom as she reminded herself that she felt their coming here was God-ordained. If that was true, the Holy Spirit would guide her.

"You're making the hot chocolate," Erin said as she came into the kitchen. "I'll pop the popcorn. Any idea where we might find a large bowl?"

"Hmmm. I think I saw some in the cabinet to the left of the sink."

Erin checked and found them. She grabbed a bowl, then found some butter in the fridge and melted it in the microwave.

By the time Kaely had the hot chocolate ready, the freshly popped popcorn was in the bowl, and Erin had poured the melted butter over the top. It smelled really good. Kaely carried the cups of hot chocolate into the living room, still praying for guidance.

Erin plopped down on the couch and tucked her legs under her while they both sipped hot chocolate and munched popcorn. Kaely noticed that Erin had put a box of Mallomars on the table. What was up with that? She seemed very attached to them, and Kaely wondered why. They'd opened the drapes next to the fireplace and could see the snow falling through the floor-to-ceiling windows on one side of the living room.

They'd just started snacking when Chester suddenly woke up from his nap. His nose sniffed the air, and he looked at them hopefully.

Kaely put her cup and bowl down. "I'll feed him. You stay there. You look so comfortable."

"Don't be silly. I'll help."

They both went into the kitchen. Kaely opened the bag of dog food while Erin filled a bowl with water. Chester had followed them, but he sat down at the entrance to the kitchen and watched. He seemed hesitant. Almost fearful.

Kaely glanced over at Erin, who appeared to have noticed the same thing she had.

"The police have been feeding him, keeping him out of the cold, so he's not starving. But he seems . . . sad," Kaely said.

"Maybe he misses his owner."

"Animals bond with people, even those who don't love them," Kaely said with a sigh. "Obviously his owner didn't care about him. How could he just leave him?"

They put the bowls of water and food on the floor. After

looking at them carefully for a moment, Chester finally got up and walked slowly into the kitchen. Then he gingerly began to eat. Erin bent down to pet him, but Chester flinched as when she reached out her hand.

"Oh, dear," Kaely said.

The dog allowed Erin to stroke his head and his back several times, but when Erin straightened up, she looked at Kaely with tears in her eyes. "Someone's been hitting him. He was afraid I was going to hurt him too."

"Well, he's safe with us now. Just give him time. He'll figure that out." She put the bag of food down on the floor. "We need a leash. Until we're sure he feels safe here, I don't want him running off when we let him out. I have a belt that should work. I'll be right back."

When Kaely left the room, Erin sat down on the floor next to Chester. She felt such a connection to this dog. He was being cared for by people, but he wasn't . . . home. That's how she felt too.

"It will be okay, Chester," she said softly. "Maybe . . ."

She couldn't finish that sentence or say what was in her heart. She couldn't promise Chester a home because she couldn't promise she'd be around. She took a deep breath and let it out. What if talking to Kaely really was her only hope? Perhaps taking a chance—trusting someone—would lead her to some kind of salvation. The therapists she'd spoken to just didn't get it. Didn't understand her. Erin hadn't been able to tell any of them the truth about how dark her life had become. What if someone at the station found out? She couldn't endure pity from those she'd worked with. Being a police officer was about being strong. About being able to deal with the daily horror they faced. Weepy police officers had no place on the force. Those who had a hard time controlling their emotions were the ones who were shunned. Who eventually left. Erin knew the mindset was wrong, but there wasn't anything she could do about it. She'd been powerless against it. That's why she had to leave. They couldn't use a broken, frightened shell of a human being.

She looked up to find Chester staring at her. When she locked eyes with him, she gasped. It was as if in that moment, something passed between them that was beyond words. Beyond description. Chester stepped away from his food bowl and came up close to her. Somehow Erin knew she shouldn't move. Then he licked her face. Just one small lick, then he backed up and went back to his bowl. But in that moment, Erin knew. This dog was going to be hers. They belonged together.

"Are you all right?"

Kaely's voice startled her. Erin realized tears were streaming down her face. She got to her feet and grabbed a tissue from the box on the small desk in the kitchen.

"Yeah, I'm fine," she said, fighting to keep her voice steady.

Kaely stared at her for a moment before saying, "No, you're not, Erin. You've locked your emotions into a room you don't want to go into. But they're beginning to leak out. The door to that room can't hold them back any longer. That's why we need to talk. I'm not a therapist, but I've been where you are." She walked up to Erin and took her hands. "I'm not going to tell you what to do—or judge you. I'm just going to listen to you. Let you unburden yourself. I've found opening that door is the first step to healing."

"Why is this so hard?" Erin asked, her voice trembling.

"Oh, my dear friend." Kaely squeezed her hands gently. "Trust is so hard. Too many times that trust is betrayed. We become afraid that it will happen again." She sighed. "Your experience with Scott made things so much worse."

Scott. The man who told me he loved me and then cheated with the woman I thought was my friend? The man I watched die right in front of me? Begging for my help?

"You were dealing with that hurt when Scott was killed, and you've also had to deal with the little girl who died. It's too much, Erin. Too much for anyone."

"There were people on the force who tried to help me," Erin said, wiping her face again. "But I felt worthless . . . embarrassed for not being strong enough."

"So you left everyone behind, not just because you couldn't trust them, but because you couldn't trust yourself."

"I killed an innocent young girl. What kind of a police officer does that?" Erin realized she'd raised her voice. She looked down to see Chester staring at her, as if confused by her reaction. She reached down again and put her hand on his head. This time he didn't pull away.

"Look, Erin," Kaely said softly, "you didn't murder anyone. It was an accident. Someone tried to kill you. You fired back. Why don't you pretend it was someone else who fired that bullet? What if it had been Scott? Would you have told him he murdered someone?"

Kaely's words made sense, but guilt still grabbed her heart with its cold, deadly hands and squeezed. If it wasn't for her, little Sarah Foster would still be alive.

Kaely let go of Erin's hands. "Look, let's take Chester outside, then we'll come back and talk, okay?" Kaely took a long leather belt and looped it around Chester's collar. "Next chance we get, we need to get this guy a new collar. It's pretty worn."

"I'll take him," Erin said, reaching for the belt.

"Okay. I'll warm up our chocolate—and our popcorn." She smiled. "Your box of Mallomars is still on the table. Meet you in the living room in a few minutes."

Erin nodded and led Chester to the front door. He seemed to be fine with the belt leash. Erin let it go while she put on her coat and then picked it up again. She opened the door, and they went outside. Erin didn't want to wander too far from the house, especially since it was so cold and it was beginning to snow harder. Thankfully, Chester didn't take long. They were headed back to the house when suddenly they were surrounded by the headlights of a vehicle that turned on its engine, backed up, and drove away from the house.

THIRTY-SIX

Adrian was fielding a lot of calls from worried residents about the storm. The department had tried to get information out to the public before the weather turned bad, but it seemed there were quite a few people who hadn't paid much attention.

Now it was all hands on deck, especially for him. His school resource officers were busy working with the local schools, and his other officers were out checking on residents and businesses, making certain everyone was prepared for bad weather. They'd set up three locations that could house anyone who lost their electricity. City Hall and two local churches had backup generators. They were prepared to take in anyone who might need help. The general store had sold out of water, ice melt, batteries, and other essentials. More supplies had been brought in from the big-box store on the edge of town. As far as Adrian could tell, the town should be pretty well equipped to weather the storm. But still, the calls came. Many folks were asking the police for weather updates. They tried to patiently explain that they weren't meteorologists, but that didn't seem to help. Tempers were frayed, and officers were exhausted. For now, everyone was on call, which kept officers from taking care of their own families.

Several times he'd wanted to call Erin and Kaely to make sure they were okay, but he hadn't gotten a break yet. Since they were both ex-law enforcement and armed, equipped with a generator, and stocked with supplies, he had no choice but to prioritize calls from residents who were in situations that were much more dire.

Still, he was having a hard time keeping them out of his mind. Especially Erin. Her deep green eyes seemed to follow him wherever he went.

"I can't get Adrian," Kaely said. "His cell phone just keeps going to voicemail."

"I'm sure he's really busy with the approaching storm," Erin said. "I remember in St. Louis when the weather forecast was bad, we'd be inundated with calls. When people are worried or frightened, they call the police, even when we couldn't really do anything for them other than to tell them what supplies they needed or where the shelters were." She sighed. "Look, the guy could have pulled over to check his map or something. There's no use worrying about some random guy. Our doors are locked. You're armed. And a storm's coming. We're fine."

"I guess so. Still, having someone parked outside the house after those murders is a little disconcerting. And this is the second time it's happened."

"I know."

"Did you happen to see what kind of car it was?" Kaely asked.

Erin shook her head. "I think it was dark. Maybe a pickup? I can't be sure. The lights blinded me, and by the time whoever it was turned around, I still couldn't see very well through the snow."

They were back in the living room. Kaely had warmed up the hot chocolate and put the popcorn in the microwave for a few seconds. Chester was back on his blanket by the fire, snoozing away. Kaely had the feeling he was simply worn out, and now that he had a place to sleep for the night and food to eat, his problems were behind him. As far as Kaely was concerned, he could stay until they left. She was a little worried about what would happen to him after that, but she had a strong feeling that Chester had just found a new home with Erin. Kaely was so happy that Chester had come along. He was just what Erin needed. Someone who would love her no matter what—and who would help her through the trauma she'd endured. Some people called dogs angels. Of course, they weren't, but right now she might not have been too surprised if Chester suddenly grew a pair of wings.

She'd been praying that God would give her the right words to say to Erin, but even more, that he would give her ears to hear Erin's heart. She'd noticed the locked gun box in Erin's room and wondered why she hadn't opened it. She'd told Kaely once that she wasn't certain she'd ever pick up a gun again. So why was it here? Locked in a box? There was one explanation, but that possibility horrified her. She was trying so hard not to feel responsible for Erin, to leave that concern to God, but ever since she'd noticed the box, fear pricked at her thoughts constantly.

Please help her, Father. Open her heart and her mind to You. You're her only true hope.

Kaely had to let the Holy Spirit lead her. If she pushed Erin too far . . . *Stop it. Put this in His hands.*

Erin took a sip of cocoa and then set her cup down on the coffee table. The snow was really starting to come down, and the wind was picking up. The outside lights showed trees whose branches were rippling in the wind. This was only the beginning. If the forecasters were correct, it was going to get much, much worse.

Kaely took a drink of her hot chocolate and slowly put it down. She was sitting in the overstuffed chair near the end of the sofa where Erin sat, a soft blue throw pulled up around her as if she were cold. But the room was nice and warm. Her reaction wasn't caused by the temperatures. It came from something else. Fear. Fear was cold and mind numbing. Kaely took a deep breath.

"So, Erin," she said. "We've talked quite a bit about your nightmares and how you have a hard time sleeping."

"Yeah. And thank you for taking my calls in the middle of the night. I'm not sure even people who called themselves my friends would have done that. I can't imagine what Noah thinks of me."

"Like I told you, when Noah goes to sleep, he's out. He could sleep through an earthquake."

Erin smiled. "I'm glad I haven't disturbed him. His work with the BAU is important."

Kaely nodded. "He loves it, and I can live through him vicariously. Although he can't discuss details of his cases, he does talk about the profiles they work." She shook her head. "Now, quit trying to make me talk about myself. You're deflecting."

Erin looked away. "Fair enough."

"Look, we came here so you could talk. I don't live in St. Louis anymore, so once we leave this place, you won't have to see me."

"I still think it's odd that you used to live there. Makes me wonder if we ever crossed paths."

"It's possible."

"I know you think it's easier for me that you live in another part of the country," Erin said, "but still, I think it would be nice if we were closer."

"You might feel that right now," Kaely said, "but knowing that you won't see me again for a while might make it easier to be honest with me."

"Maybe." Erin reached for her box of Mallomars. She took one out and then held out the box to Kaely, who shook her head. It was obvious they comforted her.

"My mom used to buy them for us as a special treat," Erin said. "They remind me of her."

That explained it. Kaely smiled. "I hear you. When I bake brownies, I think of my mother. She made them before . . . well, before my father was arrested and we went into hiding from the world. She didn't bake after that."

"I'm sorry," Erin said. "Sometimes I forget about everything you went through. You seem so . . . together."

"It took time, but God healed me. It's all due to Him." She took a deep breath and let it out. "So, tell me the things you've never said before, Erin. The things you don't want to say. What is the one memory or thought you have that you don't want to share with anyone?"

Erin's eyes filled with tears. "That's easy. The night the girl died. When I found out I killed her."

"Tell me about that."

"We've talked about that."

"True," Kaely said. "We've talked *about* that. But I want to know how you really feel—down deep inside."

"I . . . I don't know if I can." Erin got up and began to pace the floor. Chester raised his head and watched her.

"Yes. Yes, you can." Kaely paused for a moment. Then she said, "Erin, I worked for the FBI. I've seen the worst humanity has to offer. When I was with the BAU, we had cases that . . . well, let's just say that we saw and learned things about evil that shouldn't even be whispered about in the dark. Depravity that defies explanation. I had dreams too. Nightmares. And I watched coworkers take their lives because they couldn't handle it. There isn't anything you can say to me that I haven't heard before. I've also listened to other agents tell me about the innocent people who died in front of them. You're not the only one."

"Did these coworkers actually kill them?" Erin asked with anger in her voice.

"Yes. On several occasions. When firing back in self-defense, innocent people have died. I knew one guy who was trying to make a man put down the knife he held to his little boy's neck. He thought he'd talked the guy down. But as he approached him with his hand out for the knife, the man suddenly slit his own child's throat."

Erin stopped walking and looked at her. "That's horrendous."

"Yes, it is. And my friend blamed himself for it. Felt that he'd read the guy wrong. That he should have simply shot him in the head and saved the boy."

"What . . . what happened to your friend?" Erin asked.

"You may not like my answer."

"Tell me."

"Okay. He got help from the One who saved me. The One who let him know that it wasn't his fault. That he'd done everything he could to save the little boy's life. That He knew my friend would have given his own life for the boy. It was that reassurance that saved him. That made him realize that the only person responsible was the evil man who killed his son."

Erin came back over and sat down on the couch again. "Were you the friend?"

Kaely shook her head. "No, I wasn't."

"Whoever it was—that was a great friend."

"Yes, He was. And He still is."

Erin's eyebrow shot up and her eyes narrowed. "You're talking about God again."

Kaely shrugged. "Yes, I am. You asked. I'm sorry if you don't like my answer."

"You're right, I don't." She shook her head. "Kaely, you're so smart. How can you possibly believe in some kind of magical being who lives in the sky and runs everyone's life? I don't get it."

"I *don't* believe that."

Erin looked confused. "What does that mean?"

"First of all, God doesn't run anyone's life. He's not a puppet master or a dictator. And secondly, can I ask you the same question you asked me?"

Erin frowned. "I guess so."

"How can you possibly believe that the world, human beings, the universe, just happened accidentally? Out of nothing? That takes a lot more faith than I could ever muster."

Erin didn't say anything, she just looked at Kaely. Had she blown it? Had she pushed Erin too hard?

THIRTY-SEVEN

At first, he'd cursed the coming storm. It would make it harder for him to continue his mission. But then he realized that with the next offering, it could actually make it easier. She wouldn't be able to get away. She would be trapped. Of course, he would have to be able to make his escape, but he believed he could do it. He was used to bad weather. It had never stopped him before.

He'd been watching her. Planning. Waiting. That gnawing feeling was becoming stronger, as if it were eating him alive from the inside. He'd called out to his god to help him, but the only answer he received was that until he satisfied the hunger within, things wouldn't get better for him.

He had to kill her soon. Very soon.

Erin wanted to snap back at Kaely. Throw some kind of pithy response at her. But the truth was, her question was a good one. One she couldn't answer.

"Look, when I was a kid, I believed in God," Erin said. "My parents didn't take me to church, but I went a few times with a friend from school. Until they moved away. The Sunday school teacher had told us that if we prayed, God would hear us. That He answered prayer. So the night of my parents' accident, I prayed. I prayed they'd live, but they didn't. I prayed my sister would get off drugs and come home, but she didn't. So I quit praying." She sighed. "I'm sure you have some kind of pat response for something like this. But the truth is, what good is a God who ignores prayers? Who leaves someone an orphan at ten years old? If He can't do any better than that, I'm not interested."

"I don't have all the answers, Erin. But I can tell you one thing that is true. God loves you. No matter what it looks like, nothing will ever change that."

"Sure. He let my parents die, my sister disappear. And He watched while Scott and Sarah were shot to death. Great God you have there."

"He didn't cause the accident, Erin. Nor did he force your sister to take drugs. Gang members started the shooting that night Scott and Sarah died. God didn't do that. There are consequences for actions. No, Scott and Sarah shouldn't have paid for the actions of those gang members, but God didn't pull the triggers. You're blaming Him for things He had nothing to do with. And now, He wants to help you. Don't you think it's odd that the only person you're willing to talk to now is me? One of those Christians you disagree with so much? Has it ever occurred to you that He's the One who brought us together? That this is His way of reaching out to you when you need Him?" She took a deep breath. "Erin, you'll never be free if you don't take a step of faith. Just one step. Don't worry about the next ones. They'll come."

"I don't know," Erin said. "I turned my back on God because I believed He let me down."

"Okay," Kaely said. "Let me turn this around a bit. I'm certain you were a wonderful police officer. I know this because I've come to know *you*. So, why did that little girl die? Does that mean you were a bad officer? Or did you just want her to die?"

Kaely's comment felt like a punch in the stomach, and she gasped for air.

"I know that's not true, Erin," Kaely said immediately, with tears in her eyes. "But can't you see that even though terrible things happen sometimes—things we can't control—it doesn't change who we are? You were a decorated, brave, and incredible officer. Yet something terrible happened anyway. It wasn't your will, and it wasn't God's will. But it did happen. Like I said, God didn't want your parents to die. Nor did He want your sister to use drugs. The important thing to remember is that what happened to them—and to Sarah—didn't change who you are. Circumstances can't do that. This is true for you—and it's true for God. Sometimes things just happen. I know that someday God will be able to explain it to you in a way I can't. But no matter what, God is still God. He still loves us no matter what we do. And He still gave up His only Son for us." She shook her head. "But let's not get into that yet. I'll talk more about it later, but only if you ask me to. For now, I just want you to understand that no matter what, God doesn't change. He will never stop loving you. And you are still the person you used to be. The great police officer you were before that terrible night. You didn't kill that little girl, Erin. A stray bullet killed her. You weren't wrong to take that shot. The truth is, you were trained to defend yourself if your life was in danger. I know, and you should know, that you would have laid your life down for Scott, even though he'd hurt you. And you would have done the same for Sarah. That's who you really are."

Erin wanted to fire back. Wanted to shoot down Kaely's argument, but down deep inside, she knew it was true. It was as if Kaely's words had finally turned on the light inside her heart so she could see past the guilt, the pain, and the anger. It wasn't her fault. She'd only done what she was trained to do. There was no way for her to know that the bullet would penetrate the wall of that poorly constructed building and hit Sarah. She hung her head and began to sob. It was like a dam had broken inside, and she could no longer hold back the flood that poured through the cracks.

Kaely got up and came over to the couch. She opened her arms, and Erin fell into them. They stayed that way until Erin's tears finally stopped.

"Where have you been?" Adrian asked Timothy when he walked into the station.

"Checking things out at the shelters," Timothy said. "I thought that's what you wanted me to do."

"The chief didn't send that text to you, Timothy," Lisa said. "I did. I'm sorry," she said to Adrian, "but you weren't here, and I thought we should make certain they're prepared."

Adrian sighed. "Yeah, you're right. And what did you find, Tim?"

He accidentally let the nickname slip. Timothy didn't like using the less formal name, but at the moment, Adrian didn't care. They had a lot of things to do that were more important than worrying about someone's quirks.

"They need more cots," Timothy said. "I called The Salvation Army in Knoxville, and they're sending a truck with a little over a hundred more."

"Thank you," Adrian said. "I appreciate your initiative. And what about everything else?"

"We were short on blankets until Lisa called some of our churches. People began to bring in all kinds of blankets, bedspreads, and quilts. Anything they had to help."

Adrian breathed a sigh of relief. "Well, let's pray we don't need to use any of them. But at least we've done what we could."

His phone rang again. "Sorry. Just keep doing what you're doing. Excellent job. Both of you."

"Thanks, boss," Lisa said.

"And, boss," Timothy added, "in situations like this, you can call me Tim."

Adrian laughed lightly. "Thanks. A high honor indeed." The phone rang, and he picked it up. It was Merle, asking for help in case those who were trapped in his resort needed more food than he could provide. While Adrian told him about the facilities that would have food and shelter should his guests need it, he kept thinking about Erin Delaney and Kaely Hunter. For some reason, he felt unsettled about them. When he hung up with Merle, he planned to call them. Was he worrying for no reason? Kaely was ex-FBI, and Erin was an ex-cop. The skills they'd learned would be part of them the rest of their lives. Besides that, they were both smart. Savvy. They should be fine. Why couldn't he get their faces out of his mind?

THIRTY-EIGHT

Kaely was moved with compassion for her friend. What had just happened was a great step toward healing. But now Kaely would have to tread carefully.

She'd gone to the kitchen to make them both a cup of tea. While she rinsed the hot chocolate cups and put them in the dishwasher, she prayed. *Lead me, Holy Spirit. Don't let me blow this. Help me to get myself out of the way so that I can hear You.*

She'd made the mistake of getting ahead of God before, and she didn't want to do it again. Erin was fragile. More fragile than she'd realized. As a cop, Erin had been trained to protect others but not herself.

Kaely put two cups of water in the microwave and waited for it to heat up. She pulled out the Earl Grey tea, and there was milk in the fridge. Earl Grey had to be served with milk. It was the only proper way. A British friend of hers had taught her that.

As she waited for the water to heat up, a shriek from outside made her jump. Her first thought was the Woman in Watcher Woods. She stood still for a minute, and within seconds, there was another high-pitched sound. The wind. The storm was coming closer. Kaely took a deep breath to calm herself. She didn't believe in ghosts, but seeing someone out there, dressed in a dark cloak and glowing, would unnerve anyone.

As far as the storm, she was grateful that they had ample supplies and a backup generator. The only thing that bothered her was the realization that they could soon be cut off from the outside world. Still, serial killings rarely happened during bad weather. Criminals were usually concerned about having a way to escape. Being trapped in a blizzard wasn't a favorable situation to find themselves in.

Her mind drifted back to the supposed ghost wandering the woods. Who wanted them to believe there was a ghost in Watcher Woods? What was the purpose? Could the killer be dressing up as William Watcher's dead wife? But that didn't really go along with his MO or his signature. And there wasn't anything at the crime scene that connected him to the Emma Watcher ghost story. Kaely's gut told her that this killer would never do that. He lived to kill. He was driven to kill. He wasn't focused on some silly ghost story.

Although the FBI's training pointed only toward a killer's mental and emotional state, Kaely knew there was more to it. Jesus cast out demons frequently, yet today, modern thinking looked upon that explanation as ridiculous. Even some Christians laughed at the idea. However, if part of the Bible was true, then all of the Bible was true. Demons were real. Kaely had seen them in the acts of some of the criminals she'd profiled for the FBI. Unfortunately, casting out demons was frowned upon by most law enforcement agencies. She suspected the killer they were dealing with now had a spiritual problem. Using angels as his signature made this clear. She supposed that demons didn't care much for angels either—except maybe the fallen kind.

Kaely jumped when the microwave dinged. Thinking about serial killers and demons was going to make her loopy if she didn't refocus her mind on the main reason she was here. To help Erin. She was convinced that she needed to keep her talking about the night that changed her life. That had sent her spiraling. She had to find a way to move past it and live her life without that night holding her hostage. She'd taken a big step, but there was more that needed to be done in her heart and mind.

She put the tea bags in the cups, added a little milk, and carried the cups into the living room. She'd just set them down when her cell phone rang. She picked it up. Adrian again.

"Hello?"

"Things are crazy here," he said, "but I wanted to check on you and Erin. Make sure you're safely inside. The snow has started and will get heavier as the night goes on."

"We're fine. Thank you for checking. We're nice and warm and have plenty of supplies."

"Good. If you need me for any reason, you may have to leave me a message. Everyone in town seems to be calling, and we're busy setting up shelters and providing supplies for those who need them."

"Thanks for checking, but you don't need to worry about us. And I imagine your angel friend is also inside for a while too. Maybe that's a blessing in the midst of the storm."

"I agree," Adrian said. "Oh, one other thing, the first body has been identified. Knoxville had a BOLO for her. If it wasn't for the necklace she was wearing and her broken leg, it might have taken a lot longer. Turns out the necklace was a family heirloom. Very distinctive. Her family had mentioned the necklace when the BOLO was issued. She broke her leg when she was twelve. Her name is Willow Abbott. She was twenty-seven when she disappeared. She's from Memphis and rode buses from her home in Missouri, heading to Charleston, South Carolina. It was a long and arduous trip, but she was going to see an old friend who lived in Charleston. Obviously, she never made it. The last time she boarded a bus was in Knoxville. Then she just disappeared. Until now, that is."

Kaely sat down and grabbed the notebook she had on the table. "Hold on, I want to write this down." She quickly scribbled everything Adrian had told her onto a page in her notebook. "Adrian, can you give me a quick description of Miss . . . I assume it's Miss Abbott?"

"Yes. She was single." She could hear him rustle some papers. Then he said, "Medium build. Red hair. Small frame."

"Hmmm."

"Does that *hmmm* mean something?"

"Maybe," Kaely said. "Adrian, the other victims. Weren't they all small in stature?"

He was silent for several seconds. "Well, now that you mention it, you're right. I hadn't really thought about it."

"That means that our unknown subject doesn't need to be particularly large or strong. I still believe it's a man. It would still take some strength to move those bodies, and serial killers are usually male. But that fact might help you narrow your search. You'll want to add that to the profile we provided you."

"Thank you. I will. By the way, how's Ozzy doing?"

Kaely chuckled. "Well, Ozzy is now Chester. He's been fed, thanks to our friend Steve, and is sleeping in front of the fire. And I'm not sure yet, but you may have to fight Erin for him."

"I'd like nothing better than for him to go home with her," Adrian said. "Our other dogs are easy to get along with, but Ozzy—I mean, Chester—would probably be happier being the center of attention. Poor guy deserves it, don't you think?"

"Yes, I certainly do. Well, I'm sure you need to get back to work. I'll be praying for you and everyone else in town to get through this storm safely."

"Thank you," Adrian said. "We certainly need all the prayers we can get."

Kaely disconnected the call and hung up.

"You're pretty sure of yourself about Chester, aren't you?" Erin asked with a smile.

"Aren't you?"

"Maybe."

"I think it would be wonderful. Not just for you, but also for Chester. You two are going to be so good for each other. I don't know what I'd do without Mr. Hoover."

"You told me a while back that you and Noah are trying to get pregnant. You haven't said anything lately. How are things going?" Erin asked.

Kaely shrugged. "We'll get there. It's just taking longer than I anticipated." She didn't want to make her struggles part of the conversation. For now, Erin needed to be the center of attention. "Did you hear that the first victim has been identified?"

"Yeah. Who was she, and do they know why she was in the vicinity?"

"Adrian said she was traveling from her home in Missouri to Charleston, South Carolina. She was planning to meet a friend. She was supposed to change buses in Knoxville, but she didn't get on."

"Knoxville? I realize it's not that far away, but if I remember right, all the other victims were closer to Sanctuary."

Kaely picked up her notebook and looked through notes. "Yeah, you're right. Some of them lived farther away, but they all disappeared closer than Willow. Seems our UNSUB started off as far as twenty miles away, but now his comfort zone is tightening. I think Sanctuary was his intended target all along. As he perfects his murders, he seems to be focusing on this town."

THIRTY-NINE

Erin found Kaely's statement rather chilling. "So, the victims don't seem to connect to each other, but the area is important?" Erin frowned. "He has something against women, angels, and this town? Suddenly, I wish we'd picked someplace else to stay."

Kaely smiled. "What? And miss all the fun?" She shook her head. "Sorry, that was in poor taste. At the BAU we had to find something to joke about so we could get through the day. None of us took our jobs lightly. It was just . . . necessary."

"I understand. We did the same. Police officers in St. Louis see things you wouldn't believe."

Kaely took a sip of her tea and then said, "Why don't you tell me about that?"

Something inside Erin turned to ice. She felt frozen, unable or unwilling to speak about the horrors that made it impossible to sleep some nights. Hadn't she already shared enough? But why had she come here? Wasn't it to finally relieve herself of all of the shadows that had held her in limbo? She took a deep breath, as if that would help her to release the images that played in her mind.

"Look, I don't want to go into everything I've seen. Sharing what happened that night was hard enough. Suffice it to say, seeing children wasting away from a lack of food because their parents were spending their money on drugs—some of them not even wearing diapers—trying to exist in filthy conditions and housing that should have been bulldozed years ago. . . . It takes a toll on you. Sometimes we could help the children, and sometimes we couldn't. We saw women who were beaten by their boyfriends or husbands but were too afraid to leave. Gang wars that left young people lying dead in the streets." She felt her eyes fill with tears, but she didn't care. "All that potential wiped out by ignorance and violence." She shook her head. "We had to notify mothers that their children were dead. Sometimes they broke down and fell to the floor as if all the life had been drained from them. And other times, they didn't react at all. The light in their eyes had died long ago." She looked at Kaely. "I think the children bothered me the most. Maybe that's why what happened the night Scott died devastated me so much. I had so much compassion for children—and then I caused the death of an innocent girl." She shook her head. "I *accidentally* caused her death. I see that now. Thank you."

Kaely nodded. "Why don't you tell me a little more about her. You said her name was Sarah?"

Erin nodded. "Sarah Foster. Her father's name is Toby. He . . . he's a good man and was trying to raise his little girl after his wife left them both. His apartment was spotless, although like many of the buildings in that neighborhood, it needed to be updated. But you could tell he was doing his best to give Sarah a good home." She looked at Kaely with tear-filled eyes. "Sarah was a straight-A student in a Christian school. Her father worked two jobs so he could send her there. One of the teachers let Sarah come to her house after school and stay with them until Toby could pick her up after he got off work." She shrugged. "I know he tried to get them out of that neighborhood, but he didn't have any family to go to."

"Police shootings are always investigated," Kaely said. "What was the result?"

"I was cleared. I was firing back at someone trying to kill me. They said that the shooting was an accident. Just like you said."

"And did you ever talk to Mr. Foster again?"

"Yes," Erin said. "I went back to his apartment and told him it was definitely my bullet that killed Sarah."

"Did you check with the powers that be at the station before you did that?" Kaely asked.

"No."

"And why is that?"

Erin picked up her tea and sipped it. Then she put the cup back on its saucer. "Because they wouldn't have wanted me to do it. I felt . . . I knew . . . I had to." She shrugged. "I handed in my badge and gun the day before."

"And what did Mr. Foster say?"

"He . . ." Her voice caught and she cleared her throat. "He didn't say anything at first. I was waiting for him to get angry again. Like he did the night it happened. But instead, he told me he'd realized it wasn't my fault. And he thanked me for telling him the truth."

"And how did that make you feel?"

Erin crossed her hands over her chest. "How did it make me feel?"

At that moment, the wind howled loudly, almost as if it were in tune with the way Erin felt. "It made me feel even worse."

"Oh, Erin," Kaely said, her eyes filling with tears. "The police didn't blame you. In the end, even Mr. Foster didn't blame you. You just told me that you realize now that it was an accident."

Erin took a deep breath and slowly let it out. She felt better, that was true. But the pain she felt because a young girl wasn't able to fulfill her life wasn't going away any time soon.

She told that to Kaely who nodded. "I understand. A tragedy is a tragedy. But from now on, you need to remind yourself that although you witnessed it, and it's incredibly sad, the only blame there should be is toward the gang members who broke the law and then fired on the police." She met Erin's gaze.

Erin stared at her for several seconds and then dropped her head. "When it happened, I couldn't see past my own sense of guilt. My friends on the force told me the same things you have. For some reason I just couldn't accept it. It felt as if I was trying to find the easy way out." She shook her head. "I'm going to tell you something else," Erin said slowly. "But you're the only one outside of the school—and Toby Foster—who knows. You've got to keep it to yourself, okay?"

"Okay. I promise."

"I set up a foundation that works through the schools in Sarah's neighborhood to help families with children relocate to safer areas. Thankfully, other people are also donating. It's called the *Sarah Foster Foundation*."

"Oh, Erin. That's incredible," Kaely said. "You brought something wonderful out of a tragedy. I'm so proud of you."

Erin shrugged. "Thanks, but it's founded on the blood of an innocent child. The price was too high."

"I understand how you feel, but if I told you that Sarah is alive and living with God, would you be able to accept that? She's happy, safe, loved beyond measure, and blessed more than we can imagine."

Instead of being offended by what Kaely had said, Erin was actually comforted. She was actually startled by her reaction.

"I'm going to profile you, Erin," Kaely said gently. "Not an involved profile, just a brief one."

Something in Erin wanted to tell Kaely to stop. Not to do it. But even though she wanted to tell Kaely not to proceed, for some reason she couldn't.

"Erin, I suspect that you not only blame your sister for the death of your parents, you're also angry with them. Angry that they left you. And you're angry at God for not preventing their deaths—even though He had nothing to do with it. I realize your sister's drug use was the reason they went out on the roads that night of the accident. But do you really think your sister wanted that accident to happen? Of course she didn't." Kaely sighed. "Oh, Erin. You've been hard on your sister and because of that, you've been hard on yourself. In your mind, there's no room for error. No forgiveness for weakness. If you forgive your sister—and your parents—then you'd have to forgive yourself. And you haven't wanted to do that."

She paused for a moment, but Erin couldn't respond to what she'd said. She just stared down at her teacup.

"I know it's hard to face what I'm saying, but it's normal for someone who is grieving to have misplaced anger toward a loved one who dies. Rather than consciously blaming them, you find someone else to shoulder the guilt. In this case, it's your sister. And in Sarah's death—it's you. So, how do you live with it? The guilt, the anger, the blame over your parents' deaths? You join the police force. You need to fight back at the darkness that's robbed you of your parents, your sister, and your ability to believe in God. But, Erin, you carried all that guilt and false sense of responsibility over into your job."

Her eyes sought Erin's. She wanted to look away, but she couldn't. Although it was hard to hear, something told her that Kaely was speaking the truth.

"And I did the same thing with Scott?"

"What do you think? You told me that in your dream—scratch that—your *nightmare*, you tried to get to Scott, but you couldn't. You were trying to wade through blood that was so thick you could barely move?"

Erin nodded.

"Again, his blood was at your feet. You were taking the blame for him as well. My dear, dear friend. No one can handle all this guilt and be healthy. And certainly not happy." Kaely pursed her lips and blew out a quick breath of air. "You keep your gun locked in a metal box. You told me you haven't taken it out for quite some time, is that right?"

Erin could only nod.

"It's because you've had thoughts of using it on yourself, isn't it?"

"No, of course not," Erin said, her words sounding like quick bursts of gunfire.

"You just lied to me."

Erin got to her feet and walked away from the couch. This was too much. Really. She appreciated Kaely's attempts to help her, but she was getting too close.

Kaely got up and walked up to her. Then she gently took her hands. "Tell me the truth," she said gently. "I already know it, but you need to say it."

Erin tried to wrestle her hands from Kaely's, but she wouldn't let go. The harder she tried to pull away, the tighter Kaely's grip became. Finally, she cried out. "Okay, okay. You're right. I didn't believe I could go on anymore after what happened." She squeezed Kaely's hands. "But I don't feel that way anymore. I mean, I know I still have a lot to work through, but you've helped me to see a path through the pain. And . . . and I think I'm finally able to see a way out." She blinked away tears. "Thank you. Thank you so much."

"You're right. You have a long road to walk, but I think you're on the way. I'll be here for you, Erin. But please remember that God is the One who can heal you completely. Think about that?"

"I will. I promise." At one point, she might have said something like that as a way to get Kaely to back off. But now she meant it with her whole heart.

FORTY

The next day, Erin awoke to a world gone white. Everything was covered in snow, but the worst of the storm was still on the horizon. Although Kaely and Erin weren't certain Steve would want Chester on one of the beds, they decided that ignorance was bliss. Chester had followed Erin to bed as if he'd been doing it for years. He seemed to know that she needed him. It appeared she not only had a dog, but an emotional support animal. He'd cuddled up next to her in the bed, and she'd slept with her arm around him.

Kaely made waffles and sausage for breakfast. Their conversation was light and nonconfrontational. It was as if Kaely knew Erin needed a break from the heaviness of the night before. She knew Kaely had spoken truth to her. Her profile was spot on, and Erin knew she had to make some changes. But how? Was Kaely right? Was it time to give God a chance in her life?

After they ate and cleaned up the kitchen, Erin fed Chester and took him out. He was obviously potty-trained. There hadn't been any messes in the house, and he knew exactly what to do once they stepped outside. Erin took an empty plastic bag with her to pick up his waste and put the bag in the trash cart at the side of the cabin.

As they walked back toward the house, Chester suddenly stopped and stared out toward the woods.

"I'd really rather you not do that," Erin said. "With everything going on lately, it's a little spooky."

Chester stared a little longer, and then looked up at her and gave her a goofy doggy smile.

"Are you ready to go in?" she asked as if he were going to answer her.

He tugged on the belt and led her toward the front door. She was freezing and was wearing a thick coat. He had to be cold. As they approached the door, she looked up at the sky. Dark clouds were on the horizon. Probably the most serious part of the storm.

Erin wiped her snow-covered feet on the mat and opened the door. She and Chester came inside to find a towel spread out on the floor. Once again, Erin wiped her feet and then dried Chester's.

"How did he do?" Kaely asked.

"Great. He's a really smart dog. But for a minute he acted as if something in the woods caught his attention."

"I didn't hear him barking," Kaely said.

Erin took off her coat and hung it up. "No, he just seemed interested but not really upset."

"Probably an animal or something."

"Yeah, I guess."

"While you were gone, Adrian called," Kaely said.

"More dead bodies?"

Kaely shook her head. "No, thankfully. He was just check-ing on us again."

"That's nice."

Kaely went over and put several pieces of wood into the fireplace. "I think he was a little disappointed that I answered the phone."

"Don't be ridiculous."

She laughed. "Why is that ridiculous? You're single, he's single, you're cute, and he's a hunk."

Erin burst out laughing. "Did you just call Adrian a *hunk*?"

"I might be older than you, but I think that term is still used." Kaely frowned. "Right?"

"Yeah, I guess. It just sounded funny coming from you."

Kaely raised an eyebrow and gave Erin a crooked smile. "Hey, I may be married, but I'm not dead. I notice hand-some men."

"Okay, he's handsome. But he's not interested in me." She plopped down into the chair next to the couch.

"And why do you say that?"

"I'm weird looking. My nose is too small, my mouth too big, and my hair?" Erin ran her hand through her short blonde hair. "It's all over the place—like it doesn't quite know what to do with itself."

"Don't be silly. The *messy* look is all the rage. I wish I could wear it, but this super curly hair doesn't allow for anything like that."

"You're gorgeous. I'll bet Noah is a real . . . hunk too." Erin laughed.

Kaely got up and went over to the kitchen island where she grabbed her phone. She scrolled through it and brought it over to the couch.

"Here's a picture."

"Wow. He really is a hunk," Erin said. She handed it back to Kaely. "So, you two really love each other?"

Kaely looked at her with a rather odd expression. "Yeah, we really do." She frowned. "I'm sorry things didn't work out for you and Scott."

Erin shook her head. "Yeah, me too. I realized after you said something about all this guilt that I seem to enjoy dumping on myself that I also felt guilty for asking for another partner. It was . . . strained, working with him. He apologized over and over. He was drunk when . . . when it happened, and he said the girl didn't mean anything to him. Actually, that made it worse, you know? Destroying a relationship you claim to care about for someone that doesn't mean anything to you? It not only didn't make sense to me, it made me angry for the girl. No one should be treated like that. I lost all respect for him." She shook her head. "But sadly, I still loved him."

"I get it. I really do." Kaely picked up their coffee cups and went back to the kitchen. "Refill?" she asked.

"Sure."

Erin looked down to find Chester sitting next to her, watching her. She reached over to pet him. She really hoped nothing would keep her from taking Chester back to St. Louis with her. She wasn't worried about keeping him in her apartment. The landlord allowed pets. She would make sure he got to go for walks. She had nothing else to do . . . except write. Last night, she'd decided she really wanted to write another book. Maybe it wasn't what she would do for the rest of her life, but for now, it would keep her busy—and would use her law enforcement background. She'd called her agent, who was beside herself with joy. She promised to contact the publisher and start working on a contract. She told Kaely about it when she came back with the coffees.

"That's great news," she said. "If it's really what you want to do."

"For now. I enjoyed writing *Dark Matters*, I just hated all the promotion."

"Some of that might have been because of the wall you built around yourself. Someday you might actually enjoy some of that."

Erin rolled her eyes. "Now that would really be a miracle."

Kaely laughed as she carried their cups back into the living room. "So, what would you like to do today?"

"Could we just kick back some?" Erin asked. "Watch movies and eat food that's really bad for us? I brought lots of Mallomars."

Kaely grinned. "I think that sounds great. Let's do it. We still have several days to talk. Last night was pretty . . . heavy."

"Yeah, it was. But . . ." She smiled at Kaely. "It helped."

"Good." Kaely hesitated a moment. "One thing I want you to know." She cleared her throat. "We haven't talked about it a lot, but what I went through with my father . . . well, it helps me to understand the trauma you experienced. We've been through different situations, but I think childhood trauma creates so many of the same results. I blamed myself when it came to my father's actions. I felt as if I should have known. Should have realized what he was. Someone who was once a friend certainly blamed me. Like you, I had to learn to not feel responsible for his choices."

"You haven't mentioned your mother. How did she deal with it?"

"Of course, my father's proclivities reflected badly on her. Again, people decided she knew and even approved of what he did. She didn't. One thing I've learned is that some serial killers are great actors. Think about BTK—Dennis Rader. His wife and daughter had no idea what he was up to." She sighed. "My mother had a tough time. She passed her anger and sense of betrayal to my brother and me. It took her a long time to change, but she did. She married again and is very happy."

"What caused her to change?"

Kaely's eyebrows shot up. "Do you really want to know?"

Erin nodded. She was pretty sure she knew what Kaely was going to say, but she actually wanted to know the answer.

"She found God. He helped her to view her life—and herself—differently. She and her husband are very active in their church. They've been very loving to my brother and me."

"God again, huh?"

"Yes." Kaely smiled "But we'll save that for another time if you want. I promised you I wouldn't try to . . . how did you say it after we first started working together? Force God on you? We talked quite a bit about Him last night, so I'll back off today."

Erin picked up her mug and took a sip. She'd made Kaely promise not to talk about God when they had first started working together. But now . . . well, she *was* interested. She realized that being against God for no good reason didn't make sense. As a police officer, she'd tried to make facts her god. But now she was learning why someone like Kaely, so smart, educated, and talented, believed in a God that ruled the universe. Frankly, she'd begun to believe that Satan was real as well. It would explain some of the horrific things she'd seen.

"Okay, but for now, let's find some good movies and veg out. Maybe we can talk again tonight." Erin frowned. "I didn't have any nightmares last night. In fact, I got a pretty good night's sleep. Didn't wake up at 3:33, which was nice. I'm not saying it's because of being here—and talking to you—but I'm not denying it either. I feel so relaxed here. Well, except for the serial killer and the ghost."

Kaely burst out laughing. "Yeah, except for that. There is one other thing I'd like to do today. I'd like to work on the profile again. We have a new murder. And I want you to do it with me."

"You mean . . . talk to the murderer?"

Kaely nodded. "You have such great instincts. I've never worked a profile like that with someone else. How about it?"

Erin nodded. The idea was exciting.

And a little frightening.

FORTY-ONE

The day passed by quickly. As promised, the second wave of the storm moved in. The wind picked up, and the snow came down in sheets of white, mixed with pellets of ice that gleamed like diamonds. The world outside was silent and peaceful. Erin loved the feeling of being safe inside the cabin, evil held at bay. Not even a serial killer would venture out in this. His murderous spree was at a standstill, and Erin could breathe.

She, Kaely, and Chester watched three movies, *All About Eve*, *Notorious*, and *Gaslight*. Erin loved old movies and was glad to find out that Kaely did as well. Some of the newer suspense movies were too violent for her liking. When she was on the job, classic movies became an escape. Enough mystery and intrigue to keep her interested, but not so much that it reminded her of what she had to face every day on the streets.

She and Kaely could watch the snow falling through the floor-to-ceiling windows on each side of the fireplace. The porch light illuminated the white flakes as they twirled through the air, the wind pushing them into a frenzy of motion.

As they prepared dinner, Kaely found some brownie mix in the pantry and soon had them baking in the oven, the aroma of chocolate permeating the cabin.

"I'm not trying to replace your Mallomars," Kaely said. "Just give us another choice."

"You don't like my Mallomars, do you?" Erin asked with a grin.

"I actually do like them but probably not as much as you. Of course, I've never met anyone who loves them the way you do."

After they ate and as the brownies cooled, she and Kaely sat down at the table once again. They took their places at each end with an empty chair between them. Kaely had her notebook with her.

"If you don't mind, I'm going to play the recording I made last time," Kaely said. "It will help me to remember what I saw. I have my notes, but listening to me talk about him is more helpful."

Erin nodded. "I understand." She didn't really, but whatever worked for Kaely was fine with her.

Kaely lowered her head and prayed silently before turning on the recording she'd made previously.

Erin listened as Kaely's voice came over the phone. Once again, she felt something in the room. An energy. A presence. What was it? Better yet, *who* was it?

Erin listened as Kaely said, "*You're angry. You've been angry a long time. Ever since you were a child. Something happened to make you this way. You've been planning to pay someone back for a while. Not long ago, you started practicing. Practicing for vengeance. Against God. Against the angels. You're in your late twenties, early thirties. You're considered good-looking.*"

Kaely suddenly paused the recording. "I'm changing this," she said. "I think he's closer to forty."

"Why?" Erin asked.

"Hailey. Hailey Duncan. She was in her late thirties. Active in her church and by all accounts happily married. She wasn't meeting this man for a date. This was something else. It has to do with his job. She met with him because she trusted him because of that job. His position. I don't think a really young man would be able to have the kind of persona that these women, including Hailey, would trust."

"Kaely, there's something that's been bothering me."

"Tell me."

"Your profile. The last time you did this something occurred to me. I hate to even think about this but . . ."

"Profiling is educated guessing," Kaely said. "If you have a guess, I want to hear it."

"You keep talking about his job. That he has a position of respect. That these women come with him because they feel safe?"

"Yes, I stick by that."

"Wouldn't a police officer fit your profile?"

Kaely frowned. "Yes, it would. Why?"

"I don't know. I hate to bring it up since I was a police officer, but it's been on my mind."

"You think a police officer could hide his own evidence," Kaely said. "Like Sergeant Johnson?"

Erin nodded. "Or . . . or even Adrian?"

"I don't see anything in his personality that makes me

believe he's involved," Kaely said. "But no one should be off the table."

"I feel terrible pointing the finger at either one of them," Erin said. She liked Adrian and Timothy and hated to think either one of them could be a serial killer.

"I've been wrong before. Besides, you need to remember that we're not accusing anyone of anything." Kaely shook her head. "I've wondered about Steve. He fits the profile too." She sighed. "If we let our minds wander, we could start thinking everyone looks like a possible suspect. That can be dangerous."

"Okay."

"So, let's get back to the profile." She smiled. "Try not to see anyone specific sitting in the chair. Instead, let a picture come to you from the profile, not your preconceived ideas."

Erin nodded, but she wasn't sure she could do what Kaely asked.

Kaely focused her attention on the empty chair between them. "Everything else I said about you is true. You hate women, but I think you see them every day with your job. Maybe this is how you scout them out." She turned the recording back on and fast forwarded it a bit. *"The most important thing isn't the woman—it's the figurine you force them to hold. You're uncomfortable touching them. You have no physical attraction to them. You want to kill them in a certain way. You practiced it several times before you killed Chloe. However, what you did to them wasn't perfect, so you buried them. But you got it right when you killed Chloe. That's why you displayed her. She was perfection."* Kaely stopped the recording again. She clicked over to the picture of Hailey. "The connection between these women is your job. If we can figure that out, we've got you."

Kaely stared at the chair for a moment. Erin wrapped her arms around herself as the wind outside howled like a woman in pain. She shivered as a chill ran down her back. Kaely was watching the chair, but she couldn't bring herself to look. However, out of the corner of her eye, she could have sworn she saw something dark sitting there.

Kaely clicked the recording on, but once again fast forwarded it. When she stopped, her voice filled the room. She spoke distinctly, with assurance. *"You're killing because of someone else. And the angels? What does that have to do with it?"* She paused. *"Okay, let's move on. You don't mind the makeup, their shoes, or their jewelry. Why? Is it because you're not attracted to them that way?"*

She stopped the recording and stared down at her phone. It was obvious she was thinking. Once again, she skipped over some of it. When she started it again, Erin listened as she said *"They told you the angels took someone away that you loved, didn't they? And that's why you dress these women up as angels and put that figurine in their hands. You think you're paying the angels back for what they did to you."* Another pause. Fast forward. *"You don't take off their makeup or their shoes because your mother wore makeup and liked high heels. You can't remove them because it would betray her in some way. My guess is whoever told you that the angels took her also believed your mother shouldn't wear makeup or wear high heels. That's it, isn't it? Two of these women wore heels. One didn't. But that doesn't really matter. I already know about the shoes."*

Kaely stopped the tape again and looked at Erin. "Hailey

was wearing heels and makeup, so this confirms my profile. These things don't matter to him." She looked at the empty chair and sighed. "I still believe that your victims are picked at random, but now I'm thinking you use your job to lure them. I stand by my conjecture that you don't care about them, and you're not choosing them by type, job, or personality. Only by convenience. I'm not sure why you don't have elderly victims, but my guess is that unless you're stopped, that could happen."

Erin was startled to hear Kaely mention this since it was exactly what she'd thought at one time.

Kaely pushed the phone away from her as if she were finished with it. "I'm missing something," she said to the empty chair. "You hate the angels, you have a religious background, but not one that had solid doctrine. But you're smart. I've seen killers like you before. You like to play games. And you like attention. So why no letters to the local newspaper or to the police? That element should have shown itself by now. There's something . . ."

As before, Erin could swear there was a presence in the room. In that chair. She wanted to look at it, but she was afraid.

"I can see him," Kaely said, swinging her gaze toward Erin. "He's a little older. Probably late thirties, early forties. Superior. Thinks we're stupid. He may be able to hide himself from most people, but we can see him."

"I . . . I can't," Erin said. "I mean, it's like I can feel someone there, but I . . ."

"You're afraid to look. Don't be. He can't hurt you, Erin. This is just a way of profiling that helps you to move your thoughts from paper to the real world. *See* someone a little older. Create a man with a superior countenance. Someone who believes he's smarter than you."

"You think he's killed others? Before Sanctuary?" Erin asked.

Kaely shook her head. "No. I think Sanctuary is the place where he was damaged, and he has to kill here. Although most serial killers have a comfort zone, there have been exceptions to that rule. Robert Ben Rhodes was nicknamed the Truck Stop Killer. He raped and murdered women in different states. And the man known as the Train Man, traveled the rails and killed people in different parts of the country. But this man—he is tied to Sanctuary by something. There's too much symbolism in the way he kills. He's not killing for the sake of taking lives. I think he grew up here and is angry about it. Angry at the people who raised him, angry at a town that didn't protect him—and trying to avenge the person he lost."

"You said you would expect someone like him to leave messages," Erin said. "To contact the press. When writing *Dark Matters*, you told me that psychopaths crave attention. They want people to know how exceptional they are."

"Exactly." Kaely looked at the empty chair once more. "Where is it? Where's your message?"

Erin looked at the list of the women that had been found in Sanctuary. "Do you think there might be something special about the order he killed them in?"

"Possibly. Can you read me the list of the victims in order?"

Erin opened her notebook. "The oldest corpse belonged to Willow Abbot. Then there was Annie Squires."

Another gust of wind shrieked loudly and rattled the windows. Erin had the strangest feeling that something outside didn't want her to say the names out loud. *Get a grip, Erin. You're going bonkers.* She purposely refused to look at the chair she knew was empty. Why did she feel that someone sat there, staring at her? She cleared her throat. "The next victim is Terri Rupp. After that, there's Chloe Banner, the first one found with the angel figurine."

"I'm still a little surprised that he allowed us to find the first three victims without the figurine," Kaely said slowly. "Most of the time these killers are so obsessed with their signature, that they won't allow any of their failures to be discovered."

"But if there's a pattern or a signature that we're missing . . ."

Kaely nodded. "That would explain it."

"And then the most recent victim, Hailey Duncan."

Erin could have sworn she heard something coming from the empty chair. A sound, like a low growl. She looked down over by the fire and realized that Chester was staring at them. He was growling at something they couldn't see.

Erin swallowed hard. She looked down at the names again. She felt as if the blood in her body had turned to ice. She lifted her eyes to meet Kaely's.

"I know who it is," she whispered. "And it's not Detective Johnson."

Chester growled again.

"I know who the killer is, and I think I'm the next one on his list."

As soon as the words left her mouth, the lights went out.

FORTY-TWO

"Sit still," Kaely said. "The generator will kick on."

But as they sat in the dark, the only light coming from the fireplace, nothing happened. How long would it take the generator to start?

Kaely looked at Erin, whose eyes were wide with fear. How could she know who the killer was?

"If the generator doesn't come on soon . . ." Kaely started to say. But suddenly, the lights flickered back on, and noises came from the kitchen. Obviously, from appliances that had restarted.

"Now, tell me what you're thinking," Kaely said to Erin.

"It's in the names," Erin said, her voice shaking. "Think about it. Willow, Annie, Terri, Chloe, and Hailey."

"I don't understand," Kaely said. "What are you seeing . . ." And then she understood. "W, A, T, C, H. Watch. Like Watcher Woods. Then the next victim would have to be . . ." Kaely felt as if she couldn't breathe. "It doesn't mean that it's you. It could be anyone whose name starts with the letter E."

"But it isn't just anyone, and you know that."

"You said you know who the killer is. Tell me. Then we call Adrian."

"You said that his job made him someone that people would trust. Wouldn't be suspicious of. He could be in his forties. Not unattractive. And he has a signature. He likes things in order."

Kaely continued to stare at her. Then it hit her. "A certain order. Like the word *Watcher*. That's it."

"He had to have all the flyers on the bulletin board in alphabetical order."

"And the stamps were taken out of the regular booklet and put into a three-ring binder so that they would also be in order." Kaely gasped. "He knew who we were, where we're staying, and for how long. We didn't tell him that. It's Allen Dunne. Why didn't I think of him sooner? He knows where everyone lives. He delivers mail to them. He has access."

As soon as the words left her mouth, the lights went out again.

"If I cussed, I think I would be doing that now," Kaely grumbled.

Something touched her leg, and she let out a little scream. Kaely looked down to see Chester looking up at her, his head on her leg. "Chester, goodness gracious. Warn a gal first, okay?"

"So now what do we do?" Erin asked. "Just wait for the electricity to come on again?"

"I have no idea. We don't have a generator."

"My apartment complex has one," Erin said. "I've seen it, but I have no idea how it works."

"I saw some battery-powered lights in a cabinet in the kitchen," Kaely said. "I'll get them. At least we'll have them close by in case the generator doesn't come back on. Then we'll call Adrian. I'm concerned whether or not they'll be able to pick Mr. Dunne up in this weather."

"Are you sure we have enough evidence for the police to arrest him?"

Kaely sighed. "No. I doubt Adrian can arrest him, but at least he can bring him in for questioning."

"Are we really convinced it's him?" Erin shook her head. "I mean, I was when I first mentioned him, but now I'm starting to have some doubts. I mean, just because he likes to put things in order, does that make him a serial killer?"

"Remember that a profile is only supposed to narrow the search perimeters. We don't actually charge suspects. At this point, we have to hand it over to Adrian. But I've been doing this a long time. I feel confident that it's him, if that means anything."

"It does. And I realize that just because my name starts with an *E*, it doesn't mean I'm next on the list. I shouldn't have jumped to that conclusion."

"I think we should err on the side of caution," Kaely said. "I'm glad we're here together. I sincerely doubt if Allen is out in this storm, but Erin . . . I'd feel better if we were both armed."

Erin nodded. "I hear you. I—I'll get my gun."

Kaely was relieved to hear her say that she was ready to unlock her gun box. Did that mean she was no longer afraid she might use it on herself?

"I'll get mine too," she said. "Did you bring a holster?"

"No, I wasn't planning to take it out of the box."

"I have an extra," Kaely said. "I'll grab it."

Erin grinned. "You brought an extra holster? Why?"

"I have no idea. At the last moment, I just felt I should."

Erin's eyes widened. "Okay. That's . . . weird."

Kaely shrugged. She was certain the Holy Spirit had nudged her to bring it, but she didn't want Erin to feel she was being manipulative, so she stayed silent.

"After I get my gun, I'm going to look at the generator. Maybe it just needs to be reset. Hopefully, I can figure it out." She shrugged. "I doubt Allen Dunne is outside in this weather, but I'd feel better if I'm armed."

"Okay, but bundle up," Kaely said. "Maybe you should take Chester with you. It's about time for him to go out again anyway."

"I don't think he's going to like me anymore after this."

"I think he will." Kaely frowned. "Look," she said, "please watch your six. I agree that Mr. Dunne is probably not out in this storm, but . . . just be careful." She went into the kitchen and grabbed a flashlight she'd noticed earlier. "Here," she said, "use this when you go upstairs and outside. I'll have the lantern ready by the time you get back."

"I'll be careful," Erin said.

Erin took the flashlight and hurried off toward the staircase, with Chester following behind her. Kaely found four battery-powered lanterns. She also discovered a package of batteries in a kitchen drawer. She soon had the lanterns working. It helped a lot. The fire from the fireplace didn't give them much light. Now they had two lanterns for downstairs and a lantern for each of them for their bedrooms. She was hopeful that Erin would find a way to restart the generator. Being in the dark made her feel vulnerable.

She took the lanterns and went upstairs, where she found Erin with her gun. Kaely got the two holsters and her own gun and gave one of the holsters to Erin. She felt much better armed, although she was counting on the prospect that Allen Dunne was not the kind of man who would venture outside in a snowstorm.

Just then, the old post office creed jumped into her mind. *"Neither snow nor rain nor heat nor gloom of night stays these couriers from the swift completion of their appointed rounds."* The thought made her shiver, and it wasn't from the cold.

While Erin prepared to go outside, Kaely found her phone and tried to call Adrian. She wasn't completely surprised to find that she couldn't get through, but it made her uncomfortable. She and Erin were cut off from everyone. She sighed in frustration. She was definitely going to tell Steve to put a landline in the cabin so that anyone staying here would have a way to call for help if the cell towers were affected by the weather.

Kaely was relieved that Erin was able to see her weapon as something more than a means to end her life. This was a huge step. Erin had made great progress in the last couple of days. She'd finally released a lot of the pain that had held her life captive.

"God, there's still more to do. She's emptied out a lot of the hurt, but now she must fill the vacant places with You. Holy Spirit, touch her heart. She needs to know you. And keep us safe, Lord." She walked over to the window and looked out. The snow was coming down heavier now. They probably had three or four inches on the ground, and it was still accumulating. It was hard to tell because the wind blew the snow everywhere.

She was worried. She was convinced that Allen Dunne was

the killer, but she couldn't reach Adrian to let him know. She wasn't certain that Erin was his next victim, but what if she was? Was this snowstorm enough to keep them safe? It was true that most serial killers tended to lay low during bad weather because it could make it harder to get away from a crime scene. But there were exceptions. The killer called the Snowman popped into her mind again. But he was an exception. Not the rule. If Allen Dunne was smart, he'd take a break and wait for the storm to pass before striking again. With his level of fastidiousness, it seemed to her that trying to continue his plan would be too complicated and messy right now. But was she willing to stake Erin's life on that assumption?

Erin pulled her hood a little tighter. It felt even colder than the last time they'd taken Chester out. She was a little nervous after realizing that Allen Dunne was probably the UNSUB. But as she'd told Kaely, she wasn't completely convinced. He fit the profile, but they'd decided he was a serial killer because he liked things in a certain order? As a police officer, she was taught the importance of evidence—and they had none. That uncomfortable fact was the reason she'd thought Timothy Johnson was a viable suspect. No one else was better suited to hide evidence than the one collecting it. And seeing a truck like his outside the cabin? That was certainly suspicious.

Yet when she'd told Kaely she was convinced the killer was Allen Dunne, she'd been so certain. Was he the man sitting in the chair? Someone was there, she was sure of that. It had spooked her. Really spooked her.

Well, at least by now, Kaely had filled Adrian in. Maybe Sanctuary was a small town, but he appeared to be a very competent police chief. He'd know what to do. Erin just hoped he'd be able to find something solid to connect the killer to his crimes.

Chester tugged on the leash, so she stopped so he could do his business.

"You just went out an hour ago," she said. "How can you need to go again?" Chester looked at her like he was embarrassed, and it made Erin laugh. "It's okay. You're a good boy."

This time his tail wagged, and he gave her a big doggy grin.

"Come on. Let's take a look at this generator. Maybe you can figure out how to start it."

She waded through the snow, Chester behind her. She'd put their handmade leash on him because she worried about him running off. However, he seemed happy to stay by her side.

She saw the generator up ahead. As they approached it, Erin gasped. The side was open. Could the wind have done that? She looked inside. Maybe she didn't know anything about generators, but it was evident that someone had cut the power cables and rendered the unit unusable. There wasn't any way she could fix it. It was then that she saw the footprints in the snow. They led back and forth from the generator to the woods.

Suddenly, Chester began to bark, his gaze focused on the line of trees behind the house.

"Come on," she said, trying to pull him back to the house. He fought her, and she almost lost her grip on the belt. "Chester, no! Stop it!" Finally, he stopped digging his feet into the snow and let her pull him back toward the house, but she could tell he didn't want to. He looked back several times and continued to bark. It was hard to see in the snow, but a figure suddenly appeared in front of them. Erin instinctively went for her gun, but as she took it from the holster, she heard Kaely's voice.

"It's me!" she called out. "Don't shoot!"

Erin froze in place. She'd almost shot Kaely. She felt faint.

"It's okay. It's okay," Kaely said as she came up next to her. "It's hard to see, and we're both on edge. What about the generator?"

"Someone sabotaged it," Erin said. "And it wasn't that long ago. We need to get inside. Now."

The color in Kaely's face drained and her jaw tightened. "Let's get going."

Erin started to put her gun back in its holster, but she decided at the last second to keep it in her hand. They moved quickly through the snow toward the back door. Once inside, Kaely locked it immediately.

"When will Adrian be here?" Erin asked.

Kaely didn't say anything. She just took off her coat and held out her hand for Erin's. She took it off and gave it to her. Before Kaely answered her question, Erin was pretty sure what she was going to say.

"Our cell phones are out, and there's no landline," Kaely said. "We're on our own."

FORTY-THREE

He watched them from behind the trees. He laughed to himself as they discovered what he'd done to their generator. He hadn't counted on cell phone service being affected, but it only helped him. He could take his time now. He didn't have to kill her right away. He wondered how long it would take them to understand the message he was sending. Or if they even had the capacity to do so. At some point, someone would figure it out, but they still wouldn't connect it to him. He was too smart for them all.

He made his way back to his vehicle. He would stay nice, warm, and cozy while he waited for nightfall. Then he would continue with his mission. He glanced up at heaven and smiled. Were the angels crying yet? He would keep going until they did.

Kaely and Erin worked quickly to check all the doors and windows in the cabin. They also closed the drapes in the living room so no one could look inside.

"When it gets dark, we'll be at risk," Kaely said. They were back in the living room, but they'd turned off the lanterns. They needed to save the batteries just in case. "I think we need to get into one of our cars and try to make it to town. We're sitting ducks here."

"We're armed, and we're pretty sure we know who our adversary is," Erin said. "If we go outside, aren't we putting ourselves in more danger? He could be hiding in the trees. And, he could be armed too. And what if our car gets stuck?"

"I honestly don't think he wants to shoot us," Kaely said. "That would mess with his MO." She shook her head. "Maybe one of us could try to make it to the car. The other could cover her."

"I don't think we should separate. I mean, he could follow our car, if we can even get back to town, and if he doesn't do that, whoever was left here would be alone. An easier target, right?"

"You're right of course," Kaely said. "Sorry. I'm a little rattled. I left the FBI because I wanted to start a family, and I believed it would be safer for all of us. And now, here I am again." She took a deep breath and blew it out. "I guess we'd better barricade ourselves in and stay armed and watchful. Like you said, that way it's two against one."

"It's also possible that the electricity could come back on . . . and the phones. I'm certain they're both being worked on."

"One thing doesn't make sense to me," Kaely said slowly. "Why now? He could easily get trapped by the snow. I thought that would deter him. Statistically, he shouldn't be out there now."

"Maybe he has some kind of car or truck that can navigate

snow and ice." She shook her head. "Of course, 'neither snow nor rain or dark of night . . .'"

Kaely shook her head. "I thought of the same thing. Gives me the willies."

"Did you know it's not really the post office's creed? It was inscribed on New York City's James A. Farley Post Office Building in the early 1900s. It was borrowed from a passage in George Herbert Palmer's translation of Herodotus' Histories, referring to the courier service of the ancient Persian Empire."

Kaely looked at her with one eyebrow raised.

Erin sighed. "Sorry, sometimes when I get nervous, I like to quote useless facts."

Kaely smiled at her. "It's okay. And that was interesting. I had no idea."

"You're trying to appease me, aren't you?"

"Maybe. Is it working?"

Erin couldn't hold back a giggle, although she was fairly sure it was more nerves than anything else. "You're probably the only person in the world who could make me laugh at a time like this."

"I count that as a compliment," Kaely said. "Now, back to our situation." She frowned. "You know, I noticed a black SUV parked outside while we were at the post office. There was a magnetic post office sign on the side door. I'll bet that's what he's driving. If they use it to deliver mail, I'm sure it has snow tires. He might not be that worried about the weather at all."

Erin looked at her. "He . . . he wouldn't be, would he? Do you think he knows the phones are out?"

"We can't be certain, but if he has a phone, which I'm sure

he does, it certainly wouldn't be hard to figure out. I think we need to assume that he's aware of it."

"So now he knows we can't get help."

"You could be right," Kaely said. "I'll bet he disabled the generator after he knew we'd lost phone service."

"But he doesn't know when our service will be restored, does he?" Erin said. "So does that mean he feels the need to move quickly?" Even as the words left her lips, she felt her stomach flip over. It was true. He couldn't afford to wait too long. If he was determined that she would be the E in Watcher, he'd have to kill her as soon as possible, before he could move on. He wouldn't want to look for someone else. It would take too much time. She was a perfect target—and this was the perfect opportunity.

"Look, let's get this place ready," Kaely said, her expression stoic and her manner determined. "We need to make certain he can't get in, and we need to protect ourselves."

"Which means what?"

"We need to cover all the other windows. We don't want him to know where we are. There's some tin foil and scotch tape in the kitchen. We're going from room to room to close curtains, cover windows or sliding glass doors." She frowned at Erin. "How many magazines did you bring for your gun?"

Erin shook her head. "I wasn't actually planning on being targeted by a serial killer. I have one in my gun and a spare in my gun box."

"Yeah, I wasn't either. I brought three magazines. We should be okay."

Erin's mouth dropped open. "We have two guns and five magazines between us. If we need more than that to take

Allen out, we're doing something wrong. I mean, he's not superhuman." She frowned. "I always keep a spare magazine in my gun box. Why did you bring three with you? Were you planning on World War Three this week?"

Kaely shrugged. "Sorry. I fell back on my FBI training. I realized I didn't actually need three magazines when I declared my gun at the airport, but now I'm glad I brought them."

"Me too. If I miss the first thirty times, you should be able to get him."

Kaely laughed and shook her head. "It's always better to be prepared, I guess. But you're right. He should be more worried than we are. I'm going to look for candles. We have four lamps and lots of batteries. After we make certain he can't see inside the house, we'll put the lamps and candles in the most important places. We need to be able to see where we're going while we keep him from seeing us."

"Okay." Down at her feet, Chester whined. "Oh, shoot. He needs to go out again. We rushed him last time. What are we going to do?"

"We can't let him outside," Kaely said. "Even though Allen likes to stab his victims, we can't rule out the possibility that he has a gun too. I know serial killers like to stick to their MOs, but we can't take a chance."

"I have an idea," Erin said. "I'll take him out on the balcony outside my bedroom. With the lights out, I don't think he'll notice us. And unless Allen is a long way away from the house, he won't have a clear shot. I doubt he's too proficient with a gun. Doesn't seem like the type."

"Okay. Let's try it. I'm going to follow you upstairs. We can take care of the windows and doors up there while we're taking care of Chester."

Erin found the belt and attached it to Chester's collar. He immediately began tugging toward the front door. She pulled him back.

"No, Chester," she said. "Let's go upstairs." Before she headed toward the stairs, Erin said, "One thing's that's still bothering me. We believe Allen fits the profile of our killer. But what if we're wrong? I'm still wondering about Timothy."

Kaely sighed. "Well then, we're going to have to be especially careful. The unknown can be a lot scarier and unpredictable than what's known, and Timothy's been trained to shoot."

As Erin climbed the stairs with Chester beside her, Kaely's words rang in her head. Were they really prepared for what was coming? She could only hope that Kaely's God would protect them both.

FORTY-FOUR

Adrian tried several times to call Erin and Kaely, but their cell phones weren't working. The storm had affected several cell towers in the area. Thankfully, the station's landline was still working, but so few people had landlines anymore, there weren't a lot of people who could call the station if they needed help.

He was a little worried about the women since they were cut off. At least they had a generator, so they would stay warm. Quite a few people in town had lost power. The snow wasn't terribly deep yet. It was the wind that had caused so much havoc.

As it got darker, more and more residents headed to the emergency shelters to keep warm, get something to eat, and ride out the storm with friends and neighbors. Thankfully, the generator at the station was keeping up with their needs even though it was much older than the one at the cabin.

Adrian noticed Jake staring at him. Every time the wind howled and the building shook, rattling the old windows, he whined as if it was Adrian's fault.

"Just wait until it's time to go outside," he told his worried dog. "I guarantee you neither one of us will enjoy it."

Lisa came into his office. "We can't find Timothy," she said. "Not sure where he is."

"I sent him out earlier to check with anyone who lives just outside the city limits." Adrian frowned. "Maybe it's just taking him longer than we planned."

"I hope so. I'm a little worried about him. He left his radio behind again."

Adrian sighed. For some reason, Timothy had a hard time remembering his radio. He suspected his officer didn't like the rather clunky instrument and preferred to use his cell phone. Today made it clear as to why that wasn't a good idea. Police radios weren't affected by the weather the way cell phones might be. "If we don't hear from him soon, I'll go out to look for him. I'm sure he's around here somewhere." Timothy wasn't flaky. Adrian trusted him, so he wasn't really worried. Just a little annoyed.

Just then, a call came over the radio. A traffic accident near the resort. Since all of his officers were already dealing with other issues, Adrian decided to go himself. After messaging the officer who phoned it in, he put on his jacket and his radio and headed for the door. Jake came running after him. For a moment, he thought about asking Lisa to watch him, but if he tried that, Jake would be distraught. He wanted to go everywhere with Adrian, so he took him whenever he could.

"Okay, let's go. But no complaining. I mean it."

He took Jake's silly smile as his agreement to Adrian's warning. As they set off for the site of the accident, Adrian just couldn't get Erin and Kaely off his mind. If he had the time, he'd probably drive out there and check on them.

Thankfully, taking Chester out on the balcony worked. Erin noticed that he'd stopped limping. The last time they'd changed his bandages, the wound looked much better already.

It took them a couple of hours to make sure there was no way to see inside the house. They kept one of the lanterns upstairs on a hallway table. The other three were downstairs. They also set up several candles. Erin and Kaely put on a couple layers of clothing, but as long as they stayed in the living room by the fire, they were pretty warm. Kaely kept checking outside, but she couldn't see anything. If it was Allen Dunne who had disabled the generator, where was he? Of course, the post office SUV was black. Not easy to see at night.

They were both armed, and Kaely kept checking her cellphone, hoping service would be restored, but it was still out. It was almost nine o'clock when Erin reminded her that they hadn't eaten.

"I'll get us something," Kaely said. "Maybe some cheese slices and crackers?"

"Sounds good. And some Mallowmars?"

Kaely nodded. "Cheese, crackers, and Mallowmars. Sounds like a well-balanced meal. Just the thing for two growing girls."

Erin laughed. "The approved meal for those being stalked by a serial killer."

Kaely shook her head. "I'll have to remember that. Of course, this isn't my first time."

"I . . . I'm sorry. That wasn't a crack about your dad."

"I didn't take it that way at all," Kaely said with a smile. "No worries."

"You know, I honestly have no idea what I would have done without you," Erin said. Her eyes grew shiny, and she cleared her throat. "Maybe after we get through this, we could talk some more about . . . God. I'm coming to the conclusion that maybe you know something I don't."

"I can't imagine that," Kaely said with a grin.

Erin shook her head. "Point taken. The way I was raised . . ."

Before she could get the rest of her sentence out, Chester stood up and faced the front door. He began to bark. It was then that Kaely heard the sound of a motor. She quickly turned off the lantern and grabbed her gun. As she pulled the drape back just a little, she saw a vehicle pull up to the road in front of the cabin. The driver turned off his lights. It was difficult for her to see anything through the darkness, but then someone inside the vehicle turned on a flashlight. As he opened the door and got out, she was able to see that it was a dark pickup. Timothy Johnson. He began to walk toward the house but suddenly stopped. Then he turned around and headed toward the woods. Seconds later he disappeared behind the tree line.

Kaely turned her head and saw Erin's face highlighted by the flames from the fireplace. "Who is it?" she asked.

"Tim Johnson."

"Maybe he's here to help us," Erin said.

"Then why did he go into the woods? We may be wrong. It's possible that our first assumption was correct. Timothy Johnson may be our killer."

FORTY-FIVE

Erin and Kaely sat in the dark while Chester whined. No matter how hard they tried to calm him, he wouldn't settle down. Finally, Erin got up and went back over to the window. She was trying to be very careful so that no one could see them. The snow was coming down even harder, and she couldn't make out Timothy's truck now. It was too dark outside.

"I can't see anything," she said to Kaely. "Between the snow and the dark, I can't make out Tim's truck. I just want to see if it's still there. We need to know."

Kaely shook her head. "I think it's too dangerous."

Erin felt frustrated. "I promise, I'll only take a quick peek. I doubt anyone is waiting for us to open the door for a moment so they can shoot us."

Kaely sighed. "Okay, but make it fast. I'm not sure what difference it makes."

"If Timothy is the killer, why would he park where we could see him? And why would he walk into the woods? Why not stay warm inside his truck where he can get a better shot?" She shook her head. "Something doesn't feel right about this. I mean, what if Timothy actually came to check on us, and he saw or heard something in the woods? What if he's in trouble?"

"Like you said, he's a trained officer. He should be able to take care of himself."

"So was Scott."

Kaely stared at her for a moment. "Okay. But just a quick look, okay? Don't go out there. If the truck is still there, close the door. We'll decide what to do from there. Deal?"

"Deal."

As if he understood their conversation, Chester stood to his feet. "No, Chester," she said. "Stay."

Erin grabbed her coat. Although she only planned to step out on the porch, it was really cold out there. She pulled her gun from its holster, even though she didn't think she'd need it.

She pulled the door open and stepped out into the storm. It was clear very quickly that it was going to be hard to see anything through the falling and blowing snow. She held the flashlight out in front of her and held her gun in the other hand. She still couldn't see the truck, so she put the small flashlight in her mouth while she held onto the porch railing so she wouldn't fall. The steps were slippery, and she almost lost her footing a couple of times.

Suddenly, she heard Chester bark, and he shot past her, toward the figure of a woman in a cloak, light glowing from her body.

"I'm sorry," Kaely yelled from behind her, trying to be heard over the howling of the wind. "I was trying to shut the door, but he pushed past me before I could stop him."

Erin only had a moment to react. She was still a little

afraid of the ghost, but she'd fallen in love with Chester. In her mind, he was already her dog. No ghost was going to keep her from getting him back. She didn't look back, nor did she listen to Kaely's pleading, telling her not to go. She ran into the snow, headed toward the woman who stood still as if waiting for something. Chester was at her feet, barking furiously.

Before Erin could reach them, the woman turned and ran into the trees, Chester behind her.

And Erin followed.

FORTY-SIX

Erin stumbled through the snow, her heart pounding so hard she could swear she heard it beat inside her ears. She wanted to run back inside the cabin, but she couldn't. She wanted to know about the Woman in Watcher Woods, but not so much she would put herself in danger. All she really wanted was to save Chester. He'd already been abandoned once, and she couldn't let that happen again. Maybe she couldn't have saved Scott, but she wouldn't let Chester die. Not by someone pretending to be a ghost—and not by a serial killer who wouldn't think twice about killing a dog. She still had her gun, and she pulled it out of its holster. She checked her pocket for her flashlight and was relieved to find it. She turned it on and swung it around, but no one was there. Should she call Chester? Unfortunately, that would reveal her location. That would be foolish. She had to keep her location secret. Although she didn't want to do it, she turned off the flashlight. She'd only use it when she had to.

She wasn't sure who to be afraid of. Timothy Johnson? Allen Dunne? A ghost? The only thing she knew for certain was that Chester needed her. And she needed him. Maybe it sounded stupid. Risking your life for a dog, but she couldn't help it. She was tired of being afraid. And she was tired of losing those she loved. Not this time. She suddenly tripped on something. A branch hidden by the snow. The flashlight flew from her hand. She got on her hands and knees and searched for it, thinking it was close by, but she couldn't find it. Kneeling in the snow made her even colder. The flashlight was probably buried under the snow. She couldn't spend any more time looking for it. She got back to her feet and leaned against a tree, the snow blowing in her face. It was getting deeper. It covered her feet. What should she do now? She jumped when she heard a sound coming through the forest. Barking. It was Chester!

Erin stood behind the huge tree, tears pouring down her cheeks. It felt as if they were freezing on her face. It was so dark she couldn't see her hand in front of her face—until the moon peeked out from behind the clouds. She desperately needed the light to find her way back. Or to locate Chester. Yet the same thing that gave her hope also terrified her. What if the killer could see her? As if the moon had heard her, it vanished again, clouds shielding it from the earth.

Although she was afraid of a person, what if the Woman in Watcher Woods was real? Was she being targeted by a vicious serial killer or a ghost? Or both? Kaely kept telling her that ghosts weren't real. Yet, she knew what she'd seen. And she wasn't the only one. Still, it was nuts, wasn't it? At that moment, she wished she were as sure as Kaely that killer ghosts didn't exist. She wanted to call out for help, but she couldn't take the chance. One thing she was sure of, the bodies found in the woods weren't her imagination. They were very real. She also knew in her heart that she was next on the killer's list.

She held her gun out in front of her, ready to take a shot if she needed to. Of course, she couldn't shoot a ghost. But she could kill a man. A man who wanted to dress her in white and put a ceramic angel in her hands.

"Focus, Erin," she whispered in the dark. "There are no ghosts. Focus on the real threat."

She took a deep breath and squared her shoulders. She wasn't going to make it easy. She would fight for her life. A life she had been willing to throw away at one point. But now that she knew she could die, all she wanted was to live. To have a future that included the dog who had stolen her heart. Even more than that, she wanted a chance to change things. To change her life. To live without fear. She had no intention of allowing this killer to add her to his mounting death toll.

Once again, the moon snuck out from behind the clouds, and Erin looked around. She still couldn't see anyone. Should she make a run for it? Try to get back to the cabin? She shook her head in the dark. She had to keep going. She had to find Chester. Before she had the chance to do anything, the moon hid from her once again. It was as if they were playing a game of hide and seek.

Erin sighed as she leaned against the rough bark of the tree and tried to listen. Silence. Chester wasn't barking now. Where was he? Was he still alive? At first, all she could hear was the sound of owls hooting and the occasional eerie howl of a coyote.

As she waited, holding her breath, she wished she were at home in her apartment, safe and secure, Chester sitting next to her on the couch. If she couldn't be home, she wished she and Chester were back inside the cabin. It might not be completely safe, but it was better than being exposed outside. She had no idea where the cabin was. Why didn't she mark the way? Why didn't she pay more attention? As she looked around, she realized that besides the things she was already afraid of, there were also coyotes and bears in these woods.

It was then that she heard barking again. She wanted so badly to call out to him, but she couldn't. What should she do? The barking became louder and suddenly, like a miracle, there he was, at her feet, his big brown eyes staring up at her.

Then he suddenly turned around and began to growl. That's when she saw it. The figure in the dark cloak that seemed to kill all the brightness around it. Like a black hole eating all the light.

Chester put itself between Erin and the woman, baring his teeth, challenging the woman to back away. Erin couldn't stop the tears that continued to drip down her face. At that moment, she was afraid of the woman and afraid for the dog. And afraid that tonight would be her last night on earth.

Although at first, she wasn't certain what to do, she reached out with a trembling hand and took hold of Chester's collar.

"Help me," the woman said faintly before falling down in the snow and landing right in front of Erin and Chester who had fallen silent. He stared at the figure lying in front of them as if confused.

Once again, the moon slipped out from behind the windswept clouds. It was then that Erin saw the knife sticking out of her back. *He's here. He's in the woods.*

Should she run? Or should she try to help the person lying in front of her? Erin knelt down and pulled the hood off of the head of the figure lying prostate in the snow. She recognized her immediately. Not a ghost. A person. Bobbi Burke. Erin pulled back part of the cloak and found some kind of small lights sewn into the hem of the fabric. That explained it.

"What are you doing out here?" Erin asked.

"My . . . my car. Got stuck. C—couldn't leave. He . . . saw me." She turned sideways and grabbed Erin's arm. "Please . . ."

Her hand dropped, and Bobbi stopped moving. Erin put her fingers on the woman's neck and waited. Nothing. No heartbeat. She was gone.

She'd wanted to ask her who the man was, but now it was too late. Erin reached down and pulled off Bobbi's sash, fashioning it into a temporary leash. She couldn't allow Chester to run off again.

As the moon vanished once again, Erin began to lead Chester toward what she could only hope was the direction of the cabin. She had no other choice. She couldn't just wait for him to come after her. He'd killed Bobbi because she must have recognized him. But he had other plans for Erin. She squinted, trying to see through the falling snow. If only they hadn't covered the windows in the cabin. There might have been some light to help her find the way. In desperation and fear, she decided to pray to Kaely's God. What could it hurt? Maybe He had pity on fools and lost women.

"God," she whispered, "I haven't believed in You, but Kaely does. If You're real, I'd like a chance to get to know You. Please . . . please get us to safety. I have no idea where the cabin is. If You could guide me, I would really appreciate it. And if You answer me, I promise to . . ." *What could she say? She couldn't lie to God.* "If you save us," she continued,

"I promise to listen to Kaely talk about You. I mean, really listen. If You're real, of course I want to know You."

She tried to drag Chester the way she wanted them to go, the way she thought would take them back, but Chester dug his feet into the snowy ground and refused to move. Then she heard a sound that startled her. Was he actually growling at her?

Go with him.

Erin looked around her, afraid he'd found them. Afraid she would end up the next one on his ghastly list.

Go with him.

Erin stood there for a moment, looking down at Chester, though she could barely see him. As the dog stared up at her, Erin made a decision. Not a rational one—just a decision.

She loosened her hold on Chester's leash and turned the way he was pulling—the opposite direction she thought they should go. Chester forged ahead with confidence. Erin hoped he wasn't chasing a rabbit or had sniffed out something else that might lead them right into the killer's trap. But she was throwing caution to the wind—trying to listen with her heart, not her mind, and not out of past hurts. Kaely's voice rang in her head. *You'll never be free if you don't take a step of faith. Just one step. Don't worry about the next ones. They'll come.*

Although she could barely see anything in front of her, she kept going, jogging behind Chester who seemed to know exactly where he was going. The moon was still playing peekaboo with the windswept clouds. It reminded Erin of a high school dance, where the lights in the gym flickered on and off with the music. It was supposed to be a cool effect, but Erin had found it disconcerting. She pushed the thought out of her mind. She wasn't in high school, and there was nothing cool about what was happening.

As Chester wove in and out through the trees, Erin tried to keep herself from slipping on the snow. She glanced behind her to see if they were being followed, but when she did, she tripped and fell hard, slamming her knee into a fallen snow-covered branch lying on the ground, her gun flying off into the dark underbrush and out of sight.

She bit her lip, trying not to cry out in pain. Chester stopped and looked back at her as if he were trying to figure out if she could go on. Erin put her hands in the snow and pushed herself up to a sitting position. Chester whined softly, and she reached out and slowly pulled herself up to her feet. As soon as she put weight on her right foot, pain shot through her leg. She felt around on the ground and found another branch, small but sturdy. She used it as a walking stick and began to hobble as quickly as she could behind her impatient dog. Although her leg hurt, living was more important than some temporary discomfort.

Suddenly, Chester began to bark. Terrified the killer would hear and find them, Erin yanked on his leash.

"Chester. Hush! Be quiet!" She tried to keep her voice as low as she could but loud enough so Chester could hear her. When he continued to bark, she became desperate. "Ozzy! Ozzy!" she hissed, hoping he'd respond to his previous name. She hated to call him that because she was pretty sure his owner hadn't shown him much love, but she didn't know what else to do. She stumbled on something else that was covered by the snow and fell down once again. She flipped herself over on her other side before her body hit the ground.

Thankfully, she was able to protect her sore leg. The snow cushioned her fall.

As she tried to get up again, Chester suddenly tugged so hard on the sash that it slipped from her hand. She tried to grab it again, but he took off running through the woods. Before she could call him back, he was out of her limited sight. Where was he? Why had he left her? So much for some voice telling her to follow him.

Once again, she struggled to get back on her feet.

"There you are," a voice said from behind her. "Surely you didn't think you'd get away from me."

Erin turned over and found herself looking up at the man who stood over her. He wore a thick coat, gloves and a ski mask. But she knew who he was.

"You can't kill me now," she said, her mind racing. "You killed Bobbi Burke. Now everything's out of order. It's ruined."

He didn't say anything for a moment, just stared down at her. Then he cocked his head to one side as if contemplating what she'd said. Finally, he said, "But she got in the way. She doesn't count."

"Of course she does. It won't work now. People will know. They'll realize you failed. Everything is out of order."

"So, what am I supposed to do now?"

Erin could hardly believe he was serious, yet she knew he was. *Try to think the way he does. What did Kaely teach you?* Erin took a deep breath before saying, "I think you'll have to just start over. There's no other way."

Once again, he contemplated her. She was certain that to him, she was nothing more than a specimen. Like a germ under a microscope.

"You know, I think you may be right," he said with a sigh. "I need to start over. That stupid woman destroyed everything."

She'd stalled him, but how could she talk him out of killing her? He'd killed Bobbi because she recognized him. Why wouldn't he do the same to her? It was then that she saw the knife in his hand. It had blood on it. He'd taken it out of Bobbi's back. If only she hadn't dropped her gun.

"You . . . you can just leave. I don't know who you are. But I can spread your story. Make sure everyone knows there was never any ghostly woman in the woods, but that there is someone else. Someone real. You. Your story will multiply, and people will talk about you. For . . . for a lot longer than they talked about her."

This man was narcissistic. He wanted people to know how smart he was. How powerful. And he fed on their fear. She'd just appealed to all of that. Hadn't she? Had it worked?

"You're a liar, Miss Delaney," he said, his voice almost like a low growl. "Not about my starting over, but when you said you don't know who I am. Of course you do."

"No. No, I don't. I can't see your face."

"But you knew that after killing Miss Burke, I'd have to start again. You knew that because you know how important order is to me."

"No, you're wrong. Please. Just leave."

Before she could say anything else, he reached up with his left hand and pulled off his mask. The moon decided that was the moment to illuminate the area around them—as well as his face. Of course, he was right. She knew exactly who he was. Her first suspicion had been correct.

"I have no choice except to kill you," Allen said, his smile more like a grimace. "Since there's no more order, it doesn't matter. You won't stop me from starting again."

Was this the last thing she'd ever see? "Wait—wait . . ." she said. She needed to call out again to the God Kaely had told her about while she still had time. Why had she been so stubborn? Would she be able to make things right before it was too late?

"God . . ." was all she got out before he lunged toward her, his bloody knife glinting in the moonlight.

Erin's eyes were locked with his when a loud sound made them both jump. Allen's eyes widened with shock as his body collapsed, falling on the ground next to her.

"Are you all right?"

Sergeant Timothy Johnson knelt beside her, and Chester began licking the tears from her face.

FORTY-SEVEN

The roads had finally been cleared and power restored. Erin's leg was in a brace, but it was healing nicely. Dr. Gibson had even okayed her to drive back to St. Louis in four days. Noah had wanted to fly in, but Kaely had talked him out of it, choosing to spend as much time as she could with Erin before they each headed home.

Erin was sitting in the living room, a fire crackling in the fireplace, eating fried chicken, fried corn, and french fries from Dolly's Diner, specially delivered by Adrian. Of course, her Mallomars were close by.

"I thought you said you were going to take us out to dinner as a way to thank us for helping you," Kaely said, laughing.

"I'm still going to do that," Adrian said. "This is just the pre-dinner dinner."

Erin grinned. "Well, it's great. No complaints here."

"You're welcome, but I think I just heard my arteries slamming shut," Adrian said as he popped two fries into his mouth.

"But it's worth it, isn't it?" Erin said.

"Dolly may be a little weird," Kaely said, "but she hired a great cook."

Adrian nodded. "That's true, Carl is excellent."

"Carl?" Erin said. "I'm not a Dolly Parton expert, but isn't her husband's name Carl?"

Adrian laughed. "Yeah, you're right. Carl Thomas Dean. Well, if she hired him because of his name, it turned out okay. No one makes a cheeseburger like Carl."

Erin raised her eyebrows at him. "You know Dolly's husband's full name?"

He shrugged. "Hey, when you live in Tennessee, you learn all kinds of things. Dolly Parton is like royalty here. She's actually a very nice woman who gives to a lot of different charities."

"That's good to know."

Adrian nodded, but it was clear he was distracted. He stared at her for a moment before saying, "So when did you know?"

"About Allen?" Erin asked.

He nodded while Erin handed Chester a fry, which was happily accepted.

"We figured it out while we were stuck here without electricity or phone service," Kaely said. "Actually, we were writing the names of Allen's victims on a list, trying to see what connected them. Once we began doing that . . ."

Erin jumped in. "I realized that the first letter of each first name spelled . . ."

"Watch," Kaely finished for her.

"And then we wondered if he was purposely trying to spell something. Obviously, it was Watcher. That's when we became concerned."

"But not so concerned that you didn't think twice about

dashing off into the night?" Adrian asked, his tone incredulous.

Erin shrugged. "When we saw the woman in the woods again, and Chester ran off . . ."

"You had to go after them?" Adrian said.

"Yeah. . . . Look, it might not sound like a smart thing to do, but I was afraid for Chester. I was also a little concerned for Timothy. But to be honest, I still wasn't completely sure it was Allen. Until the last moment."

"So you actually thought Timothy might be a serial killer?"

Erin smiled and looked at Kaely. "Well, we were pretty sure it wasn't him. But we saw a truck like his parked outside the cabin two different times. That seemed suspicious."

"I asked him to check on you," Adrian said, shaking his head. "This cabin is on his way home. It never occurred to me that you'd think he was up to no good. He would have knocked on your door, but he saw something in the woods. He went to check it out. We know now that it was Bobbi."

"I thank God he was there," Kaely said. "His quick thinking saved Erin's life. I just wish he'd been able to help Bobbi."

"She was trying to scare people away from the cabin," Adrian said. "Her partner at the real estate company knew what she was doing. She should have tried to stop her. It cost Bobbi her life." He shook his head. "She should never have been out there. I guess she planned to drive away before the snow got too deep, but her car got stuck. I have to wonder if she was coming to you for help."

"Well, if she was, why didn't she take that ridiculous costume off?" Erin asked.

Adrian shrugged. "I guess we'll never know."

"So she wanted to buy the cabin herself?" Kaely asked.

Adrian nodded. "She thought that if people believed there was a ghost in the woods, they wouldn't want to stay here. She planned to drive the price way down and buy the cabin from Steve for a pittance. After that, the Woman in Watcher Woods would disappear, and Bobbi would rake in a fortune through rentals." He sighed. "Poor Timothy didn't even know Bobbi had been attacked. Not until you found her body."

"What made her glow?" Kaely asked.

"Just some lights she'd wired inside the cloak," Erin said. "I saw them while we were out there."

"Yeah, she had them connected to a battery," Adrian said. "Pretty spooky looking."

"I'm so grateful that Chester knew Timothy was in the woods and led me to him," Erin said, "or I could have ended up just like Bobbi."

"So, you two didn't trust Timothy completely but Chester did?"

Erin laughed. "Yes, Chester was smarter than an ex-cop and an ex-FBI agent."

"Well, he knew Timothy," Adrian said. "They were pretty good friends."

Erin took a drink of her soda before saying, "I have to admit that, at first, I thought Kaely had fired the shot that killed Allen."

"I got there right after Timothy did," Kaely said. "But it still might have been too late."

"You realize that we all know the police department isn't getting that dog, right?" Adrian asked, looking at Chester.

Erin looked down at the border collie curled up next to

her on the couch, his paw on her leg. "Yeah, but I don't think any of your fellow officers will really mind."

Adrian shook his head. "I'm sure they'll all be happy that Ozzy—I mean Chester—has found a good home. Chester won't mind either. He's obviously chosen his person."

Erin reached over and stroked his soft head. "He's so very special," she said softly. "I believe we need each other."

"So back to realizing that Allen Dunne was our killer," Adrian said. "How did you tie that in to seeing that the murderer was spelling Watcher?"

"It was at the post office," Erin said.

"We noticed that when someone tried to put up a flyer on the bulletin board, Allen freaked out," Kaely said. "He came from behind the counter and grabbed it. Said the man was going to make things *out of order*. When he moved the other flyers, we realized he had them in alphabetical order. Then, when I was looking over the stamps, I saw that the pages had been cut out of the usual booklet and put into a spiral notebook. I didn't realize until we were talking about the killer, that those pages were also in alphabetical order. You see, some people, like Allen Dunne, are driven to try to control everything. The obsession to put things in order is part of their psychological makeup."

"I always thought he was strange, but I never saw him as a serial killer." Adrian frowned. "I guess we'll never know how he approached those women, but we know where they met him. He delivered their mail. And who would suspect a mail carrier? We found his phone. He took pictures of his victims. He may have been too smart to leave evidence at the scene, but he was dumb enough to keep photos that tied him to the murders. At least we can completely close this case."

"Something else we'll never know," Kaely said, "is whether he asked Chloe for a date and then punctured her tires or if he just picked her up once her tires went flat."

Erin nodded. "Maybe he asked her out, and she turned him down? Disabling her car might have been his backup plan. He needed that *C*."

"That's really disturbing," Adrian said. He paused for a moment. "Why did he wait so long to start killing? He's lived here since he was a kid. His grandparents raised him after his mother died. Then when he was older . . ." He stopped and stared at Kaely. "Oh, man. He didn't start killing with Willow Abbott did he?"

Erin shook her head. "No. He probably killed his grandparents."

"How could you possibly know that?"

"Because that's who he was," Kaely said. "I'm certain they did something that triggered his behavior. I'm pretty sure it had to do with his mother. My guess is that he felt they hurt her in some way. I'm also confident that she wore high heels, makeup, and blue ribbons in her hair. That's why he added the ribbon and never removed his victims' makeup, jewelry, or high heels. I know serial killers who were very triggered by those things. But Allen? No, they didn't bother him at all. The white dress symbolized purity, either his mother's or he put it on his victims because he believed angels wear them. I would lean toward the latter because of the figurines." She sighed. "We'll never know exactly what he was thinking."

"So, he was trying to spell out Watcher with his kills?" Adrian asked. "Why? What does that have to do with anything?"

Kaely shook her head. "He was trying to send a message.

Like a challenge. It's a common thing with serial killers. Think of the Zodiac. Jack the Ripper. There are more. He probably picked the words Watcher Woods for his puzzle because people were afraid of the ghost that supposedly roamed there. It might also be that he felt connected to William Watcher in some way. A lot of serial killers pattern themselves after other murderers."

"Why didn't he include his grandparents' initials in his puzzle?"

"Because they weren't important," Erin said. "They were just obstacles to get out of the way so he could begin his quest for what he considered to be his fight against God—or the angels."

Kaely nodded. "Yes, I agree."

"I still can't believe you thought Timothy was a serial killer," Adrian said with a smile. "He's one of the most moral people I've ever met. I trust him with my life."

Kaely smiled. "Yes, I understand. But think about it. He's attractive. Has a very respectable job. Knows how to hide evidence. He was in a position to tell you what he wanted you to know, but not necessarily what you needed to know."

"Maybe you should have told us Timothy was going to be checking on us?" Erin said. "I mean, we knew there was a serial killer running around and a strange vehicle keeps showing up?"

"Yeah, I get it. Sorry." Adrian popped another fry in his mouth, chewed, and then swallowed. "So now what?"

"Well, we're leaving in four . . . well, three days after today," Kaely said. "I'm going home to Virginia, and Erin will be going back to St. Louis."

"You're right," Erin said. "But I won't be there long."

Kaely frowned. "Why?"

"Well, I decided that I need to leave St. Louis," Erin said slowly. "Too many bad memories there. I need a fresh start."

"I think that sounds like a great idea," Adrian said. "Where will you go?"

Erin laughed and looked at Kaely.

Kaely's sudden, wide smile told her she'd figured it out.

"I made Steve an offer he couldn't refuse," Erin said.

"You bought the cabin," Adrian said. He said it more as a statement than a question. "But aren't there bad memories here as well?"

"I would say that this experience has been . . . challenging. But something good happened too. Something I needed. Being here—with Kaely—has allowed me to start over. Besides, the peace and quiet will help me with my writing." She smiled at Kaely. "Our little adventure has given me ideas. I'm ready to write another book."

"I think that's wonderful," Kaely said. She looked over at Adrian. "And you already have a friend here."

Adrian's face flushed and he picked up his drink. Erin noticed it and wondered why he'd reacted that way. Strange. Hopefully, he didn't mind that she was moving to Sanctuary.

"I hope you'll come back," Erin said to Kaely.

Kaely nodded. "I think we should make this a yearly thing at least, don't you?"

"Absolutely," Erin replied. "But . . ."

"But perhaps without a crazed serial killer next time?"

Adrian grinned at them. "I would certainly appreciate that."

Erin shrugged. "We'll do our best, but we certainly can't promise anything."

"No, we certainly can't," Kaely said, smiling.

NOTE FROM THE AUTHOR

Dear Reader,

I hope you've enjoyed this book. I try hard to write stories that will entertain you, but even more importantly, I pray that something I've written will touch your heart. If you find yourself relating to my characters who struggle with fear, loneliness, and sorrow, just like the rest of us, I want to give you some good news. God has the answer to every problem you face, and He loves you with a love that is deep, eternal, and boundless. If you've never asked him into your life, you can take care of that today. John 3:16 says: "For God so loved the world that he gave his one and only Son, that whoever believes in him shall not perish but have eternal life" (NIV). Below, is a prayer you can use to change your life forever.

"Lord Jesus, I turn to You in my time of need. I believe that You are the Son of God and that You died on the cross to pay the price for my sins. Lord, I receive You as my Savior, and I want You to be my Lord. Wash me clean with Your blood and fill me with Your Holy Spirit. Help me to follow You the rest of my life. Amen."

If you've prayed this prayer, will you let me know? You can contact me through my website, NancyMehl.com. Please find a good local church where you can become part of a family that will help you on your journey. May God bless you abundantly.

DISCUSSION QUESTIONS FOR *SHATTERED SANCTUARY*

1. Erin Delaney is grappling with a tragic incident from her past. How does this trauma shape her character and influence the story?

2. Kaely Quinn-Hunter is a Christian, and Erin isn't. Kaely approaches their relationship with caution, not wanting to push Erin away by being too forceful with her faith. Does she handle it correctly? Is this how you would have done it?

3. Why do you think Erin is dealing with agoraphobia after that fateful night in St. Louis?

4. Erin and Police Chief Adrian Nightengale have both relocated to Sanctuary in an attempt to find a more peaceful life. Do you think changing locations makes

it easier to deal with trauma? Or do you just end up taking your problems with you?

5. Of all the characters in *Shattered Sanctuary*, which one did you relate to the most? Why?

6. Did any of the characters remind you of someone you know? Who and why?

7. Would you like to live in a cabin in the Smoky Mountains? Why or why not?

8. How much do you think the setting affected the plot?

9. If you were making a movie of this book, who would you cast in the main roles?

10. What was the main spiritual theme of *Shattered Sanctuary*? Were you able to apply it to your own life?

ACKNOWLEDGMENTS

As always, my thanks to my editors: Jessica Sharpe, Susan Downs, and Kate Jameson. I couldn't do this without you.

Thank you also to Supervisory Special Agent Drucilla Wells (retired), Federal Bureau of Investigations, Behavioral Analysis Unit. Your help is invaluable.

My appreciation to retired police officer Darin Hickey. Thank you for your willingness to answer my questions.

My unending thanks to my friend and assistant, Zac Weikal. Thank you for making me look much better than I really am.

Thank you to all the readers who keep me going. Without readers, there would be no writers. Never forget how important you are.

Most of all, thank you to my Father, who has never deserted me, even when I gave Him plenty of reasons to do so. I love You.

READ ON FOR A *SNEAK PEEK* AT
THE NEXT BOOK IN

THE
ERIN DELANEY
MYSTERIES
SERIES.

AVAILABLE OCTOBER 2025.

ONE

I was only nine years old when I knew I was destined to be a serial killer. My best friend and I watched a show on TV that talked about them. I'd never felt more excited about anything in my entire life. When I was ten, I almost changed my mind. I went to my friend's church, and the pastor talked about Jesus. I wondered if there was another way for me to go, but when the pastor told us that Jesus wanted us to love everyone, I knew I could never live that way. Hate filled my heart and my mind so strongly that there wasn't room for anything else. The only thing I truly loved was my hate, and I had no desire to let it go.

Now that I'm older, I'm ready to fulfill my destiny.

And I know just where to start.

At the beginning.

It was a cold and rainy night. Alex Caine stared at himself in the mirror. He looked as tired as he felt. His hazel eyes narrowed as he gazed at his chiseled features. His dark hair was beginning to gray and needed to be cut.

Erin Delaney stared at the words on her first page and laughed quietly. "Never open with weather," she said under her breath. "Never describe a character by having him look in a mirror." She sighed loudly. "How many other writerly taboos can I break?"

She got up from the couch and headed into the kitchen for another cup of coffee. Chester, her border collie, jumped down and followed her, his nails clicking on the wooden floors. Wherever she went, he was right beside her. Since she'd moved from St. Louis, she'd noticed that he'd become a little clingy. He'd been with her almost five months, but he still had trust issues. Just like she did. They really were a perfect match. In St. Louis, he'd watched her carefully whenever she had to leave him in the apartment, his large brown eyes echoing the fear that someone else had caused by abandoning him. Eventually, he began to relax a bit, but they obviously had a way to go until the shadows of the past no longer held him in their grasp. Now that they'd left St. Louis for good and arrived back in Sanctuary, Erin hoped he would finally believe he was loved and that he would never be left behind again. She wasn't certain what she would have done without him over the past several months. He was her best friend and her constant companion. Together, they were facing the ghosts of their former lives.

She'd just plopped back down on the couch, Chester jumping up next to her, when her phone rang. Kaely. It had been a while. She answered it.

"Hey," she said. "Glad to hear from you."

She expected Kaely's greeting to be equally cheery, but her response seemed guarded, careful.

"Everything okay?" she asked.

Kaely's sigh came through the phone. "No, it isn't. We need you to come to Quantico. There's . . . a situation."

Erin's body stiffened. "What . . . what kind of situation?"

Kaely cleared her throat before saying, "The BAU is working on a case. Someone is killing women, and they're using MOs they picked up from several mystery and suspense novels."

"I don't understand," she said, although in the back of her mind, she did.

"The third murder copies the killings in your book, Erin. We want you to come here so we can keep you safe—and so you can help us find this guy."

NANCY MEHL is the author of more than fifty books, a Parable and ECPA bestseller, and the winner of an ACFW Book of the Year Award, a Carol Award, and the Daphne du Maurier Award. She has also been a finalist for the Christy Award. Nancy writes from her home in Missouri, where she lives with her husband. To learn more, visit NancyMehl .com.

Sign Up for Nancy's Newsletter

Keep up to date with Nancy's latest news on book releases and events by signing up for her email list at the website below.

NancyMehl.com

FOLLOW NANCY ON SOCIAL MEDIA

Nancy Mehl Author Page   @NancyMehl1

More from Nancy Mehl

Former FBI profiler River Ryland suffers from PTSD after a serial killer case gone wrong and has opened a private investigation firm with Tony, her former colleague. Their first job is a cold case, but when they race to stop the killer before he strikes again, an even more dangerous threat emerges, stirring up the past and plotting to end River's future.

Cold Pursuit
RYLAND & ST. CLAIR #1

Former FBI behavioral analysts River Ryland and Tony St. Clair are asked to assist on a profile to catch the Snowman, a serial killer who has stayed hidden for over twenty years. As the killer's pattern emerges and danger mounts, River and Tony are in a race against the clock to catch a killer before he catches one of them.

Cold Threat
RYLAND & ST. CLAIR #2

As former FBI analysts turned private investigators, River Ryland and Tony St. Clair are hired to find a missing crime blogger known for investigating cold cases. As they work through the woman's latest case, they awaken an unknown killer who will stop at nothing to carry out a deadly plan.

Cold Vengeance
RYLAND & ST. CLAIR #3

◊ BETHANYHOUSE

 Bethany House Fiction

 @BethanyHouseFiction

 @Bethany_House

 @BethanyHouseFiction

 Free exclusive resources for your book group at BethanyHouseOpenBook.com

 Sign up for our fiction newsletter today at BethanyHouse.com